P9-DMH-670

PENGUIN BOOKS

GIRL WITH GREEN EYES

Edna O'Brien was born in the West of Ireland and now lives in London. One of Britain's most popular and respected contemporary writers, she is author of *The Country Girls*, *Girl with Green Eyes* (first published as *The Lonely Girl*), *Girls in their Married Bliss*, *August is a Wicked Month*, *Casualties of Peace*, *The Love Object* (short stories), *A Pagan Place*, *Zee and Co.*, *Mother Ireland*, *Night*, *A Scandalous Woman and Other Stories*, *Johnny I hardly knew you*, *Arabian Knights* (photography by Gerard Klijn), *Mrs Reinhardt and Other Stories*, *Returning*, *A Christmas Treat* and *A Fanatic Heart*. Edna O'Brien was awarded the *Yorkshire Post* Novel Award in 1971. *The Collected Edna O'Brien*, containing nine novels, was published in 1978, and *Some Irish Loving*, an anthology of prose and poetry, in 1979.

EDNA O'BRIEN

GIRL WITH GREEN EYES

PENGUIN BOOKS

IN ASSOCIATION WITH

JONATHAN CAPE

Penguin Books Ltd, 27 Wrights Lane, London w8 5tz (Publishing and Editorial)
and Harmondsworth, Middlesex, England (Distribution and Warehouse)
Viking Penguin Inc., 40 West 23rd Street, New York, New York 10010, USA
Penguin Books Australia Ltd, Ringwood, Victoria, Australia
Penguin Books Canada Ltd, 2801 John Street, Markham, Ontario, Canada L3R 1B4
Penguin Books (NZ) Ltd, 182–190 Wairau Road, Auckland 10, New Zealand

First published as *The Lonely Girl* by Jonathan Cape in 1962
Published as *Girl with Green Eyes* in Penguin Books 1964
Reprinted 1964 (twice), 1965, 1966, 1967, 1968 (twice), 1970,
1971, 1972, 1974, 1975, 1976, 1977, 1978, 1980, 1981, 1982, 1983, 1984,
1985, 1986, 1987

Made and printed in Great Britain by
Hazell Watson & Viney Limited,
Member of the BPCC Group,
Aylesbury, Bucks
Set in Linotype Georgian

For

ERNEST GÉBLER

Chapter One

It was a wet afternoon in October, as I copied out the September accounts from the big grey ledger. I worked in a grocery shop in the north of Dublin and had been there for two years.

My employer and his wife were country people; like myself. They were kind but they liked me to work hard and promised me a rise in the new year. Little did I know that I would be gone by then, to a different life.

Because of the rain, not many customers came in and out, so I wrote the bills quickly and then got on with my reading. I had a book hidden in the ledger, so that I could read without fear of being caught.

It was a beautiful book, but sad. It was called *Tender is the Night*. I skipped half of the words in my anxiety to read it quickly, because I wanted to know if the man would leave the woman or not. All the nicest men were in books – the strange, complex, romantic men; the ones I admired most.

I knew no one like that except Mr Gentleman; and I had not seen him for two years. He was only a shadow now and I remembered him the way one remembers a nice dress that one has grown out of.

At half four I put on the lights. The shop looked shabbier in artificial light too, the shelves were dusty and the ceiling hadn't been painted since I went there. It was full of cracks. I looked in the mirror to see how my hair was. We were going somewhere that night, my friend Baba and me. My face in the mirror looked round and smooth. I sucked my cheeks in, to make them thinner. I longed to be thin, like Baba.

'You look like you were going to have a child,' Baba said to me the night before, when I was in my nightgown.

'You're raving,' I said to her. Even the thought of such a thing worried me. Baba was always teasing me, although she knew I'd never done more than kiss Mr Gentleman.

'It happens to country mopes like you, soon as you dance with a fellow,' Baba said, as she held an imaginary man in her arms and waltzed between the two iron beds. Then she burst into one of her mad laughs and poured gin into the transparent plastic tooth-mugs on the bedside table.

Lately Baba had taken to carrying a baby gin in her handbag. We didn't like the taste of gin and tonic so much, but we loved the look of it, we loved its cool blue complexion as we sprawled on our hard beds, drinking and pretending to be fast.

Baba had come back to Joanna's boarding-house from the sanatorium and it was like the old days except that neither of us had men. We had dates of course – no steady men – but dates are risky.

Only the Sunday before Baba had a date with a man who sold cosmetics. He came to collect her in a car painted all over with slogans: 'Give her pink satin', 'Lovely pink satin for that schoolgirl bloom'. It was a blue, flashy car and the slogans were in silver. Baba heard him honk and she looked out to see what kind of car he had.

'Oh Holy God! I'm not going out in *that* circus wagon. Go down and tell him I'm having a haemmoridge.'

I hated the word haemmoridge, it was one of her new words to sound tough. I went down and told him that she had a headache.

'Would you like to come instead?'

I said no.

On the back seat there were advertisement cards and little sample bottles of 'pink satin face lotion', packed in boxes. I thought he might offer me a sample but he didn't.

'Sure you wouldn't like to see a show?'

I said that I couldn't.

Without another word he started up the car, and backed out of the cul-de-sac.

'He was very disappointed,' I said when I got back upstairs.

'That'll shake him. Feck any samples? I could do with a bit of sun-tan stuff for my legs.'

'How could I take samples with him sitting there in the car?'

'Distract him. Get him interested in your bust or the sunset or something.'

Baba is unreasonable. She thinks people are more stupid than they are. Those flashy fellows who sell things and own shops, they can probably count and add up.

'He hardly spoke two words,' I said.

'Oh the silent type!' Baba said, making a long face. 'You can imagine what an evening with him would be like! Get your mink on, we're going to a hop,' and I put on a light dress and we went down town to a Sunday-night dance.

'Don't take cigarettes from those Indian fellows with turbans; they might be doped,' Baba said.

There was a rumour that two girls were doped and brought up the Dublin mountains the week before.

Doped cigarettes! We didn't even get asked up for one dance; there wasn't enough men. We could have danced with each other but Baba said that was the end. So we just sat there, rubbing the goose-flesh off our arms and passing remarks about the men who stood at one end of the hall, sizing up the various girls who sat, waiting, on long stools. They never asked a girl to dance, until the music started up, and then they seemed to pick girls who were near. We moved down to that end of the hall, but had no luck there either.

Baba said that we ought never go to a hop again; she said that we'd have to meet new people, diplomats and people like that.

It was my constant wish. Some mornings I used to get up, convinced that I would meet a new, wonderful man. I used to make my face up specially and take short breaths to prepare myself for the excitement of it. But I never met anyone except customers, or students that Baba knew.

I thought of all this in the shop as I gummed red stickers on any bills which were due for over three months and addressed them hurriedly. We never posted bills, because Mrs Burns said it was cheaper to have Willie, the messenger boy, deliver them. Just then he came in, shaking rain from his sou'wester.

'Where were you?'

'Nowhere.'

As usual at that time of evening, he and I had a snack, before the shop got busy. We ate broken biscuits, raisins, dried prunes, and some cherries. His hands were blue and red with cold.

'Do you like them, Will?' I said, as he made a face at my new white shoes. The toes were so long that I had to walk sideways going upstairs. I put them on because Baba and I were going to a wine-tasting reception that night. We read about it in the papers and Baba said that we'd crash it. We had crashed two other functions – a fashion show and a private showing of a travel film of Ireland. (All lies, about dark-haired girls roaming around Connemara in red petti-coats. No wonder they had to show it in private.)

At half five, customers began to flock in on their way from work, and around six Mrs Burns came out, to let me go off.

'Very stuffy here,' she said to Willie. A hint to mean that we shouldn't have the oil heater on. Stuffy! There were draughts everywhere and a great division between the floor and the wainscoting.

I made my face up in the hall and put on rouge, eye-shadow, and lashings of ashes-of-roses perfume. The very name ashes-of-roses made me feel alluring. Willie sneaked me in a good sugar bag, so that I could bring my shoes in the bag, and wear my wellingtons. The gutters were over-flowing outside, and rain beat against the skylight in the upstairs hall.

'Don't do anything I wouldn't do,' he said, as he let me out by the hall door and whistled as I ran to the bus shelter a few yards down the road. It was raining madly.

The bus was empty, as there were very few people going down to the centre of the city at that hour of evening. It was too early for the pictures. There were toffee papers and cigarette packets on the floor and the bus had a sweaty smell. It was a poor neighbourhood.

I read a paper which I found on the seat beside me. There was a long article by a priest, telling how he'd been tortured in China. I knew a lot about that sort of thing, because in the convent where I went to school the nun used to read those stories to us on Saturday nights. As a treat she used to read a paper called *The Standard*. It was full of stories about priests' toe-nails being pulled off and nuns shut up in dark rooms with rats.

I almost missed my stop, because I had been engrossed in this long article by the Irish priest.

Baba was waiting for me outside the hotel. She looked like something off a Christmas tree. She had a new fur muff and her hair-set was held in place with lacquer.

'Mother o' God where are you off to in your wellingtons?' she asked.

I looked down at my feet and realized with desolation that I'd left my shoes on the bus.

There was nothing for it but to cross the road and wait for the bus on its return journey. It was an unsheltered bus-stop and Baba's hair style got flattened. Then, to make everything worse, my shoes were not on the bus and there was a different conductor. He said that the other conductor must have handed them in to the lost property office on the way to his tea.

'Call there any time after ten in the morning,' he said, and when Baba heard that, she said, 'Turalu,' and ran across the road back to the hotel. I followed, dispiritedly.

We had trouble getting in to the banquet room, even though Baba told the girl at the entrance door that we were journalists. She rooted in her bag for the invitation cards and said that she must have forgotten them. She said they were pink cards edged with gold. She knew because the girl at the door held a pile of them in her hand and flicked their gold edges impatiently. Baba's hands trembled as she searched, and her cheeks looked flushed. The two spots of rouge on her cheekbones had been washed unevenly by the rain.

'What paper do you represent?' the girl asked. A small queue had gathered behind us.

'*Woman's Night*,' Baba said. It was what she planned to say. There is no such magazine.

'Go ahead,' the girl said grudgingly, and we went in.

As we walked across the polished floor, my rubber boots squeaked loudly and I imagined that everyone was staring at me. It was a very rich room – chandeliers alight, dusky-blue, velvet curtains drawn across, and dance music playing softly.

Baba saw our friend Tod Mead and went towards him. He was a public relations officer who worked for a big wool company and we had met him at a fashion show a few weeks before. He took us for coffee then and tried to get off with Baba. He affected a casual world-weary manner, but it was only put on, because he ate loads of bread and jam. We knew he was married but we hadn't met his wife.

'Tod!' Baba hobbled over to him on her high heels. He kissed her hand and introduced us to the two people with him. One was a lady journalist in a big black hat and the other a strange man with a sallow face. His name was Eugene Gaillard. He said 'Pleased to meet you', but he didn't look very pleased. He had a sad face and Tod told us that he was a film director. Baba began to smirk and show her dimples and the gold tooth, all at once.

'He made so and so,' Tod said, mentioning a picture I'd never heard of.

'A classic documentary, a classic,' the lady journalist said.

Mr Gaillard looked at her earnestly, and said, 'Yes, really splendid; shatteringly realistic poverty.' His long face had an odd expression of contempt as he spoke.

'What are you doing now?' she asked.

'I've become a farmer,' he told her.

'A squire,' Tod corrected.

The lady journalist suggested that she go out there some day and do an article on him. She was nicely dressed and reeked of perfume but she was over fifty.

'We might as well get some red ink,' Baba told me. She was disappointed when neither of the men had offered to get it for her. I followed her across towards the long row of tables which were placed end to end along the length of the room. There were white cloths on each table and waiters stood behind, pouring half glasses of red and white wine.

'They weren't very pally,' Baba said.

Their voices reached me and I heard Tod say, 'That's the literary fat girl I was telling you about.'

'Which one?' Eugene Gaillard asked, idly.

'Long hair and rubber boots,' Tod said, and I heard him laughing.

I ran and got myself a drink. There were plates of water biscuits but I couldn't reach them and I felt hungry, having had no tea.

'Literary fat girl!' It really stabbed me.

'Your fashions are original – rubber boots and a feather hat,' Eugene said behind my back, and I knew his soft voice without even turning round to look at him.

'You brave coward,' he said. He was tall, about the same height as my father.

'It's nothing to laugh at – I lost my shoes,' I said.

'But it is so original, to come in your rubber boots. You could start a whole trend with that kind of thing. Have you heard of the men who can only make love to girls in their plastic macs?'

'I haven't heard,' I said sadly, ashamed at knowing so little.

'Tell me about you,' he said, and I felt suddenly at home with him, I don't know why. He wasn't like anyone I knew, his face was long and had a grey colour. It reminded me of a saint's face carved out of grey stone which I saw in the church every Sunday.

'Who are you, what do you do?' he asked, but when he saw that I was shy, he began to talk himself. He said that he had come because he met Tod Mead in Grafton Street and Tod dragged him along.

'I came for the scenery – not the wine,' he said, looking round at the gilt wall-brackets, the plush curtains, and at a tall, intense woman with black earrings, who stood alone near the window. If only I could say something interesting to him.

'What's the difference between white wine and red wine?' I asked. He wasn't drinking.

'One is red and one is white,' he laughed.

But Baba came along, with the white muff and a bunch of potato crisps.

'Has Mary of the Sorrows been telling you a lot of drip about her awful childhood?' She meant me.

'Everything. From the very beginning,' he said.

Baba started to frown, then quickly gave one of her big false laughs and moved her hands up and down in front of her eyes. 'What's that?' she asked. She did it three times but he could not guess it.

'Past your eyes – milk – pasteurized milk. Ha, ha, ha.' She told Eugene Gaillard that she worked on the lonely-hearts' column of *Woman's Night* and had a great time reading hilarious letters.

'Only yesterday,' she ran on, 'I had a letter from a poor woman in Ballinasloe, who said, "Dear Madam, my husband makes love to me on Sunday nights and I find this very inconvenient as I have a big wash on Mondays and am dog tired. What can I do without hurting my husband's feelings?"

'I told Mrs Ballinasloe,' Baba said, ' "Wash on Tuesdays." ' She threw her little hands out to emphasize the simple way she dealt with life's problems, and he laughed obligingly.

'Baba is a funny girl,' he said to me, still smiling. As if I ought to rejoice! It was my joke. I read it in a magazine one day when I had to wait two hours in the dental hospital to have a tooth filled. I read it and came home and told Baba; and after that she told it to everyone. Baba had got so smart in the last year – she knew about different wines, and had taken up fencing. She said that the fencing class was full of women in trousers asking her home for cocoa.

Just then Tod Mead came up waving an empty glass.

'The drink is running out, why don't we all go somewhere?' he said to Eugene.

'Those are two nice girls you found,' Eugene said, and Baba began to hum, 'Nice people with nice manners that have got no money at all ...'

'All right,' Eugene said. 'We'll have dinner.'

On the way out, Baba ordered twelve bottles of hock to be sent C.O.D. to Joanna – our landlady. The idea was that, having tasted the wine, people would order some. I knew that Joanna would have a fit over it.

'Who is Joanna?' Eugene asked, as we moved towards the door. We waved to the lady journalist and one or two other people.

'I'll tell you all about her at dinner,' Baba said.

My elbows touched his; and I had that paralysing sensation in my legs which I hadn't felt since I'd parted from Mr Gentleman.

Chapter Two

WE had dinner in the hotel. Eugene left word with one of the page-boys that he would be in the dining-room if there should be a telephone call for him. All through dinner I felt anxious and wished that he would be called, so that he could go away and then come back to us. Needless to say, I thought it must be a woman.

We had thin soup, lamb cutlets coated in breadcrumbs, and french fried potatoes. He didn't eat much. He had a habit of pulling his sleeves down over his wrists. His wrists and hands were hairy. Black, luxuriant hairs. Baba never stopped talking. I didn't say much, I couldn't balance the pleasure of seeing him and talking at the same moment. He said that I had a face like the girl on the Irish pound note.

'I never had a pound note long enough to look at it,' Baba said.

'You look at it next time,' he said, and then the waiter came over and refilled our glasses with wine. I felt very happy and the food was nice.

'Mister Gay-Lord, Mister Gay-Lord,' a page-boy called. My heart jumped with pain and relief.

'You, you, you,' I said to him, and Baba kicked me to stop being so excited and making a fool of myself. He excused himself and went out very slowly.

He looked nice from the back: tall and lean, with a bald patch on the very top of his head.

'He's a smasher,' Baba said.

'Rich!' Tod added, and smiled peculiarly. He was jealous of something, I felt.

'He's a good catch,' Baba said.

'Har, har, har,' Tod said, but I knew by the look in his small blue eyes that he withheld something. It occurred to me that maybe Eugene was engaged or married.

When he came back we tried to pretend that we had not been discussing him.

'I'm very sorry,' he said, 'but I shall have to leave you. I have to go out to the airport to see someone off, to America. It's important, otherwise I would not do this.'

My heart sank and Baba dropped her spoon full of ice-cream back on the glass dish. I think she said 'Oh'.

Tod stood up, very worried, thinking, I suppose, that he might have to pay the bill.

'Actually I have to be getting along myself, Eugene. Little old Sally is expecting me in for tea,' and he got red around the collar as he spoke. 'I'll run you out to the airport, it's on my way.'

I nearly died, thinking that Baba and I might have to pay for the dinner by washing up for the next ten or eleven years; but Eugene paid it all right.

He shook hands, apologized, and left us there to drink a liqueur with our coffee. The waiters looked puzzled – the men's departure and my rubber boots made them think we were very eccentric.

'Jesus, just our luck,' Baba said when they had gone.

'I suppose lots of women have *died* for him,' I said.

'He's classy,' she said. 'I'd like to get going with him.'

All I wondered was, would we ever see him again.

'We could write to him,' Baba said. 'You could draft a letter and I'd sign it.'

'Saying what?'

'I don't know.' She shrugged, and read the menu. There was a notice printed at the bottom of the menu which said that clients could inspect the kitchen if they wished.

'Let's do it for gas,' Baba said.

'No.' I had no inclination to do anything but just sit there and sip coffee and beckon to the puzzled waiter to bring more when my cup was empty. Would we see him again, ever?'

'Hold on for your life,' Baba said at last, 'I have a marvellous idea.' She suggested that we should buy tickets for a dress-dance and invite him. She said that we could pretend that we got the tickets for nothing, or had won them at a raffle or something.

'We'll get you a partner; Tod or The Body or something.'

The Body was a friend of hers who trained greyhounds in Blanchardstown. His real name was Bertie Counihan but we nicknamed him The Body because he hardly ever washed. He said washing harmed the skin. He was big and broad-shouldered with black curly hair and a happy, reddish face.

We did exactly as Baba planned. At the end of the week (when I got paid) we bought four tickets for a grocers' dance which was to be held in Cleary's ballroom in October. Then we got Eugene's address from Tod and drafted a letter to him. Neither of us paid Joanna that week.

We waited anxiously for his reply, and when it came I nearly cried. He wrote and told Baba that he hadn't danced for years and feared that he would be dull company at such a jolly outing. Very politely, he declined.

'Christ, we're done for,' Baba said as she handed me the letter. His handwriting was difficult to make out.

'Oh God!' I said, more disappointed than I had expected to be. All my hopes had hinged on that dance, on seeing him again.

'What a life,' I said. We had the tickets but no men, no money, no dance dresses.

'We'll have to go, we can't bloody well let those tickets go to waste,' Baba said.

'We've no fur coat,' I said. Often when we went down town at night to look at people going in to dress-dances, we saw that most of the women had fur coats, or fur stoles over their long dresses.

'We'll hire dresses from that hire place in Dame Street,' Baba said.

'It's morbid.'

'It's twice as morbid to sit in this dump with four bloody tickets going to waste on the mantelshelf.'

'We've no money to hire dresses,' I said, pleased at such an easy solution to the whole thing. I had no interest in going now.

'We'll sell our bodies to the College of Surgeons!' she said. 'They come and collect when you're dead, and the students put you on a table, with no clothes, and take you to pieces.'

I said that she couldn't be serious. She said she'd do anything for a few bob.

I thought of him out there in his large house, unaware of the misery he had caused us. I imagined a brown leather-topped desk, with numerous pens and pencils, and two colours of ink in special glass bottles.

'You can steal in that joint where you work, they're underpaying you,' Baba said.

'It's a sin.'

'It's not a sin. Aquinas says you can steal from an employer if he underpays you.'

'Who's Aquinas?'

'I don't know, but he's something in the Church.'

Finally we managed it. We borrowed five and ten shilling amounts from various people and hired long dresses and silver dance shoes. Baba's dress was white net and mine a lurid purple. It was the only one they had which fitted me.

We got quite excited on the evening of the dance. We bought half a pound of scented bath crystals and bathed in the same water. I put pancake on Baba's back to hide her spots and she put pancake on mine and hooked my dress up. I could scarcely breathe in it, it was so tight.

'Bee-beep, bee-beep,' The Body's horn hooted at nine o'clock, and we went down holding our dresses up so that the tails would not get dirty. He had come in the blue van, which he uses to take greyhounds to the veterinary surgeon and such places. It smelled of that kind of life.

Then we collected Eamonn White, a chemist's apprentice who was to be my partner for the night. He was a nice boy except that he kept saying 'great gas', 'great style', 'great fun', 'great van', 'great gas', all the time.

On the way down we stopped at a pub in North Frederick Street to have a few drinks. The customers stared at Baba and me, in our long tatty dresses with tweed coats over our shoulders. Baba was miserable because she hadn't been able to borrow a fur.

'Name your poison,' The Body said, clapping Eamonn on the back.

Eamonn was a Pioneer, and wore a total abstinence badge

which he must have transferred from the lapel of his ordinary suit to his hired black suit. He said he'd have tomato juice and The Body was very offended by this, but Baba said *we'd* have large ones to make up for it.

I danced with Eamonn for most of the night, because he was my partner. 'Great gas, great gas,' he kept saying. It was his first dress-dance. He marvelled at the slipperiness of the floor, the pink lighting, two bands, paper roses hanging from the ceiling, and tables beautifully laid for supper. My frock was strapless and his warm, pink hands seemed to be on my bare back all night. He had blond hair and blond eyelashes and the pinkness of his skin reminded me of young pigs at home.

The Body was different:

'You're a noble woman,' he said to me later as I danced with him in my hired silver shoes and wondered if I would ever waltz with Eugene Gaillard. I was glad that he hadn't come, because he would have seen me in my foolish dusty dress, saying foolish tittery things to amuse the others.

We drank wine with our supper and then as usual The Body took too much and got obstreperous and started to shout. He rolled the menu up and bellowed through it:

'Up the Republic, Up Noel Browne, Up Castro, Up me.'

Eamonn was frightened and left the table. He never returned. Being a Pioneer, he did not understand the happy madness which drink could induce in others.

At two o'clock, just when everybody was getting very merry and the band players had begun to toss paper hats around, Baba and I brought The Body home. He was too drunk to drive so we left his blue van there and hired a taxi. We had no idea where he lived. It's funny that we should have known him for a year but did not know where he lived. Dublin is like that. We knew his local pub but not his house. We brought him home and put him on the horsehair sofa in Joanna's drawing-room.

'Baba, Caithleen, I wan't'tell you something, you're two noble women, two noble women, and Parnell was a proud man as proud as trod the ground, and a proud man's a lovely man, so pass the bottle round. What about a little drink, waiter, waiter ...' He waved a pound note in the air, still thinking he was at the dance.

'Have a sleep,' Baba said, and she put out the light. His voice faded with it and within a minute he was breathing heavily.

We knew that we would have to be up at half six to get The Body out of the house before Joanna's alarm went off at seven.

'We've just three hours' sleep,' Baba said, as she unhooked my dress and helped me out of it. A new boned brassière had made red welts on my skin.

'We'll sue,' she said when she saw the welts. We went to bed without washing our faces, and when I wakened the pancake make-up felt like mud on my face.

'Oh God,' I said to Baba, as I heard The Body shouting downstairs: 'Girls, les girls, there's no "Gents", there's no bloody service here – where do I *go*?'

We both ran out to the landing to shut him up but Joanna had got there before us.

'Jesus meets his afflicted mother,' The Body said as Joanna came down the stairs towards him in her big red nightdress, with her grey hair in a plait down her back.

'Thief, thief,' she shouted, and before we even knew it she had pressed the button of the small fire-extinguisher that was fixed to the wall at the end of the stairs and trained the liquid on him.

'I want police,' she yelled, and he was struggling to explain things to her but he couldn't make himself heard.

'Stop that bloody thing, he's our friend,' Baba said, running downstairs.

The Body was covered with white, sticky liquid which looked like hair shampoo, and his dress-shirt was drenched. His wet hair fell over his face in oily curls.

'He's our friend,' Baba said, sadly. 'God protect us from our friends.'

'You call him a friend, hah?' Joanna said. He put his hand on the banister and proceeded to go upstairs. Joanna blocked the way.

'I want to see a man about a dog,' he said, wiping the wet off his face with a handkerchief.

'What dog? I have no dog, I say,' she shouted, but he pushed past her.

'Gustav, Gustav,' she called, but I knew that cowardly Gustav would not come out.

'Jesus falls the first time,' The Body chanted as he tripped on a tear in the brown linoleum.

Baba ran to him and got him up. A little later we helped him into the bathroom to wipe the stuff off his hair and face.

'Who's that cow out there, who the hell is she?' he asked as he looked into the bathroom mirror and saw his wild, bloodshot eyes and oily ringlets. He beamed when he saw himself:

'Look at that jaw-line, look at it, Baba, Caithleen; I should have been a film star or a boxer,' he said. 'Me and Jack Doyle and Movita. Oh Movita, oh Movita, you're the lady with the mystic smile. ... Who's that cow out there? ...'

Joanna rapped on the bathroom door. 'You leave my house. I come from good Austrian family, my brathers doctors and Civil Service.'

'Balls,' he said.

'What ball you say?'

Baba stuffed the white towel over his mouth to shut him up and through it he murmured: 'Veronica wipes the face of Jesus. ...'

'Come on, we'll dance down the road,' Baba said, and somehow she got him out of the house and up to the bus-stop. By then it was half seven.

Joanna found twelve eggs in a pot on the gas stove. The Body had apparently been boiling eggs and the water had boiled off. She flew into a fresh rage when she saw that the saucepan had got burnt.

'You leave my house this day,' she said to us. 'My good, best saucepan. One dozen country eggs for nogg for Gustav and my fire-extinguisher. I am not spending all this money on frivolous. I tell you this if I go poor I am better dead.' She almost cried as she held the pot of brown eggs for us to see.

'All right,' Baba said. 'We'll leave.' She proceeded to go

upstairs, but Joanna caught the cord of her dressing-gown.

'You cannot leave me, eh? I am gutt to you like a mother. I stitch your clothes and your ironing.'

'We're leaving,' Baba said.

'Oh please.' There were tears in Joanna's eyes by now.

'We'll think it over,' Baba said, and then Joanna caught her winking at me, so that she knew we would not leave. She got abusive again.

All I wanted was to go back to bed, but it was morning and I had to dress myself and face the day.

Chapter Three

LUCKILY for me, that day was Wednesday and (as usual)
the shop closed in the afternoon.

I took the dance dresses and shoes back to the hire shop,
and then collected photos of myself which had been taken
by a street photographer the previous Wednesday. I felt
tired and nervous from the short sleep and the mixture of
drinks which we had had. I wished that I were rich and
could drink coffee all afternoon or buy new clothes to cheer
myself up.

As usual I went to the bookshop at the bottom of Dawson
Street where I had a free read every week. I read twenty-
eight pages of *The Charwoman's Daughter* without being
disturbed, and then came out, as I had an appointment to
meet Baba in O'Connell Street.

Coming down the stone steps from the bookshop I met
him, point-blank. I saw him in that instant before he saw
me and I was so astonished that I almost ran away.

'Oh you!' he said as he looked up in surprise. He must
have forgotten my name.

'Mr Gaillard, hello,' I said, trying to conceal my excitement. In daylight his face looked different – longer and
more melancholy. A shower of rain had brought us together. He came up to shelter in the porch and I stood in
with him. My body became as jelly just from standing close
to him, smelling his nice smell. I kept staring down at the
long, absurd toe of my white shoe which had got blackened
from rain and wear.

'What have you been doing since, besides going to
dances?' he said.

'Yes, we went last night, it was marvellous, a marvellous
band and supper and everything.' Oh God, I thought, I
am as dull as old dishwater. Why can't I say something exciting, why can't I tell him what I feel about
him?

'The rain sparkles on the brown pavement,' I said in a false fit of eloquence.

'Sparkles?' he said, and smiled curiously.

'Yes, it's a nice word.'

'Indeed.' He nodded. I felt that he was bored and I prayed that there would be a deluge and that we would have to stay there for ever. I imagined the water rising inch by inch, covering the road, the pavement, the steps, our ankles, our legs, our bodies, drawing us together as in a dream, all other life cut off from us.

'It's getting worse,' I said, pointing to a black cloud that hung over the darkening city of Dublin.

'It's only a shower,' he said, shattering all my mad hopes. 'What about a cup of tea, would you like some tea?' he asked.

'I'd love it.' And in the rain we crossed the road to a tea-shop.

I forget what we talked about. I remember being speechless with happiness and feeling that God, or someone, had brought us together. I ate three cakes; he pressed me to have a fourth but I didn't, in case it was vulgar. It was then he asked my name. So he *had* forgotten it.

'Tell me, what do you read?' he asked. He had a habit of smiling whenever I caught his eye, and though his eyes were sad he smiled nicely.

'Chekhov and James Joyce and James Stephens, and ...' I stopped suddenly in case he should think that I was showing off.

'I must loan you a book some time,' he said.

Some time? When is some time, I thought as I looked at the tea-leaves in the bottom of his cup. I poured him a second cup, through the little strainer which the waitress had belatedly brought. The tea dripped very slowly through the fine strainer.

'Oh that fiddle-faddle,' he said, so we discarded the strainer and left it on a side plate to drip.

I knew that Baba would be waiting and that I should go to her, but I could not stand up and leave him. I loved his long, sad face and his strong hands.

'I often wonder what young girls like you think. What *do* you think of?' he asked, after he had been looking steadily at me for a few seconds.

I think about you, I thought, and blushed a bit. To him, I said in a dull stupid voice, 'I don't think very much really; I think about getting new clothes or going on my holidays or what we'll have for lunch.'

It seems to me now that he sighed and that I tittered to hide my embarrassment and told him that some girls thought of marrying rich men, and one I knew of, thought only of her hair; she washed it every night and measured how much it grew in a week and it was half way down her back like a golden cape. But it gave her no pleasure because she worried about it too much.

'Where do you go on holiday?' he asked, and I sighed, because I longed to stay in a hotel and have breakfast in bed. I never had breakfast in bed, except once or twice in the convent when I was sick, and then there was a cup of hot senna which I had to drink down first. Sister Margaret always stood there while you drank the hot senna, telling you that it was good for the soul as well as the body.

'I go home.'

'Where's home?'

I told him.

My father had gone back from the gate-lodge to our own house and he lived there with my aunt. I described it as best I could.

'You like your home?'

'There's a lot of trees. It's lonesome.'

'I like trees,' he said. 'I sow them all the time – I've got thousands of trees.'

'Have you?' I said. I felt that he was bluffing and I don't like bluffing.

He looked at his watch and inevitably he had to go.

'I'm sorry, but I was to see somebody at four.'

'I'm sorry for keeping you,' I said as we stood up. He paid the bill and took his corduroy cap off the mahogany hat-rack inside the door.

'Thank you. A pleasant encounter,' he said as we stood

26

on the stone step. I thanked him, he raised his cap and went away from me. I watched him go. I saw him as a dark-faced God turning his back on me. I put out my hand to recall him and caught only the rain. I felt that it would rain for ever, noiselessly. The buses were full, as it was after five o'clock, and Baba was furious when I got there an hour late.

'Blithering eejit,' she said. I did not tell her that I had met him.

We had coffee, and later, as arranged, The Body came. We had more coffee, he apologized for everything and gave us five pounds to cover the cost of the dance tickets. Then he took us by taxi to the greyhound track at Harold's Cross.

On the following Wednesday I went to Dawson Street and stood outside the bookshop for two hours, but Eugene Gaillard did not come, nor the next Wednesday nor the one following.

I waited for four Wednesdays and walked around searching for a sight of him, in his long black coat with the astrakhan collar. I imagined him sitting in Robert's café looking at dark-haired girls. He said that he liked dark hair and dark eyes and very pale skin; he said these things had a quietness which he liked. I sat in Robert's too and thought of him – he didn't eat potatoes and he drank water with his dinner, so I took to drinking water with my meals. Tap-water in Joanna's was never cold or sparkling the way you imagine water should be, but it was nice to do something that he did.

I waited and walked around, certain that I would meet him, and the wild hope made my spirits soar. I could almost smell him, see the black hairs on his hands, his proud walk. But for a whole month I did not see him. Once I saw his car parked in Molesworth Street and I waited for ages in the doorway of a wool shop which had closed down. Finally the hunger drove me home, and next day I wrote to him and asked him to have tea with me the following Wednesday.

The week went round and I came to the restaurant feeling mortified. He was there all right, sitting at a table inside the door, reading a paper.

27

'Caithleen,' he said when I came in. It was the first time he ever said my name.

'Hello,' I said, trembling, and wondered if I ought to apologize for having written. I sat down in my old coat with a new blue chiffon scarf around my neck.

'Take off your coat,' he said, and I slipped it off and let it hang on the back of the chair.

'I always forget how pretty you are, until I see you again,' he said as he looked carefully at my face. 'Ah, the bloom of you, I love your North-Circular-Road-Bicycle-Riding-Cheeks.'

My cheeks were always pink no matter how much powder I used. He ordered sandwiches, cakes, scones, and biscuits. I worried, fearing that I would have to pay the bill, being as I had invited him and I had only ten shillings in my purse. He put his elbows on the table, his fist under his chin. In repose his eyelids were lowered partly, and when he made the effort of raising them you were surprised by the tender expression in his great brown eyes. His face was hard and formidable but his eyes were compassionate.

'Well?' he said, smiling up at me. 'So here we are.' There was a spot of dried blood on his jaw where he had cut himself shaving.

'I hope you didn't mind coming,' I said.

'No, I didn't mind. I was very happy in fact, I thought of you on and off during the past few weeks.'

'Five,' I said, hastily.

'Five what?'

'Five weeks. You know me five weeks.' He laughed, and asked if I kept a diary, and I thought to myself, he's a sly one.

'Tell me more about your social life?' he asked as I bit into a cream slice and then licked my lips clean.

'I thought I'd see you,' I said, openly.

'I know, but ...' He halted, and played with the sugar-tongs. 'You see, it's difficult, I'll be quite honest, I don't want to get involved. It must be my natural, puritan caution, because Baba and you are two lovely girls, and I'm a man more than old enough to know better.'

Keep Baba out of this, I thought as I said to him 'What do you mean "involved"?' – my voice choked, my heart pounding.

'You are a nice girl,' he said, and he put his hand across and petted my wrist, and I asked then if we could have tea once in a while.

'We're having tea now,' he said, nodding towards the silver pot. 'We might even have dinner.'

'Dinner!'

'Dinner!' he said, mimicking my breathless, surprised voice.

We had dinner that evening and afterwards we drove out to Clontarf and walked down by the Bull Wall, as it was a mild, misty November night. He held my hand; he did not squeeze my fingers or plait them in his, he just held my hand very naturally, the way you'd hold a child's hand or your mother's.

He talked about America, where he had lived for some years. He had lived in New York and in Hollywood.

The sea was calm, the waves breaking calmly over the boulders and a strong, unpleasant smell of ozone in the air. I could not tell whether the tide was coming in or going out. It is always hard to tell at first.

'It's going out,' he said; and I believed him. I believed everything he said.

Walking down over the concrete pier we shared a cigarette. There were fog-horns blowing out at sea and a chain of lights across the harbour that curved like a bright necklace, beyond the mist. Lighthouses blinked and signalled on all sides and I loved watching the rhythm of their flashes, blinking to ships in the lonely sea. They made me think of all the people in the world, waiting for all the other people to come to them. For once I was not lonely, because I was with someone that I wanted to be with. We walked to the end of the pier, and looked at the rocks and the pools and the straps of seaweed on everything. He talked about another sea – the far-away Pacific.

'I used to drive out there on week-days, when things became too much in Los Angeles. The sky is always blue in

California, a piercing blue, and the pavements hot, and the tanned, predatory faces booming out their hearty nothings. I like rain and isolation. . . .' He spoke very quietly, using his hands in gestures all the time. I could just see the outline of his face, greenish from moonlight and the glow of the tipped cigarette which we shared.

'And you drove out there?' I said, hoping that accidentally, or otherwise, he would tell me something of his personal life.

'I drove out there and walked over this great, white, Pacific beach, edged so delicately with tar-oil on the one side and oil-derricks on the other. I kicked the empty beer cans and wanted to go home.'

I thought it odd that no other people occurred in his reminiscences. It was only the place he described, the white beach, the beer cans, the ripe and rotting oranges along the roadside.

'You always talk of places as if only *you* had been in them,' I said.

'Yes, I was born to be a monk.'

'But you're not a Catholic,' I said immediately.

He laughed loudly. It was strangely disturbing to hear his laugh above the noise of the washing waves and the anxious breathing of two people who lay between the rocks, making love. He said that Catholics were the most opinionated people on earth – their self-mania, he said, frightened him.

At the end of the pier we looked down at the water as it lapped against the concrete wall and he told me that he had won cups and medals for swimming when he was a boy. He had lived most of his life in Dublin, with his mother, and had gone to work at twelve or thirteen. His father had left them when he was a small boy, and as a child he had combed the beaches looking for scrap.

'I found shillings often,' he said. 'I've always been lucky, I've always found things. I've even found you with your large, lemur eyes. D'you know what a lemur is?'

'Yes,' I lied, and then terrified that he might ask, I talked rapidly about something else.

Driving me home he said:

'It's a long time since I've spent an evening with such a nice girl.'

'Go on,' I said, looking at his fine profile and longing to know of all the other women he had been with and their perfume and what they said and how it had ended. He said that up to the age of twenty-five while he was apprenticed to various trades – cinema operator, gardener, electrician – he could only afford to look at girls, the way one looks at flowers or boats in Dun-Laoghaire harbour.

'It's true,' he said, turning to smile at me.

The smile was nice and I moved nearer and touched with my cheek the cloth of his grey, hairy overcoat.

He did not kiss me that night.

Chapter Four

WE met three evenings a week, after that. In between he
wrote me postcards, and as time went on he wrote letters.
He called me Kate, as he said that Caithleen was too 'Kil-
tartan' for his liking – whatever that meant.

Each Monday, Wednesday, and Saturday he waited outside the shop for me in his car, and each time as I sat in
near him, I trembled with a fantastic happiness. Then one
night he stayed in a hotel in Harcourt Street and planned
to meet me at lunch-time next day in order to buy me a
coat. It was coming near Christmas-time, and anyhow my
old green coat was shabby. He bought me a grey astrakhan
with a red velvet collar, and a flared skirt.

'I'm stuck with you now,' he said as I walked around the
shop, while he surveyed the coat from behind. I wished that
he wouldn't scrutinize so much, because I have a stiff walk
and become ashamed when people look after me.

'It suits you,' he said, but I thought that it made me look
fatter.

We bought it. I asked the assistant to wrap up my old
one. She was very posh with moonlight dye in her hair and
a pale lavender shop-coat which buttoned right up to her
throat. Then he bought me six pairs of stockings and we
were given one free pair as a bonus. He said that it was
immoral to get a free pair just because we could afford six
pairs, but I was delighted.

I thought of Mama and of how she would love it, and I
knew that if she could she would come back from her cold
grave in the Shannon lake to avail herself of such a bar-
gain. She was drowned when I was fourteen. I felt guilty on
and off, because I was so happy with him and because I had
never seen my mother happy or laughing. Being in the posh
shop reminded me of her. A few weeks before she was
drowned, she and I went to Limerick for a day's shopping.
She had saved up egg money for several weeks, because

32

although we had a lot of land, we never had much ready cash; Dada drank a lot, and money was always owing – and also she sold off old hens to a man who came around buying feathers and junk. In Limerick she bought a lipstick. I remembered her trying the various shades on the back of her hand and debating for a long time before deciding on one. It was an orange-tinted lipstick in a black and gold case.

'My mother is dead,' I said to him as we waited for our change. I wanted to say something else, something that would convey the commonplace sacrifice of her life: of her with one shoulder permanently drooping from carrying buckets of hen food, of her keeping bars of chocolate under the bolster so that I could eat them in bed if I got frightened of Dada or of the wind.

'Your poor mother,' he said, 'I expect she was a good woman.'

We lunched in the restaurant off the shop and I worried about being late back to work.

As he followed me through a narrow, cobbled cul-de-sac towards where the car was parked, he said, 'You're like Anna Karenina in that coat.'

I thought she must be some girl-friend of his, or an actress.

Driving back, I said rashly, 'Would you like to come and have tea this evening, in the house where I stay?' Baba had been pestering me to invite him home to tea so that she could flirt with him.

He said he would, and promised to be there at seven.

As I hurried towards the shop he called after me, laughing, to take care of the new coat. I blew him a kiss.

'Your old bottom's getting fat,' he shouted. I nearly died. There were customers waiting around the door and they heard him.

When Mrs Burns wasn't looking I wrote a note to Joanna to ask if we could have something special for tea. It was Friday and always on Friday we had roly-poly pudding. We had the same things on the same successive days of each week. Joanna called it her 'New systematic'.

Willie took the note over and returned with Joanna's

reply on his blue, hungry lips. 'Mine Got, I am not spending any luxury for this rich man.'

I bought her a cake in the bakery two doors away. It was an expensive cake topped with shredded coconut. I sent it over along with a bag of biscuits and a sample jar of cranberry jelly. Willie came back and reported that she had put the cake in a tin, which meant that she had put it away for Christmas. Christmas was five weeks away. All afternoon my heart was bubbling with excitement; happiness, unhappiness. Twice I gave wrong change, and Mrs Burns asked me if it was my bad time. In the end I got so worked up that I hoped he wouldn't come at all. I could see his face all the time, and his grave eyes, and a vein in the side of his temple that stood out. Then I became terrified that once having seen where I lived, he would no longer ask me out.

Joanna's house was clean but shabby. It was a terraced, brick house, linoleumed from top to bottom. She had a strip of matting (which she got cheap) on the downstairs hall. The furniture was dark and heavy and the front room was stuffed with china dogs and ornaments and knick-knacks. There was a green rubber plant in a pot on the piano.

When I got home Baba was there, all dressed up. Joanna must have told her that he was coming. She wore her tartan slacks and a chunky cardigan back to front. The V-neck and the buttons were down her back.

As I went into the room I heard Joanna say, 'It is not good to the floor these girls with spiked shoes.'

Our stiletto heels had marked the linoleum.

'I have no other shoes,' Baba said in her brazen, go-to-hell voice.

'Mine Got, upstairs is full of shoes, under the beds, the dressing table, I see nothing but shoes, shoes, shoes.'

They both noticed my new coat.

'Where d'you feck it?' Baba asked.

'A new coat! Astrakhan,' Joanna said. And she touched the cuff with her hand and said, 'Rich, you are a rich girl. I had not a new coat since I left my own country nine years ago.' She held up nine fingers as if I didn't know numbers.

'You give me your old one, hah?' she said, grinning at me.

'What's for tea?' I asked. I had cycled home so quickly that my chest pained. He was due any minute.

'You ask me what's for tea! You know what is for tea,' Joanna said.

'But look, Joanna, he's awful special and rich and everything. He knows film stars, he met Joan Crawford, oh Joanna, please, please.' I exaggerated to impress her.

'Rich!' Joanna said, rolling the R of that word, her favourite word, the only poem she knew.

'I tell you this I am not rich. I am a poor woman but I come from good home, good respectable Austrian family, and driven out of my own country.'

'He's from around there too,' I said, hoping to soften her.

'Where?' she asked as if I had just insulted her.

'Bavaria or Rumania or some place,' I said.

'Is he a Jew, eh?' Her eyes narrowed. 'I do not like Jews, they are a little bit mean.'

'I don't know what he is, but he's not mean, honest,' I said, and I almost told her that he had bought the coat for me.

Baba, quick to deduce things, sang 'Where did you get that coat?' to the air of 'Where did you get that hat?'

'My father sent me the money,' I lied.

'Your aul fella is in the workhouse!' She had no brassière on, and you could see the shape of her nipples through the white jumper.

'What's for tea?' I asked again.

'Roly-poly pud,' Baba said. The sudden ring of the door-bell impinged on her high voice and I ran upstairs to put some powder on.

Baba let him in.

I put on a pale blue dress, because pale colours suit me. It had a silver, crystalline pattern like snow falling, and the neck was low. It was a summer dress but I wanted to look nice for him.

Outside the dining-room door I rubbed the goose-flesh on my arms and paused to hear what they were saying to him. I could hear his low voice, and Baba using his Christian name already. Awkwardly I went in.

'Hello,' he said, as he stood up to shake hands with me. Baba sat next to him, her elbow resting on the curved back of his chair. He looked very tall under the low ceiling and I was ashamed of the little room. It seemed more shabby with him in it; the lace curtains were grey from smoke, and the smiling china dogs on the sideboard looked idiotic.

'You found us easily enough?' I said, pretending not to be shy. It's funny that you're more shy with people in your own house. Out on the street I could talk to him, but in the house I was ashamed of something.

Joanna carried in the roly-poly pudding – wrapped in muslin – on a dish.

'Mine Got, *is*, is so hot,' she said, as she laid the plate down on a pile of home-made table mats which Gustav had cut from a spare piece of linoleum. She unwrapped the wet muslin.

'Hot cuisine,' Baba said to Eugene and winked. The pudding looked white and greasy; it reminded me of a corpse.

'My own, home-make,' Joanna said proudly. She cut the pudding into sections and as she cut it trickles of hot raspberry jam flowed on to the dish; then she respooned the jam back on to each portion.

'For my nice new guest,' she said, giving him the first helping. He declined it, saying that he never ate pastry.

'No, no, is no pastry,' Joanna said, 'good Austrian receipt.'

'The seeds of raspberry jam get stuck between my teeth,' he said, half joking.

'Take your teeth out, eh?' she suggested.

'They're my own teeth,' he laughed. 'Let's just have a nice cup of tea?'

'You not eat my food.' Her poor face looked hurt and she grinned stupidly at him.

'It's my stomach,' he explained. 'I've got a hole in it, in there,' and he put his hand over his black pullover and tapped his stomach. Earlier on he had asked Joanna's permission to take off his jacket. The black pullover suited him. It gave him a thin, religious look.

'Constipate?' Joanna asked. 'I have the bag upstairs brought with me from my own country, what d'you call, enema?'

'Holy God,' Baba said. 'Let him have his tea first.'

'It's just a pain I have,' Eugene told her, 'anxiety . . .'

'Anxiety – a rich man?' Joanna said. 'What anxiety can a rich man have?'

'The world,' he said.

'The world,' she shouted. 'You are a little bit mad I think.' Then, fearing that she had overstepped her place, she said, 'It is so terrible for your poor stomach, you poor man,' and she touched the bald patch in the centre of his head and petted it as if she had known him all her life. Within a minute she fetched dill pickles, salame, black olives, smoked ham and a dish of home-made macaroons.

'Oh goodie,' Baba said, cooing. She took a moist black olive and held it between her fingers while she kissed it.

'No, a mistake,' Joanna said, taking it back, 'these are special for Mr Eugene.'

'That's right, Joanna, we foreigners must stick together,' he said – but when she went out to make tea he made us a ham sandwich each.

'What made me think that girls ate delicately?' he said to the jam dish, and this set Baba off on one of her laughing fits. Baba had developed a new, loud laugh. She turned to Eugene and said:

'There's nothing I like so much as a cultivated man.'

He bowed from the waist and smiled at her.

Baba looked very nice that particular evening. She has a small, neat face with dark skin. Her eyes are small too, and shiny and very alert. They remind you of a bird, darting from one thing to another. Her thoughts also dart, and she gives the impression of having great energy.

'I used to know a girl like you once,' he said to her, and Baba just went on smiling.

'Good, best tea,' Joanna said as she came in with the silver teapot and a dented tin hot-water jug.

'Nice? Good? Eh?' she asked before he brought the cup to his lips.

'Breathtaking,' he said.

He inquired about her country, her family, and if she intended going back there. She answered with the long rigmarole about brothers and good family which Baba and I have heard five thousand times.

'Open the hootch,' Baba said to me, nodding towards the bottle of wine which Eugene had brought.

'She'll open it soon as she gets sentimental,' I said. Joanna was so busy talking that she did not hear us.

'She's at the height of her sentimental now, she's passed that slob bit about her slob brother changing her napkin when she was two and he was four,' Baba said.

'My brothers spent me a night at the opera ...' Joanna rambled on, then Baba tapped her elbow, and pointing to the wine, said:

'Give the man a drink.'

Joanna's face fell, she got confused, she said, 'You like tea, eh?'

'Yes,' he said, 'I don't drink wine really.'

'Wise man, I like you,' she beamed at him, and Baba sighed out loud.

'You must not marry a shop girl from Ireland,' Joanna said. 'You must marry somebody from your own country, a countess.' Joanna was so stupid that she didn't think I'd mind her saying a thing like that. I singed the hair on her bare arms with my cigarette.

'Mine Got, you are burning me.' She jumped up.

'Sorry.'

Then, Gianni, the other lodger, came in and in the confusion of introducing Eugene, I did not have to apologize any further.

When Joanna stood up to get his cup and saucer she hid the wine behind one of the china dogs.

'That's that,' Baba said, and poured herself some cold tea.

'Mi scusi,' Gianni, the lodger, was saying as he asked Baba to pass the sugar. He was showing off, using his hands and making false, conceited faces – I didn't like him. He had arrived at Joanna's the day I hoped to go to Vienna with Mr Gentleman, and at first I helped him with his English and we went to *Bicycle Thieves* together. Later he gave me a necklace and thought that he could make very free with me because of that. When I wouldn't kiss him on the landing one night, he got huffed and said the necklace cost a lot of money. I offered to give it back but he asked for the money instead and we remained cool ever since.

'Some more dirty, foreign blood,' Eugene said good-humouredly.

'I come from Milano,' Gianni said, offended. He had the least sense of humour of anyone I ever met.

'She can't inhale,' Baba said when Eugene passed me another cigarette. I took one anyhow. Holding the match for me he whispered, 'You've polished your eyes and everything,' and I thought of the delicate moist kisses which he had placed upon my eyelids and of the things he whispered to me when we were alone.

'You know Italy well?' Gianni asked then.

Eugene turned away from me and let the match die in the glass ashtray which Gustav had pinched from Mooney's snug. 'Guinness is good for you' was written in red on the gold-painted ashtray.

'I worked in Sicily once. We were making a picture there about fishermen and I lived in Palermo for a couple of months.'

'Sicily is not good,' Gianni said, making his boyish, contemptuous face.

He's a selfish fool, I thought as I watched him pack sausages into his mouth. He got sausages because he was a male lodger. Joanna had some idea that male lodgers should get better food. I was watching him when it happened. My cigarette fell inside my low-necked dress. I don't know how, but it did; it just slipped from between my fingers and next thing I was burning. I yelled as I felt my chest sting and saw the smoke rising towards my chin.

'I'm on fire, I'm on fire.' I jumped up. The cigarette had lodged at the base of my brassière and the pain was awful.

'Mine Got, quench her,' Joanna said as she dragged my dress and tried to pull it away from me.

'Jesus,' Baba said, and she roared laughing.

'Do something, hah,' Joanna shouted, and Eugene turned to me and immediately began to smile.

'She did it for notice,' Baba said, picking up the jug of milk and proceeding to pour it down inside my dress.

'The good, best milk,' Joanna said, but it was too late, I was already sogging from half a jug of milk, and the cigarette went out, naturally.

'Honestly I thought it was some joke you were playing,' Eugene said to me.

He was trying to control his laughing in case I should be offended.

'You *are* a silly girls,' Joanna said to either Baba or me. I went out to change my dress.

'What'n the name of Christ were you doing, mooning like that?' Baba said out in the hall. 'You're a right looking eejit.'

'I was just thinking,' I said. I had been thinking of a plan to get Eugene to bring me out, away from them so that we could kiss in the motor-car.

'Of what may I ask?' I did not tell her. I had been thinking of the first night he kissed me. Suddenly one rainy night as we walked down by the side of the Liffey towards the Customs House to the city, he said, 'Have I ever kissed you?' and he kissed me quite abruptly, just as people flocked out of a cinema. I felt faintly sick and giddy and I have no idea whether that kiss was quick or prolonged. I loved that part of Dublin then and for ever, because it was there I laid my lips to the image of him that I had created, and the pigeons' droppings on the Customs House were white flowers which splashed the dark, ancient stone of the steps and porch. Afterwards in the car, I tasted his tongue and we explored each other's faces in the way that dogs do when they meet, and he said, 'Wanton,' to me. While I had been thinking of all this, Baba looked inside my dress to see what damage the cigarette had done. It lay there, all grey and soggy, and my chest had got burnt.

'Go up and change your dress,' she said.

'Come up with me.' I did not want her with Eugene. Already I was jealous of the way she said, 'Absolutely,' to everything he said and showed her dimples.

'Not on your life,' she said as she held the door-knob and patted her dark bouffant of hair before going back in to the room, to sit near him. She looked silly from behind with the cardigan on back to front and the buttons running down her back and a V of darkly flushed back.

I put on lashings of her perfume upstairs, and more powder and another dress.

When I came down Gianni was sitting at the old piano, striking chords softly from its yellowed keys and humming something amid the talk which had arisen in the room. The table was pushed back near the window, and Baba told me that we were going to have a sing-song. She leaned on the corner of the sideboard and in her light, girlish, early-morning voice she began to sing:

> 'I wish, I wish, I wish in vain,
> I wish I was a child again,
> But this I know it never will be,
> Till apples grow on a willow tree. . . .'

And then before we could clap she began another song which was incredibly sweet and sad. It was about a man who had seen a girl in the woods of his childhood and had gone out into the world, haunted by her image. The refrain was, 'Remember me, remember me, remember for the rest of your life. . . .' Towards the end Baba's voice quavered as if the words meant something very special to her, and Eugene said that she sang like a honey bird. She blushed a bit, and pushed her sleeves above her elbows, because the room was warm. Her bare arm with the fuzz of gold hair looked dainty as she rested it on the sideboard and murmured about being hot. I saw him look at her and knew that her singing would often dance across his memory.

Gustav came in and Joanna opened the wine and served it in liqueur glasses to make it go far. On and off, Baba or

Gianni sang. Baba then said that I would have to recite, being as I couldn't sing.

'I can't,' I said.

'Oh please, Kate.'

'Go on,' Eugene said. He had sung 'Johnnie I hardly knew you', in a pleasant, careless voice.

I recited 'The Mother' by Patrick Pearse, which was the only poem I knew. It was far too emotional for that small, hot room. As I recited:

> 'Lord thou art hard on mothers
> We suffer in their coming and their going. . . .'

Baba sniggered and said aloud, 'What about the children's allowance?' Everyone laughed then, and I felt a fool, and though he said, 'Bravo, bravo,' I hated him for laughing with the others.

Baba sang several more songs and Eugene wrote the words of some on a piece of paper which he put into his wallet. Her cheeks were red, not with rouge but with a flush of happiness.

'You're warm,' he said to her and stood in front of the fire to keep the heat away from her.

Greater love than this, no man hath, I thought bitterly as he stood in front of the fire and grinned at Baba, because of the duet which Gustav and Joanna had begun to sing.

For me the night was long and disappointing. When he left around eleven, he did not kiss me or say anything special.

Even in sleep I worried about losing him. First thing when I wakened I remembered Baba singing 'Scarlet Ribbons' and the way he smiled at her. It was cold, so I stood on my nightdress and put my clothes on. The window was white with frost and uneven icicles clung to the top part of the frame.

I went to work early as it was Saturday, our busy day; and I wanted to have the shelves well stocked with provisions.

'Oh darling,' Mrs Burns said when I let myself in. She had come out to get sausages and rashers from the tray of meat-things which were kept on the marble shelf behind the counter. I was wearing the coat which he had given me and she admired it. I told her that Eugene Gaillard had given it to me and she stared and said, 'What! Him!'

I guessed what she had to say, even before she began. He was a married man, she warned, and God only knew the number of innocent little girls whom he had started on the road to ruin.

There are no innocent girls, I thought. They're all scarlet girls like Baba, with guile in their eyes; and I asked if he was really married.

She said she had read all about it in the paper a year or two before. She remembered reading it the time she was in hospital having her veins cut, and the woman in the bed next to her commented on him and said that *she* knew him when he had holes in his shoes.

'He married some American girl. She was a painter or an actress or something,' Mrs Burns said, and I took the coat off and let it fall in a heap on the floor. I hated it, then.

'A good job I told you,' she said, as she went inside with black-pudding, two eggs and some back rashers.

I closed my eyes and felt my stomach sinking down and down. That explained everything – his reserve, the house in the country, those stories of deserted Californian beaches with beer cans and rotting oranges, his aloneness.

One sadness recalls another: I stood there beside the new crumpled coat and remembered the night my mother was drowned and how I had clung to the foolish hope that it was all a mistake and that she would walk into the room, asking people why they mourned her. I prayed that he would not be married.

'Oh please God, let him not be married,' I begged, but I knew that my prayers were hopeless.

Automatically I filled shelves with tins of things and I took eggs from a wooden crate and cleaned them one by one with a damp cloth. I put a pinch of bread soda on the stains which would not come out easily, and then I counted half-dozens of clean eggs into sectioned boxes that were marked 'Fresh country eggs'.

Two eggs cracked in my hand; they were going off slightly,

and that strange, sulphurous smell of rotting eggs has for ever been connected in my mind with misery.

At times I felt violent and wanted to scream but the Burnses were in the kitchen eating a fry and there was nothing I could do.

He rang me at eleven o'clock. The shop was packed and both Mr and Mrs Burns were serving at the counter.

He sounded very cheerful. He rang to invite me to his house the following day. He had talked of inviting me once or twice before.

'I'd love to meet your wife. It was a wonder you didn't tell me you were married,' I said.

'You never asked me,' he said. He was not apologetic. His voice sounded sharp and I imagined that he was going to put the telephone down.

'Do you wish to come tomorrow?' he asked. My legs began to tremble. I knew that customers were looking at my back, listening to what I said. They used to joke me about boys.

'I don't know ... maybe ... Will your wife be there?'

'No.' Pause ... 'She's not there now.'

'Oh.' Suddenly I was filled with hope and vague rapture. 'She isn't dead, by any chance?' I asked.

'No, she's in America.'

I heard the ring of the cash register behind my back and knew that Mrs Burns would sulk for the day if I stayed any longer on the phone.

'I have to go now, we're busy,' I said, my voice high and nervous.

He said that, if I wished, he could collect me at nine the following morning.

'All right, at nine,' I said.

He put the telephone down before I did.

On and off throughout the day, I cried, in the lavatory and places. I rang Tod Mead to ask all about the marriage but he was not in his office so I learnt nothing that day.

Chapter Five

I set out early on Sunday morning, as the church bells of Dublin clanged and clashed through the clear, bright air. Other people were on their way to Mass but I was going to visit him in his own home. I did not feel sinful about missing Mass, because it was early morning and I had washed my hair. The city was white with frost and the road looked slippy in places.

I went up to the corner of the avenue to wait for him because Joanna had threatened to send Gustav with me.

'A chaperon you need,' she said. She said that it was not right for me to be alone with a strange man in his home. She said that he might be a spy or a maniac. She called it a meaniac.

'I'm going alone and that's that,' I said. I wanted to hear about his marriage.

'Gustav will not be in the way,' she said. She was really worried about me. She polished Gustav's brown leather boots and put them beside the fire along with his clean grey socks. He always put on his shoes and socks at the fire, having warmed his feet first.

'Oh all right, so,' I said and I got out of the house on the excuse that I was going to early Mass.

Eugene was ten minutes late. He was lined and grey as if from lack of sleep. He just looked at me and breathed on my face in welcome.

'Wow!' he said to the wide straw hat that I wore. It was a summer hat really, with a bunch of wax rosebuds on it.

'You look like a child bride – it must be that hat,' he said, and grinned at it. I suppose he thought it was foolish. My long, clean, bright hair fell down over both shoulders and I had put on very white make-up. I told him about Gustav wanting to come with us. He just smiled. I thought the smile peculiar and wondered if I should have brought someone

45

after all. I said a prayer to my Angel Guardian to protect me:

> Oh angel of God, my guardian dear,
> To whom God's love commits me here;
> Ever this day be at my side
> To light and guard, to rule and guide.

He asked me if I had had breakfast. I said no. I had been too excited to eat. Then he reached to the back seat and got a fawn wool scarf, which he put around me. He tied a soft knot under my chin and kissed me before we set out.

We drove through the city and past suburbs and then along a wide road with ditches and trees on either side. Sometimes we came into a village – houses, a few shops, a pump, a chapel.

'I usually go to Mass,' I said as we slowed down to let people come out the chapel gates and cross the road.

'I have a few prepaid indulgence forms and excommunication applications at home somewhere, which may fix you up,' he said, and I laughed it off and said how nice the country looked. Branches and little dark, delicate twigs formed a fretwork of black lace against a cold, silver sky. I hadn't been in the country for months, not since I was home the previous summer: and I thought of my aunt and my father settling to the Sunday papers and a long sleep after their Sunday lunch. My aunt looked after my father now and they lived in our old house, occupying one or two of the large, damp rooms.

'Feel your ears clicking,' he said as we climbed a long rocky hill towards bleak mountain land. There were no trees on that stretch – just gorse bushes and granite rocks. Sheep moved between the marbled rocks, and I felt my ears buzzing, just as he said. We got to his house around eleven. The frost had melted by then and the laurel hedge was a dark, glossy green; the house itself was white, with french windows downstairs, and trees all around it.

A big sheep-dog ran to us and Anna opened the door. I had heard of her – she looked after him in a haphazard sort

46

of way, and lived downstairs at the back of the house. She was married and had a baby.

'Well, at long last,' she said, almost insolently.

'Hello, Anna.' He handed her the parcels from the car and introduced me. There were chops, a sheep's head for the dog, a bottle of gin and a new coffee-pot.

'Booze,' she said. She was a weedy woman with a greasy face and long straight hair. She looked sleepy or drugged or something.

Even though it was winter, flowers were blooming on the rockery – a mist of small blue flowers trailed over the marbled rocks. I felt that he was excited about showing me his house; he hummed as we climbed the stone steps to the door.

The front hall was clean and bright, with cream paint-work, black antique furniture, and walking-sticks in a big china holder.

' 'Tis a divil to keep clean,' Anna said as she led the way down to the kitchen, and just as we went in by one door, we heard her husband go out by another. She said that he was shy.

'Now aren't you glad you came?' Eugene said to me when Anna went into the dairy for a jug of cream. He made coffee.

'Yes, it's lovely,' I said, looking around the large, stone-flagged kitchen, and at the set of green house-bells high on the wall which looked as if they hadn't been in use for years. Small logs were stacked to dry at one end of the black-leaded range, and a boiling kettle let out its own familiar sigh. It was a nice kitchen.

He changed into an old oatmeal jacket and went out to saw some wood, as Anna said that Denis had gone off for the day to count sheep and mend a fence. I longed to follow Eugene but she drew a chair over near the fire for me, so I sat and talked to her, while she chopped cabbage on the big kitchen table. She looked sluttish in a black cotton skirt and a shapeless grey jumper. She wore a man's hat and had stuck a duck's feather into the brown, stained band.

'Are you an actress?' she asked, soon as we were alone.

'No.'

'He knows a lot of actresses.'

She poured herself some gin from the bottle he had brought and told me that she wasn't a servant really and that I mustn't think so. A caretaker she called herself, nodding to the backstairs, where her apartments were and where her baby slept. She had a baby, nine months old. She talked about her womb, and about her husband.

'The only woman he ever warmed to was Mrs Gaillard – Laura,' she said, looking into my eyes. Her own eyes were a bright, malignant yellow.

'He has a little blue stone upstairs that he's keeping for her. He found it out on the mountain.'

She talked of great times and big parties they'd had in Laura's time, and I imagined the front rooms filled with people, candles on the mahogany tables, and lanterns in the beech trees down the avenue. I had not fully believed that Laura existed up till then, but I believed it now, because Anna said so – 'Laura was great sport; she had a big fur coat and her own car and everything. The place is like a churchyard now' – she poured herself more gin and squeezed some lemon into it.

There were a lot of slugs in the cabbage and she just tipped them into the fire from the blade of the knife.

Eugene wheeled a barrow of logs in, and she went off on the excuse that she had to do something upstairs.

'Is she drinking?' he asked. The bottle of gin was on the table with the cut lemon beside it. He took away the bottle, and told me about a new power-saw which he would like me to see. He had just cut the wood and you could see the bright knots of amber resin in it and smell its fresh resin odour.

'That would be lovely,' I said, though machinery bores me. He tiptoed over and kissed me and asked if something worried me, because my face looked tense.

'Has she been telling you a whole long saga?' he asked.

I nodded.

'Don't believe a word of it, she's invented a big fairy-tale. Did she say we had a Rolls-Royce and a butler?'

48

I nodded again, and smiled at the tuft of his hair which stuck out foolishly over one ear. He wore his cap sideways and he looked pale in the oatmeal jacket.

'I'll tell you about it later,' he said, and though I dreaded him having to tell me, I also wanted desperately to know everything, so that Anna could not surprise me with anything new.

We ate lunch off a little circular table in his study and it was late, as Anna had got slightly merry from the gin and did not put on the vegetables until after two o'clock.

'To Plough the Rocks of Bawn,' she hummed as she came in, carrying plates. She still kept on the man's hat, which made me wonder if she had shingles or something. The bacon was sliced on our plates and she also carried a big napkin of steaming, floury potatoes.

'That's a nice bacon,' she winked at him, and he smiled into her yellow face. She had put on some violet eye-shadow which didn't enhance her appearance, because there were black circles under her eyes anyhow. He said that she had appropriated all the cosmetics which 'your woman' left behind. He rarely called Laura by name.

'Will you be my amanuensis, in this shooting-lodge?' he joked as I looked around the room to admire it. The walls were a faded blue, the paintwork cream. There were no curtains on the french windows (just shutters which had been drawn back), and the light came in, in abundance, so that you could see where Anna had dragged a cloth over the pieces of brown mahogany furniture and only half dusted them. The view through the long window was magical. Beyond the paling wire was the front field, below it a forest of trees and in the distance a valley of dreaming purple. He said that it was a valley of birch trees and that in wintertime the twigs of birch always had this odd, flushed purple colour. He suggested that we drive down there after lunch but I did not want to go and spoil the beautiful illusion.

'Tell me, what sort of food do you like?' he asked as he put butter on my cabbage and passed me a tube of mustard. At home we always mixed mustard in egg-cups.

'I like everything.'

'Everything?' He looked appalled.

I was sorry then that I didn't pretend to have some taste. He talked about his work; he had just finished a script for a picture on the world's starving people. He had travelled all over the world, to India, China, Sicily, Africa – gathering information for it. On his desk were photographs of tumble-down cities and slums with hungry children in doorways. It made me hungry just to look at them.

'Bengal, Honolulu, Tanganyika,' I repeated after him in a dreamy voice, recounting the cities where he had been. I had no idea where those places were.

'You make a lot of pictures?' I asked.

'No. I make odd little pictures; I made one I think you'd like, about a Maori child.'

'Is your name on the screen?' I longed to be able to tell my aunt.

'It's such small print,' he said, measuring its depth by holding his thumb and forefinger slightly apart, 'no one ever reads it. I made *one* picture in Hollywood – a Romance – and I bought this house with the earnings from it.'

That would be in Laura's time, I thought, as he went on talking about one he made on sewerage-systems.

'Sewerage?'

'Yes, you know, water sewerage, it's a very exciting business.'

I looked at him and saw that he was quite serious and I knew that I could never tell my aunt about him now.

'They're charming films. I used to think of my life as a failure, purposeless ... until I got older and became aware of things. I now know that the problem of life is not solved by success but by failure: struggle and achievement and failure ... on and on.' He said the last words almost to himself.

What he said reminded me of a film I had seen, of a turtle laying her eggs on the sands and then labouring her way back to the sea, crying with exhaustion as she went.

'I'd like to see some of your films,' I said.

'You will.' But he did not make any plans then. There was a bed in the room with a rug thrown over it. He said that

50

it had been brought down from upstairs once when somebody was ill. He didn't say who.

We went for a walk so that I could see the woods before
it got dark. He loaned me a raincoat that was lined with
honey-coloured fur and a pair of woman's wellingtons from
under the stairs. I turned them upside down before putting
them on, because once I found a dead mouse in a welling-
ton. Some corn seeds dropped out of them.

'All right?' he asked.

'Lovely, thank you.' They pinched a bit. She must have
had smaller feet than me. Baba always says I probably have
bigger feet than any girl in Ireland.

We went up by the wood at the back of the house to
shelter from the misting rain. There were all kinds of trees
and the ground was soggy with leaf mould. He said that
huge red and purple mushrooms grew in the wood in
summer. It was very quiet except for the rain and our feet
breaking twigs. Even though it was winter the wood was
green and sheltered, because there were many big Christ-
mas-trees.

'So you heard that I'm married,' he said, as I stood to
admire the startling red berries on a holly tree.

'Yes, the boss's wife told me.'

He smiled and seemed almost flattered that anyone should
know about his private life.

'And *you* think this is a very bad thing?'

'Oh no,' I said, staring straight ahead at a split oak that
looked like the legs of a giant. He went on:

'Yes, I married an American girl when I was over there.
She was a nice girl, very personable, but after a couple of
years she didn't care for me. I wasn't "fun". A privileged
girl, brought up to believe that she is special, changes an
unsatisfactory husband as she might change her bath salts.
She believes that happiness is her right.'

'That's a pity,' I said. It was a stupid thing for me to say,
but I was afraid that I might cry, so I had to say something.

'She was a failed painter. We lived in Hollywood in a
plaster mansion-cottage – they're going cheap there in the
last few years,' he said aside as if he were addressing the

holly tree. 'The unending blue sky nearly drove me mad
did the people – "Hi Joe, Hi Al, Hi Art". We came to Irela
and bought this house. I had money from the pictur
made and she had an income. She had gone to school i
gold-plated Rolls. She hated everyone.'

It occurred to me that he was secretly proud of tl
though he may not have known it.

'She had big plans,' he said, 'hunting and shooting. !
thought we might invite film directors here and writers.
did, but they never came. It rained, I got my rheumati
back.' He moved his neck stiffly, as if there was rheur
tism always waiting to be summoned. 'I put on my lc
underpants and my long face and she said that I hae
feudal attitude to women because I let her carry in a log
the fire. She left one day when I was out, mowing hay w
Denis ... there was a note on the table and ...' He stopp
and withdrew whatever it was he had intended to say.

'I'm sorry,' I said. I *was* actually sorry.

'Oh ... thank you.' He smiled, and put out his hand
catch the drips of rain that fell from the trees. It was
first time he looked shy or ill at ease.

The dark, polished green of holly leaves was reflected
his pale skin so that he looked a little green and unheal
and I longed to take him in my arms and console him.
walked on.

At the top of the wood he climbed on to a grass di
and pulled me up by the hand to show me the view.

'Ah,' he said, breathing in the wonderful remoteness
the place.

'You mustn't worry about my being married.'

'I'm not worrying,' I lied.

'I would have told you about it, eventually,' he said
don't talk about some things easily. Guilt and failure
painful topics, and as you get older you try and put th
out of your mind.'

I shivered slightly; I don't know why, and he put an a
round me, thinking that I was dizzy from standing on
height.

Underneath, sheep grazed on the rough, yellowish g

which stretched towards a low mountain. Some gorse had been burnt, and in the fading light the charred, bent branches looked like skeletons of ghosts. The view depressed me.

'That was why I did not want to get involved with you in the very beginning,' he said quietly.

'I know now,' I said, and he turned sharply to see if I were crying or something.

Then he smiled at me. 'You're wild, you must have grown up out in the open.'

I thought of our front field at home with pools of muddy water lodged around the base of trees and I felt desolate.

'You have a look of mystique on your face,' I said.

His pale expression fell to pieces and he hollered with laughter and asked where I had picked up such a word. I realized that it must have been a wrong word, but I had read it in some book and liked its sound.

'Dear girl, you'll have to give up reading books.' He took my hand and we ran down the slope of the ditch and back into the wood. We had a quick look at a plantation of young pine trees which he had put down. A netting wire fence ran all around them to keep out rabbits and deer. He reached in and touched the tip of the trees and said that he must sow one for my coming. I wondered if he had sown trees for his wife and if he still loved her.

Anna and her husband went out after tea to play cards, and took their baby, though Eugene said it would get pneumonia.

I felt uneasy being alone with him in that large house. He lit two Tilley lamps, drew the shutters in the study, and said, 'Let's have a little music.'

There were records in small piles on the floor and books everywhere, and antlers sprung at me from one wall. He said that the previous owner, who had been keen on slaughter, had left traces of himself behind – horns and heads, and dried skins on the floor. A strange music filled the room and he moved around, beating time to it and pausing to see how I liked it. It had no words.

'Well, what do you think of that? What does it remind

you of?' he asked when the record had played itself out. It reminded me of birds making a brown V in the sky.

'Birds,' I said.

'Birds!' He did not know what I meant, so he put on another and this one sounded much the same.

'More birds?' he said, laughing, and I nodded. I think he was disappointed, because he did not play any more records that night.

'Let's look at the fire upstairs,' he said, but I did not want to go up there. I feared that it might be a plan to lure me up to his bedroom. He had lit a fire there, earlier on – because of a damp patch over the mantelshelf, he said.

'I'll sit here,' I said as he went off, carrying a brass candlestick and a new, unlighted candle. I looked at his desk, to try and find out things about him. It was littered with papers, letters, air-mail envelopes, packets of flower seed, stiffeners from a man's collar, copper nails in a jam jar, and ashtrays with funny drawings on them.

'Could you bring up the bellows, please?' he called down to me.

The fire in the bedroom had gone out. It was a large room with a double bed and dark mahogany furniture. Four pillows on the bed – two at either side – caught my eye.

'Well, sometimes I sleep on one side and sometimes I sleep on the other; it makes a change,' he said, divining my thoughts.

'Stay,' he said as he worked the bellows up and down, and caused ashes to rise towards the picture over the fireplace – a naked woman lying on her side.

'I'll have to be off,' I said, trying to sound casual. A naked woman was no thing to have staring at him every night in his bed. A gust of smoke blew down the chimney into his face and made him cough.

'Could you open the window, please?' he asked, as the coughing almost took his breath away. The window was stiff so I had to tap it; it opened suddenly and unexpectedly and the sudden draught quenched the candle.

'I'm afraid I have to go home now, it's eight o'clock,' I

said in a slightly hysterical voice as I groped my way to-wards the door.

'Go,' he said. 'But my dear girl I haven't seduced you yet!' He laughed and I thought of a portrait of him down-stairs which looked sinister. I groped for the doorknob (the wind had caused the door to slam) but could not turn it. My hands became powerless. He relit the candle and stood there, near the fireplace, holding it.

'Stop trembling,' he said, and then he said that there was nothing to be afraid of and that he had been joking. I realized that I was being silly and I began to cry.

'There, there,' he said, coming over to pet me. 'You are a silly girl.' He bent down and kissed my wet mouth more tenderly than he had ever kissed me before.

We went downstairs and made tea and talked and then he said that he would take me home. I combed my hair which had become tossed while he kissed me.

Outside, the stars were fierce with frost, the ground hardened with it, the pine trees very still and very beauti-ful. In the greenish moonlight, I turned to him to say that I did not really want to leave so early. The place looked enchanting in the frost; inside in the study a warm fire blazed behind a guard, the lamp was lowered and the last record lay on the green baize of the wind-up gramophone, silent.

'I hate going now,' I said, but we had put on our coats and he had brought the car around to the front of the house, and anyhow he said that we would have to drive slowly because of ice patches reported on the nine-o'clock news.

'Back to the village,' he said. It was a phrase he used whenever he drove me home.

Chapter Six

I w: went most Sundays after that, and then, one Sunday night I stayed.

I slept in the guest-room, where the floor and wood work had been newly varnished. Everything was a little sticky.

In fact I didn't sleep, I kept thinking of him. I could hear him whistling downstairs and moving around until after three o'clock. He had left me a magazine to read. It contained a lot of drawings – people with peaked noses and staircases growing out of their ears, which I did not understand. I kept the light on because Anna said a woman had died in that room just before Eugene bought the house. A colonel's wife who took digitalis pills.

Towards morning I dozed, but the alarm-clock went off at seven and I had to get up to go back to work.

'Did you sleep?' he asked. We met going down the stairs and he yawned and pretended to stagger.

'No, not very well.'

'Nonsense, isn't it! Two people at opposite wings of the house, lying awake.'

'Next time we'll keep each other company and put a bolster in the bed between us, won't we?' he said, as he kissed me. I looked away. I had been brought up to think of it as something unmentionable, which a woman had to pretend to like, to please *a husband*.

He brought a rug for my knees and a flask of tea which I drank in the car, as there was no time for breakfast.

The next Sunday I stayed, and I still went to my own room. I did not want to sleep in *his* bed; he put it down to scruples but actually I was afraid. Early next morning he tapped on my door and as I was awake I got up, and we went out for a stroll through the woods.

There are moments in our lives we can never forget: I remember that early morning and the white limbs of young birches in the early mist, and later the sun coming up behind the mountain in crimson splendour as if it were the first day of the world. I remember the sudden brightness of everything and the effect of suffused light as the sun came through the mist, and the dew lifted, and later the green of the grass showed forth very vividly, radiating energy in the form of colour.

'I wish we could be together,' he said, his arm round my neck.

'Will we be?' I said.

'It seems so natural now, so inevitable. I was never one for necking in backs of cars, it strikes me as being so *sick*,' he said.

Kissing, or 'necking' as he called it, suited me nicely, but I could not tell him that.

But I could only postpone it until Christmas-time.

He invited Baba, Joanna, and Gustav for Christmas dinner so that I would feel at ease, as his friends terrified me. They were mostly people from other countries who told each other obscure jokes and I felt that they looked on me as some sort of curiosity brought in for amusement.

It was a pleasant dinner, with red candles along the table and presents for everyone on the tree; Joanna was in her element, she got an old gilt frame to bring home and some logs for the dining-room grate. Baba waltzed with Eugene after dinner to gramophone music, and everybody had plenty to drink.

At midnight the guests went home but I stayed. It looked quite respectable really, because Eugene's mother was also staying. She was a frail, argumentative little woman, with a craggy face and a big forehead like his. She coughed a lot.

Eugene helped her upstairs to the guest-room (the room I usually slept in) and brought her hot whisky and a little mug for her teeth. Then he came down and we ate cold turkey and cream crackers.

'I hardly saw you all day, and you looked so pretty at dinner,' he said as we sat on the sheepskin rug in front of the fire, eating. He read to me, poems by Lorca, which I didn't understand, but he read nicely. He wanted me to read one but I felt shy, sometimes I became very shy in his company. One side of my face got very hot so I took off one of my red lantern earrings. Raising his eyes from the book, he saw the warm lobe blackened a little by the cheap tin of the earring-clip, and he groaned.

'Your ears could go septic,' he said as he examined the red earrings which I had bought on Christmas Eve so that I would look glamorous for him.

'Made in Hong Kong!' he said as he threw them in the fire. I tried to rescue them with the tongs but it was too late; they had sunk into the red ashes.

I sulked for a bit but he said that he would buy me a gold pair.

'If I didn't care about you I wouldn't worry about your ears,' he said. I laughed at that. His compliments were so odd.

'You soft, daft, wanton thing, you've got one mad eye,' he said, looking into my eyes, which he decided were green.

'Green eyes and coppered hair, my mother wouldn't trust you,' he said. His mother had cold, blue eyes which were very piercing and shrewd. A smell of eucalyptus oil surrounded her.

I lay back on the woolly rug and he kissed my warmed face.

After a while he said, 'Will we go to bed, Miss Potts?' I was happy lying there, just kissing him; bed was too final for me, so I sat up and put my hands around my knees.

'It's too early,' I said. It was about two in the morning.

'We'll wash our teeth,' he said, so we went upstairs and washed our teeth. 'You're not washing your teeth properly, you should brush them up and down as well as back and forth.'

I think he just said that to put me at my ease. I had stopped talking and my eyes were owlish, as they always are when I am frightened. I knew that I was about to do something terrible. I believed in hell, in eternal torment by fire. But it could be postponed.

The bedroom was cold. Normally Anna lit a fire there, but in the excitement of dinner and presents she had forgotten about it.

He undressed quickly and put his clothes on a wing-backed armchair. I stood watching him, too self-conscious to move. My teeth chattered, from fear or cold.

'Hop in before you get cold,' he said as he got something out of the wall press. His long back had one vivid strawberry-mark. Dark tufts of hair stuck out under his arms, and in the lamplight the smooth parts of his body were a glowing honey colour.

He got into bed and propped his head on one fist while he waited for me.

'Don't look at me,' I asked.

He put his hand across his eyes, the fingers were spread out so that there were slits between them. While I undressed, he recited:

> 'Mrs White had a fright
> In the middle of the night,
> Saw a ghost, eating toast
> Half-way up a lamp post....'

Then he asked me to unscrew the Tilley lamp. A trickle of paraffin flowed out from the metal cap and mingled with the toilet-water, which I had poured on my hands and wrists.

'You're such a nice plump girl,' he said as I came towards him. The light took a few seconds to fade out completely.

I took off the coat which I had been using as a dressing-gown, and he raised the covers up and gathered me in near him.

I shivered but he thought it was with cold. He rubbed my skin briskly to warm it and said that my knees were like ice. He did everything to make me feel at ease.

'Have you fluff in your belly-button?' he asked as he poked fun at it with his fingers. It was one thing I was very squeamish about, and instantly (I began to tighten with fear), my whole body stiffened.

'What's wrong?' he said as he kissed my closed lips. He noticed things very quickly. 'Are you filled with remorse?'

It was not remorse. Even if I were married I would have been afraid.

'What is it, darling, little soft skin?' If he had not been so tender I might have been brave. I cried on to his bare shoulder.

'I don't know,' I said hopelessly. I felt such a fool crying in bed, especially as I laughed so much in the day-time and gave the impression of being thoughtlessly happy.

'Have you some terrible traumatic experience?' he asked.

Traumatic? I had never heard that word before, I didn't know what to say.

'I don't know,' I said. 'I don't know' was the only sentence which formed itself in my crying brain.

He tried to assure me, to say that I need not worry, that there was nothing to be afraid of, that surely I was not afraid of him. He caressed me slowly and gently and I was still afraid. Before that, on armchairs, in the motor-car, in restaurants, I touched his hands, kissed the hairs on his wrists, longed for the feel of his fingers on my soft secret flesh, but now everything had changed.

He said that I should talk about it, tell him what exactly appalled me, discuss it. But I couldn't do that. I just wanted to go to sleep and waken up, finding that it was all over, the way you waken up after an operation.

I lay in his arms crying and he said that I must not cry and that we would do nothing but have a big, long sleep and wake up full of energy. He was a little quiet. He blamed himself for being so stupid, so unthinking, for not having known that I would be nervous and afraid.

Eventually he turned over on his other side to go to sleep. He took a sleeping-pill with a glass of water.

'I'm sorry, Eugene. ... I do love you,' I said.

'That's all right, sweetling,' he said, patting my warm bottom with his hand. At least we had got warm.

'I won't be afraid tomorrow,' I said, knowing that I would.

'I know that,' he said. 'You're just tired, now go to sleep and don't worry about a thing.'

We joined hands. I wanted to blow my nose, as I could scarcely breathe from all that crying. I was ashamed to blow it, in case it was vulgar.

I went to sleep, mortified.

Some time towards morning we must have come together again, because I wakened up to find myself refusing his love.

Immediately afterwards he got up and dressed. I apologized.

'Stop saying you're sorry,' he said as he drew his braces up. 'There's no need to be sorry, it's a perfectly natural thing,' he said. He sat on the armchair and put on his socks.

'Are you getting up?' I asked.

'Yes, I often get up at dawn when I don't sleep very well; I go out for a walk or do some work. . . .'

'It's my fault.'

'Stop saying it's your fault, stop *worrying*,' he said. I was glad that it was too dark for me to see the expression on his face; I could not have looked at him.

He left the room, and later I heard his steps outside on the gravel.

I lay on, and wept. I had never felt so ashamed in my whole life; I felt certain now that he was finished with me because I had been so childish. When daylight came, about half past eight, there were a few stars left in the heavens. They looked wan and faint as stars do in the morning.

'Go home . . . vanish,' I said to the stars or to myself, and I got up and dressed when I heard Anna poke the range downstairs. I did not know how I would face her, or Denis or his mother or him. My black, sequined jumper which I thought so charming at the dinner table felt idiotic in the early morning. I wished that I could get out of the house and escape back to Joanna's without being seen. I looked in the mirror. My face was red, blotchy, swollen. Everyone would know!

It began to snow. It came very fast and sudden and it fell slantwise on the front field but did not lodge there. It melted as it touched the ground. I stuck my head out, hoping that the sleet might change my face, and then I went to the second guest-room to toss the bed which I should have slept in. It seemed foolish and sad to have to do such a thing, but Anna was very observant and would have noticed. Under that divan bed I found a box of old toys, and torn books.

'This book belongs to Baby Frances Gaillard,' I read on the fly-leaf of an animal book. I nearly died. He had never said that he had a child, but I ought to have wondered why he was so tender with Anna's baby. It made everything worse; I looked at the toys, torn and chewed, and cried over them. The sleet, my red, unslept cheeks, the silly sequined jumper, the cold green porcelain of an unlit anthracite stove in the room, all seemed to multiply my sense of shame. I sat there, weeping, until Anna knocked on the door to say breakfast was ready.

Down in the kitchen I could not bring myself to look at him. I held my head down. He handed me a cup of tea and said, 'Did you sleep well, Miss Caithleen Brady?'

Anna was there, watching.

'Yes, thank you.'

He bent his head and looked sideways at my face, hung in shame. He was laughing.

'I'm very glad that you slept well,' he said, as he brought me over to the table and buttered some toast for me.

Later his mother came down and we had breakfast together. She complained about the porridge being lumpy. She lived with a sister in Dublin, and said that there was one thing she could not stand, and that was lumpy porridge.

He drove her back around noon and I thought I should go too, but he asked me to stay a while longer, as he said he wanted to talk to me. I stayed.

'See you again, dear,' his mother said as he helped her into the car. She had a shawl over her fur coat and a hot-water bottle for her knees. She looked rather happy, because he had given her whisky and chocolates and white turkey meat, wrapped in butter paper. She liked to be pampered, she was making up for all the years when she had worked as a waitress to rear her son. He was quite distant with her and she was sharp with him. But she liked it when he fussed over her.

When they had gone I went up the woods. The sleet had stopped and now it rained mildly. I did not know whether I should risk staying another night or not. I was trying to decide – the gently falling rain made a background of vague soothing noise for my muddled thoughts. I thought of other woods, dampness, cowslips in a field of high grass, all the imaginary men I had ever talked to and into whose strong arms I had swooned in a moment of ecstatic reconciliation. But I could not decide; I had never made decisions in my life. My clothes had always been bought for me, my food decided on, even my outings were decided by Baba. I walked round and round, touching the damp trees, inhaling the strange, wild smell of the damp wood.

When I heard the car come back I walked towards the house and then I heard him whistle as he came up the woods to find me. He wore an old brown hat which made him look rakish, and as he came towards me I knew that I would stay another night and risk making a fool of myself again.

'I'll stay,' I said instantly, and he was pleased. He said that I looked a lot better since I came out and that rain suited me and that I must always live in rainy country and wear my hair long, like that, and wear a dark macintosh.

'And I won't be afraid,' I said, as we ran down the wooded hill towards the yard in order to make some tea. He was dying for tea. I did not feel sleepy any more. We spotted Anna looking at us through his field-glasses.

'She'll break those glasses,' he said, but by the time he got in the house she had restored them to their brown leather case which hung on the end of the curtain pole in his study. When he complained, Anna said that he must have been seeing things. He prepared a turkey hash, while Anna and I chopped vegetables.

Before dinner he carried a white china lamp upstairs to the dressing-table in his room so that I could make up my face. He stayed there, watching, while I applied pancake make-up with a damp sponge and spread it over my face evenly. It made me pale. In the mirror my face looked round and childlike.

'The old man and the girl,' he said to the spotted mirror, which was wedged at the right angle by a face-cream jar – one of Laura's no doubt. He debated whether or not he should shave.

'Am I likely to be kissing anybody?' he asked the mirror as he stroked the stubble on his chin.

I laughed.

'Well am I?' he asked again. I loved kissing him. I thought, if only people just kissed, if all love stopped at that.

He picked up my hairbrush and began to brush my hair very slowly. I liked the slow, firm strokes of the brush on my scalp and after a while I felt exhilarated from it. He smiled a lot at me in the mirror.

'I have too much chin and you have a shade too little. We should make perfectly chinned children,' he said. He expected me to laugh, but I didn't. There were some things which I was very touchy about: babies for instance. Babies terrified me. Then I remembered the box of toys; I had never forgotten it really, just postponed thinking about it.

'There is a box of toys in my room, under the bed,' I said.

'Yes, I know, they're mine. I had a child.'

'Oh.'

'I had a daughter, she's three now.' I thought his voice changed, but I could not be certain. I imagined him giving a little girl a pick-a-back, and the thought stabbed me with jealous pain.

'Do you miss her?' I asked.

'I miss her very much, almost every minute of the day I think of her, or think that I'm hearing her. Once you've had a child you want to live with it and watch it grow.'

He went on brushing my hair but it was not the same after that.

*

I slept in his bed that night, and he loaned me a white flannel nightdress with rosebuds on it, which was exactly like one my mother kept in a trunk at home, in case she ever had to go to hospital. He set the alarm-clock for seven and put it on the bedside table, and put the lamp out. I thought of Laura, because he said that he had bought the clock in New York, one night when he was walking around, very late. He said you could buy things in the middle of the night there, or go to the pictures. I longed to go with him to

64

London – where he was going in a day or two. During dinner a telegram had been delivered, asking him to go to London as soon as possible. I read it in the study after dinner, when we were eating mandarin oranges. It said: 'YOU OLD SOD CAN YOU COME OVER AND DO SOMETHING TO THIS LOUSY SCRIPT ON SEWERAGE. IT STINKS.' It was from somebody called Sam, and Eugene said that he would have to go there for a few days. He took a canvas travel bag from the gun bureau to remind him to pack.

' 'Tis well for you,' I said, and I thought that he might bring me, but instead he asked me what I did with orange pips.

'I swallow them,' I said. There were so many that it would have been a day's work to remove them.

'You swallow them,' he repeated, raising his eyes to the cracked ceiling. 'How am I ever going to take *you* into society?'

'I'll be very polite,' I said, sure that he would invite me to London, but he didn't.

We went to bed early and he got me the nightdress from the hot press and set the clock for seven.

'Not so cold tonight,' he said when we got into bed. There had been an oil-heater on in the room for several hours and the air was fuggy.

'Not so strange, either, is it?' he asked as he rubbed my cold knees briskly and asked if I usually slept with half a dozen hot-water bottles. Baba and I had one stone bottle between us and we were always threatening to buy a second one, but it seemed such a waste of good money. We fought over it a lot and sometimes I went to bed very early to have the first of it.

'Not so strange,' I lied as his hand roamed over my body and his fingers searched for the places I liked most to be caressed. I was thinking that by next day he would be off in London, far away from me, and already I had begun to tighten with fear and nervousness. I drew my nightdress down over my knees and said that we would just talk about things.

'But I want to love you,' he said. 'I've been thinking all

65

day of how I shall make love to you and make you happy.'
He went on caressing me, and in a half-hearted way I
caressed him and wished that I could stop myself from
being so afraid. But that night was a failure too.

We were up and ready to leave for Dublin long before the
alarm went off. I heard it ring when I was putting on my
coat; but I was too downcast to go up and press in the
button.

In the motor-car he hardly spoke. His profile looked grey
and forbidding and I thought, he has a hard, unforgiving
face.

'I hope you enjoy London,' I said.

'I hope so,' he said, and asked if I had the two books he
loaned me. He loaned them to me the previous night, before
we went up to bed. One was a novel, and the other was
called *The Body and Mature Behaviour*.

'I have them here,' I said, kicking my bag to indicate
where they were. I thought for one minute that he was
going to ask me to give them back, but he didn't.

'Will you write to me from London?' I asked.

'Of course,' he said, but coolly. 'I'll send you a card.' And
I thought with desolation of how different it would have
been between us if I had not been afraid in bed.

I longed to do something dramatic, to scream or throw
his new coat back at him, or jump out of the car while it was
moving. A minute later, I longed to be in his arms, un-
afraid, pleasing him. More than anything I longed to please
him. It seemed like weeks since he had put my hair behind
my ear and whispered, 'I am never going to let you go.' In
fact it had only been nine or ten hours before, that we had
got into bed and he had kissed my frightened nipples and
they had sprouted like seed potatoes – before I got the fit of
shivering.

*

He drove me right up outside the shop. I asked him not
to, in case Mrs Burns should be looking out the bedroom
window, but he ignored it, or else he did not hear me.

I got out quickly, said good-bye, and thanked him.

'Good-bye,' he said. He was as off-hand as if I were some stranger to whom he had given a lift. I ran to the shop door, and unlocked it with the key, which I had ready in my hand. I went inside, without turning back to wave.

*

A moment later when I drew up the blind of the shop window, there was no sign of his car. I knew that he was gone. It was all over, Christmas, kissing, everything....

Chapter Seven

HE had gone five days now and there was no news of him. Baba said that he had probably arranged to meet his wife in London and that we would never see him again.

'You got a coat out of him,' she said, 'I got sweet damn all.'

'It wasn't his wife,' I said angrily. 'I read the telegram myself, it was about his work.'

'It's bound to be that bitch he married,' Baba said. Baba maintained that all wives were bitches.

Anyhow she said that we would soon know, because we were on our way to a fortune-teller in Donnybrook. At Donnybrook Church we got out of the bus, and as we had never been in that church before, we nipped in for three wishes. Two women who were filling lemonade bottles with Holy Water from a tub inside the door, directed us to the fortune-teller's house.

It was a large brick house. In the cold tiled hallway, seven or eight girls waited. Three of them told us that they came regularly every week and each of the others had been to the fortune-teller at least once before.

'She's marvellous,' they said. They also said that she was moody. The place reminded me of the convent – the walls tiled half-way, the group of girls with their various smells of sweat, and perfume, and soap; the absence of cigarette smoke. A home-made, inked sign said 'No smoking'. It didn't even say 'please'. I had only to close my eyes to smell again the convent cabbage and hear a nun admonishing Baba about the hole in her sock.

'Come in to the place,' Baba said to me, and together we went into the downstairs lavatory to have a smoke. A block of pearl-coloured disinfectant was placed in a saucer on the ledge – it gave the place a hygienic smell.

'Jesus, this place gives me the creeps,' Baba said, and we debated whether or not we should leave. But I wanted to know very badly about Eugene so we stayed. When we came out, and took our places on the stool, four more girls had arrived. To many of the girls it was a recreation; they came once a week, instead of going to the pictures or to a dance.

'Now don't give her any clues, about any damn thing,' Baba warned me, and just then a middle-aged woman came out of the fortune-teller's room, crying. We all stared at her. I supposed that she had heard something awful, such as that her husband was leaving her for another woman.

'We'll go in together,' Baba whispered, and I said yes.

We had to wait an hour.

'Sit down,' the fortune-teller said in a disinterested voice as we went into her room. We guessed that she must be in one of her bad moods because the others had told us that if she didn't talk, it meant bad humour. She sat beside an electric fire, drinking tea and warming one hand around the cup. She was dressed completely in black and her pale face suggested that she never had any fresh air. The room was large and draughty, with a faded screen dividing it into two. Baba nudged me as much as to say, it's awful.

'Well,' the fortune-teller said at last, picking up Baba's hand as if it were some loose object which was not joined to Baba's arm.

'Why are you wearing an engagement ring, *you're* not engaged.'

It was her mother's engagement ring which Baba wore. She took it off and gave it to me to hold.

'There's trouble in store for you,' the fortune-teller said, staring into the palm of Baba's neat hand. Poor Baba looked very frightened and sat with her shoulders tensed up.

'You'll marry a rich man,' she went on, 'that is, when you give up this married man.'

Baba blushed. I knew that it must be Tod Mead.

'You have one brother and your birthday is in June,' she said as she dropped Baba's hand abruptly and asked us to change places. The routine was that she read hands first, then read the cards, and finally the crystal. A beautiful crystal of green glass rested on a side table.

'You'll make a journey,' she said to me. She had a black

scarf tied around her head so that you couldn't see her hair. Her voice was low, extraordinarily flat, and uneventful. She had no interest in the things she told me.

'It's an unpleasant journey,' she noted, 'and before the new year is out, you'll marry an eccentric man, you'll have to marry him, because you will be the mother of twins.'

'Twins,' Baba said, and fell into a fit of laughing and could not stop. So did I. It wasn't just my face that laughed, my whole body shook with it. She waited for us to stop, but it became worse and finally she dropped my hand and asked us to leave the room.

Baba stood up, delighted, as she felt that she had heard enough about herself. I tried to apologize but the fortune-teller would not listen.

'A refund,' Baba said gaily as she retrieved the two ten-shilling notes which we had put on a plate when we came in.

'Put that money down, young lady,' the fortune-teller shouted; so Baba dropped the money and we ran out of the room, laughing.

Just as we approached the hall, a man stuck his head out of a side door and said, 'Excuse me, Missy, how do you spell umbrelley?'

He talked through his nose, and of course this made us hysterical with laughter.

'I don't know,' Baba said, talking through *her* nose. 'Why don't you go up the river on a bicycle?'

He laughed too, he even laughed through his nose.

'Talk about the loony bin,' Baba said as we ran down the avenue. Baba said that she might set mad dogs on us, so we ran the whole way to the road.

*

We took a bus to Grafton Street and then got out to look at the shop windows, because the sales were on.

Then we went to Davy Byrnes's cocktail bar and ordered a pernod between us. We hadn't enough money to buy two drinks.

'Look *fast*,' Baba said. We sat near the door and Baba said that some moron was bound to buy us a drink. She beamed at a man in a leather jacket who had an absurdly curling moustache.

'That drink has to last two hours, till closing time,' she said as I took a swig of pernod. It was like liquorice cough bottle mixture and it looked cloudy when she added water to it. She kept adding water all the time, to make it go far. The bar-boy asked if we were all right.

'We're broke,' Baba said, and he went off and got us two glasses of beer.

'That's the best I can do,' he said, placing the glasses down on little blotting-paper mats that bore an advertisement for something.

'I won't forget you,' Baba said. He was a young boy, just up from Tipperary and we had spoken to him one night before.

'Right,' he said in a falsely brave voice.

'I'll send you my garter in the post,' Baba said, and he went off, blushing and grinning.

'Decent of him,' I said to Baba. The beer tasted insipid after the pernod.

'Decent! It's my charm that gets us these sort of favours,' Baba said, and then she turned to look at the man with the moustache. He stood by the counter, drinking alone. I suppose with that moustache no one could sit or stand opposite him without laughing.

'Excuse me, have you got the right time on you?' Baba leaned over and asked him.

Right time! There was a wall clock staring her in the face. It was twenty minutes past nine o'clock.

He moved away, agitated. A tremor began in a tick in his right cheek. I suppose he thought we might damage his good name, just by talking to him. I knew him well by sight, as he sold scooters in a shop in D'Olier Street. Suddenly I felt cheap and humiliated and I wished that Eugene would come and take me to the cathedral of tall green trees behind his house.

'We'll ring The Body,' Baba said. It was what she always said – ring someone, anyone – when we had nothing special to do. He drank in his local pub in Blanchardstown most

71

nights from nine o'clock on. She got three pennies, and
went off to telephone.

*

A country-looking boy came over to me and said, 'I was
looking for Bovril.'

'Were you?' I said, cutting him dead with my cheeky
look. My hair was loose around my face and I tossed it out
of one eye at regular intervals. He just stood there, looking
at me, with his coat open and his jacket open, and a glaring
yellow pullover inside it. Baba came back and he repeated
to her that he had come in to get some Bovril.

'Have a whisky,' she said.

'I never broke my Confirmation pledge,' he said in a
rough, humourless voice. He sat at our table.

'Where's The Body?' I asked Baba.

'He's gone to Mount Mellory to Confession.' Every
January The Body went to the Cistercian Monastery at
Mount Mellory to fast and pray. He always returned full
of good resolutions but after a week or two he was on the
drink again.

The country boy told us that he was from Oranmore
and that he had come to Dublin for treatment, because
he had an accident the summer before and was still lame
from it.

'I'm going in to the Rotunda tomorrow,' he said, and
Baba laughed, because the Rotunda is a maternity hospital.
He rooted in his pocket for an envelope and we saw that it
was addressed to the Richmond hospital. The envelope was
black with finger-marks and you could see that it had been
opened and restuck.

'Poor you,' Baba said falsely. He bought us a whisky each,
and a pork pie, and coffee for himself.

' 'Twas an aul' tractor,' he said, 'it rolled over me. I was
nearly in pulp only for me father –'

Baba flapped her hands behind his back and signalled to
me to shut him up. He was talking loud and everyone could
hear him.

At closing time we left and walked with him to his hotel.

We promised to visit him in hospital but we didn't think we would.

'We'll write t'him care of the Rotunda,' Baba said, as we ran up Amiens Street to catch the last bus.

*

At home, we heated soup.

'You're getting dull,' Baba said.

'I know,' I said. The night had been stupid, boring, paltry. Nothing interested me now, unless it had to do with Eugene; I thought of him and of his sudden outbursts of nervous energy which made him dance around and conduct an imaginary orchestra or chop wood for an hour. It even gave me pleasure to think of his sheep-dog, and of the old house with its dark wood always creaking and shutters rattling at night.

'It's Eugene?' Baba said.

'Yes,' I said despairingly.

Then the soup began to boil and a nice smell pervaded the small kitchen. We had to open the window to let the smell out, otherwise Joanna might have come down, as the soup was part of next day's lunch.

'Did he try it on?' Baba said. The two drinks had made her outspoken.

'Sort of,' I said. Shame stifled me as I remembered the soft bed, with the nice smell of clean linen and an owl crying in one of the pine trees.

'How far did he go?' Baba asked.

'Oh don't ask me such a thing!' I drank the soup and remembered back to the evening at dinner, when the telegram asking him to go to London had been delivered. Anna, who is cursed with the curiosity of the lonely, had said:

'No one dead?'

'No one dead,' he had said, and gone on with his dinner. Anna had sulked. She had looked funny that night, because she'd taken her curling-pins out for dinner (he would have remarked on them), and her long dark hair was neither straight nor curly, but quiffed in places. I thought of every detail of my visit – even the kind of soap he used, and the colour of his face-cloth.

'You'll never hear from him again,' Baba predicted, but she was mistaken.

Next morning I had a letter, and Baba had a card.

'How dare you read my correspondence,' she said, snatching the card from me, 'sly bitch.'

I read my own letter upstairs:

Dear Sweetling,

How are you? We parted bad friends and don't think I didn't notice the resentment in your fat bottom as you hurried in to your huckster shop.

Anyhow I've been thinking of you and I forgive you everything. I'm working very hard on those glorious sewerages which I told you about; and I'm staying in a hotel, which is full of young American girls! Makes me nostalgic for the old days, but have no fears, none are as awkward or as pretty as you. You are a nice, kind, dear, sweet, round-faced pollop and now that I'm all mixed up in you and your mad hair, don't set fire to yourself until I come back to you.

If you have any days off, please go out and light fires in the bedrooms and open windows, as I'm sure A. won't.

Good night from your devoted

E.

It was written on hotel paper and I read it several times.

On the way to work I could see his face as clearly as if he were walking with me – his long, unyielding face with the well-defined bones and the fine skin that came away from the bone when you pinched it. I could see his body too, his nakedness; the curious elegance with which he walked across the room. I remembered the funny hang of the pouch between his hairy thighs and how I had been afraid.

'It won't bite you,' he said, and to the touch it grew miraculously like a flower between the clasp of my fingers.

I wondered if I would be afraid next time.

*

In the shop I wrote to him and posted it at lunch-time.

As I came in to lunch there was a smell of stew in the

hall and a typed letter on the table for me. My heart leaped with pleasure as I thought it was a second letter from him, but it had a Dublin postmark.

It read:

Are you aware that this man is evil and has lived with numerous women and then walked out on them. If you cease to disregard this information I shall have to secure your parents' address and inform them.

A friend

I nearly fainted black out when I read it. I reread it, and noticed that two words had been crossed out before the word 'evil'. At first, 'treacherous' had been put down, then 'bad', and finally 'evil'. It was a typed letter. I had no idea who could have sent it.

I could not eat any lunch. I knew that something was going to happen.

Chapter Eight

It happened at four o'clock, as I packed an order of groceries into a cardboard box.

It was New Year's Eve and we were busy with orders. Suddenly the shop door was pushed open with a bang, and two very small men helped my father in to the shop. He had been drinking.

'Happy New Year,' he said to me.

'Hello,' I said. My breathing quickened and I began to shake all over. He introduced me to the two men and told them how clever I was, and that later on I would do an examination for the civil service.

'No future in this place, no future in it....' His eyes roamed around the dusty shelves and spotted the cartons of Hall's Wine along the top ledge of a glass case.

'They're empty,' I said. They were empty. We just put the cartons on display, and kept the bottles in a press under the counter.

'Give me a bottle,' he said, his eyes red-rimmed and frantic. I got a half-bottle from the press and said that we had no more in stock. He tore the paper seal, and uncorked it and drank. He had a new hat. Always when he set out on a binge he bought a new brown hat. Our wardrobes were stacked with brown hats.

His friends were smaller than me – they were jockeys. They asked if they could weigh themselves, but my father was leaning against the porcelain scales and it did not register properly. Soon after, they left.

'Good friends of mine, they gave me a good tip for the Curragh Races,' he said as they walked towards the door, and I knew that the minute they were out of sight he would turn on me.

'I wasn't expecting you,' I said.

'I wasn't expecting this,' he said, searching in his overcoat pocket. He took a letter out and said, 'I want to talk to you, my lady; you living like a heathen. ...'

'What's that?' I said, snatching the letter. It was a typed letter and I read it feverishly.

Dear Mr Brady,

It is high time you knew about your daughter and the company she keeps. For over two months now she's having to do with a married man, who is not living with his wife. He is well known in this city as a dangerous type. No one knows where he gets his money and he has no religion. He shipped his wife to America and the house is a blind to get young girls out there and dope them. Your daughter goes there alone. I hope I am not too late in warning you as I would not like to see a nice Catholic Irish girl ruined by a dirty foreigner.

A friend

I read it again through a mist of tears, not only because my father stood over me bursting with temper but because someone thought of Eugene as being like that.

'Nice thing for your poor father to get in his old age.' I had forgotten how tall my father stood, and how harsh his voice sounded.

'It's not true,' I said. 'None of it is true. I know this man' – I couldn't bring myself to say Eugene's name – 'but Baba knows him too and my landlady, and everybody.'

'Is he a divorced man?'

'He is, but ...'

His thin face was very red. 'Where is he? I'll hammer the life out of him.'

'He's gone away,' I said.

'He's having nothing more to do with you,' my father said. 'You'll never set eyes on him again.'

That was too much to hear. 'I'm my own boss, I'll do what I like.'

'I'll have no impertinence!' he shouted.

Mrs Burns rushed out to see what all the commotion was about. She told my father what a nice girl I was and suggested that I take him over to Joanna's for a cup of tea. She did not want him in the shop, because he was shouting and he looked wild.

Joanna did not want him either.

'Maybe throw sick on the best carpet and Gustav out,' Joanna said to me in the kitchen, as we made a pot of tea. My father sat in the dining-room, drinking the Hall's Wine and threatening what he would do to Eugene.

I took three pounds from his old overcoat, which was hanging on the hall-stand. It had a smell of stale drink and cigarettes. There were pound notes in various pockets, so that I didn't think he'd miss the few pounds I took. He must have got the money for grazing, because although Jack Holland owned most of our land my father had kept some fields at the far end of the boundary.

After he'd had the tea, Joanna asked me to take him away, as he was falling asleep on the chair.

I took him up the road, towards the phone booth, so as to ring for a taxi, to go to the railway station.

'You're coming home with me, you know that?' he said.

I walked in front, to separate myself from him. 'I can't leave my job,' I said.

'Don't think you're fooling me,' he said. 'You're coming with me, and that's that.' He pushed his new hat back on his head and scratched the top of his forehead where the hat-band had made a red rim.

'Stop shouting on the road,' I said. A lot of customers lived on that road and I did not want to be disgraced.

'You're coming home,' he said.

I did not want to go home. Even at the best of times the house saddened me. After my mother was drowned, our place was mortgaged and Jack Holland bought it. My father moved to the gate-lodge and Jack let our big house to an order of nuns. The nuns left after a year or so, because the house was too damp and too expensive. While it was idle, stories began to circulate about my mother's ghost being seen there. A bank official who was to have rented the house changed his mind when he heard about the ghost, so in desperation Jack Holland asked my father to go back for a few months, to dispel the foolish rumours about Mama. My father was there for over a year now, and my Aunt Molly (my mother's sister) came to look after him when her own father died. She had but the wind and a few bantams to talk to, in her house in the Shannon island, so that she liked caring for my father and seeing the postman and an occasional visitor.

I rang the nearest taxi rank, and asked the driver to collect us, outside the phone booth, then waited, stiffly, my face turned away.

'You haven't a lot to say to your father.'

'Should I have?' I said bitterly.

I was planning something. I decided that just as he got into the taxi I would run away, on the excuse that I had left something important in Joanna's. But even as I planned it, I saw how fruitless it would be.

We waited. My toes felt cold and I curled and uncurled them to try and keep warm.

'Here it is,' I said, putting up my hand, and the taxi slowed down.

I opened the door and he got in awkwardly. He was too tall for getting in and out of motor-cars.

'Oh I forgot my bag of clothes, I'll have to run back for it,' I said.

'What run? We'll drive back for it,' he said, with suspicion.

'No, there's no need,' I said, 'anyhow the taxi couldn't turn round in the cul-de-sac, I won't be a sec.' And I closed the door on his shouting voice and ran back in the direction of Joanna's house. I knew that it would take the driver a few minutes to turn round on the main road, so I reckoned that if I got to Joanna's side-road in time, I could knock at the first house and hide. I knew the woman there as I often gave sweets to her two children.

I ran recklessly, bumped into a lame man and didn't even wait to apologize. I was nearly at the corner of Joanna's road when I heard the car close behind me.

'Come back here,' my father called. I ran faster, knowing that he was too drunk to catch up with me. But the car drove on a little, passed me by, and then he jumped out just as I turned to run the other way. He caught me by the belt of my coat.

'I tell you, you won't do this again.'

79

'I'm not going home, I'm not going home,' I screamed, hoping that some passing stranger might rescue me.

'Get in that car,' he said. I held on to a railing.

'I'll tell the police,' I said, and by now the taxi-driver had come out of the car and both of them hustled me towards the door which was swinging open.

They pulled me across, and I was afraid that my new coat (Eugene's) would get torn. Children gathered across the road to look at us, and the taxi-driver said I ought to have more sense and why would I not go with my father who wanted to save me from the streets.

I sat as far away from my father as I could, and during the ride he abused me and told the taxi-driver what an impossible girl I had been, and how I had driven my mother to an early grave.

'Good beating she wants,' he said, as I cried to myself.

At the station he bought two single tickets and we passed through the ticket barrier and down the platform towards the train, which was due to leave in about twenty minutes.

'D'you want a cup of tea?' he asked as the train began to move. It was the first word we had spoken since we got in. I knew that he suggested it so that he could go to the bar; the bar and the restaurant adjoined each other on those trains.

'No, thanks,' I said to spite him. I was wondering how I'd escape; whether I'd get off at the first stop or pull the communication cord when he wasn't looking and jump off. In my mind I planned very brave things, but the moment he spoke to me I quavered.

'You go and have a cup of tea,' I said, but he guessed my motives and told me to come with him. I followed him up the open corridor, between the rows of seats, in search of the bar.

He ordered a double whisky for himself, and tea and a ham sandwich for me. The tea was served in a plastic carton which was so hot that I had to hold it with my handkerchief.

'Well, I declare to Christ if it isn't Jimmy Brady,' a voice said behind my back.

'Tim,' my father said, standing up to greet an old friend.

They grabbed each other's coat collars and looked into each other's red, drinking faces and swore about the coincidences of life.

I simply said, 'Oh, God!' – knowing now that everything would be worse and that my father would drink twice as much. The man's name was Tim Healy and he had played hurley with my father at school.

They went across to the counter and Dada bought drinks for Tim Healy, and for two other friends who had been drinking with Tim before we arrived.

'That's my youngster, I'm bringing her home.' Dada nodded towards me, and the three strange men clasped my hand and one man squeezed it until the signet ring on my little finger dug a mark into the next finger. Tim Healy ordered orangeade for me, and came and sat with me.

'Move up there,' he said, and I moved to a new part of the stool where it felt cold. He sat on the space I had nicely warmed.

'Well, Caithleen? Caithleen, isn't it? How are you? You're a fine girl, and so well you ought to be, you have a decent father and a lovely mother. How's your mother?'

'She's dead,' I said. 'She got drowned.'

Sudden tragedy filled his bull-like face and he looked as if he was going to cry. He caught my elbow and said that he wouldn't have wished it for twenty thousand pounds.

'The best go first,' he said, sniffling to control his tears.

'Yes.' Stupid Christmas streamers were hanging from the windows and a tinselled 'Peace on earth to men of goodwill' was on the wall underneath a caption to drink more porter.

Tim Healy wanted to go over and sympathize with Dada, but I asked him not to. I knew that they would drink very much more, if Dada was reminded at that moment of my mother's death.

'You know me,' Tim Healy said, 'I wouldn't hurt a fly.'

Later on he told me that he inspected sausage factories and was on his way to Maraborough, to do a job there next morning.

'If you saw a sausage made!' he said, opening his mouth wide and drawing his head back to indicate some unmentionable scandals in sausage factories. He bored me, but I put up with it because I saw in him a fresh chance of escape. I decided that when he and my father started reminiscing about hurling matches, and goals scored, I'd slip away, hide in a lavatory, and get off at the next stop.

My father spoke out bravely about the blackguard who had tried to ruin me. They shook their heads, saying that I was only a child and had no sense. Four glasses of orangeade were lined up for me.

'Givvus an aul' song there,' Tim said to my father.

'I can't,' my father said, 'I'm getting old – we'll all sing something,' and they sang 'Kevin Barry'. Some were a few words ahead of others but that did not matter. The young bar-boy looked uneasy, as if he should stop them, but Dada shook a friendly fist at him and asked him to sing up.

'The bloody English,' Tim said when they had finished. A sigh of agreement went around the bar.

Without warning, my father started to sing, 'I sigh for Jeannie with the nut-brown hair', and all the time he kept raising his chin and pulling his shirt collar away from his Adam's apple, as if it were choking him. His eyes filled with tears and I supposed that he thought of Mama, because he used to sing that song at Christmas when we had a card party and Mama gave two geese as a prize.

I looked out the window and saw the dark, formless fields slipping past me as we sped farther and farther from Dublin, towards the central plain of Ireland.

I could go now, I thought, so I stood up, ready to slip towards the exit.

'Where are you off to?' my father called.

'To the cloakroom,' I said. I didn't like to say lavatory.

'Oh, a natural requirement, a natural requirement,' Tim said, and then winking at my father he said, 'I'll show the lady' and he linked me up the corridor. My father must have told him to keep an eye on me.

'Don't worry,' he said as we stumbled along, over the jolting floor, 'you'll meet a nice boy yet, one of your own kind.'

I did not tell him this but I now knew that I would never marry one of my own kind.

Passing through the restaurant car, I saw with longing people eating rashers and eggs; tucking clean napkins under their chins; saying ordinary, pleasant things to one another. The calm of their lives made me furious with my own fate.

'We'll be "bona-fide" if we walk much farther,' Tim Healy said as we went through the eating-car and past a row of first-class carriages where people lolled their heads against linen head-rests, and three priests played cards.

'I'll wait for you,' he said. I did not manage to escape that time.

At Maraborough, Tim Healy and his two friends got out. There were big, maudlin farewells and large whiskies all round.

Then I was alone with my father again.

He was quite drunk now, swaying on the high stool. He took a box of squashed cigarettes from his pocket:

'Here, have one, have one of mine,' he said to the bar-boy who linked him up the corridor, back to the enclosed carriage, where I had left my gloves and an evening paper. Some carriages were open, but ours was an enclosed one.

'I can walk on my own two feet,' he kept saying.

'Of course you can,' the bar-boy replied, but still linked him.

Dada sat in a corner seat, and closed his eyes instantly.

Roscrea was the next stop, but I knew that it was not for thirty minutes or more, by which time he might have wakened up. Still seated, I edged up near the window, above which was the communication cord and the red sign, saying 'Five pound penalty for improper use'. I was going to pull it. As I prayed for courage I tried to think of the fun of it, of him being wakened up suddenly by a guard, and asked for five pounds. By then I would be gone; vanished into the dark fields. It looked very dark outside and I hoped that there would be a house somewhere near. Then I thought of savage dogs, guarding a farm-house gate, but I still decided to go.

I stood up, quietly; and took one last look to make sure he was asleep. A quenched cigarette was hanging slackly from his lower lip and he slept with his head tilted backwards. I felt a little sorry for him – so weak and broken, and unlovely.

Don't be an ass, stop pitying him, that's what ruined your mother's life, I told myself as I raised my hand, to the black communication chain. I was shaking like a leaf.

'Pull it, pull it quickly,' I whispered to myself.

Either my anxious whisper wakened him, or else he had not been asleep at all, because suddenly he sat up and said:

'Where are we, where are we?'

I took my hand down and collapsed on to the seat, pleased almost that I had been saved the ordeal of pulling the cord.

'I was just looking out to see where we were,' I said, hating myself for being so cowardly.

'You've travelled this long enough to know where you are.'

He lit a cigarette, and by some manner of means stayed awake for the rest of the journey. A hackney-car met us at our own, dimly-lit station. I had sent my aunt a telegram earlier in the evening.

*

Our kitchen was as dismal as I had remembered it – old clothes of Dada's across a chair, a faded piece of palm stuck behind the picture of the Sacred Heart and before it a small red lamp burning. We put him to bed, and my aunt then lectured me, as I knew she would.

She made some tea and we ate the remains of a Christmas cake which was kept in a rusty biscuit-tin. It was awful, but I ate it to please her. She rambled on and on about the good education I'd had, and the shock it was for my father to get such a letter.

*

Later she stole his shoes and hid them, so that he could not go out next day and raise the wind for more drink. We said the rosary, aloud.

We could not go to bed, in case he might set fire to the

blankets; so we sat there, and after a while she dozed on the card chair. It was a chair my mother got for cigarette coupons before the last war. I was four or five when the war began, and it meant nothing to me except that the cigarette people stopped putting coupons in the packets and we got no more of those folding chairs with the green canvas seats.

*

While she dozed, I planned what I would do – leave on the first bus the following morning, before my father wakened up. I knew that it was disloyal to her, but I was determined to go back to Eugene, Eternal Damnation or not.

I counted my money, counted the hours, heard her snore slightly, and sometimes from my father's room I heard a moan or the gluggle of drink being poured. He had left the light on.

I was going away again, going away, for ever.

Chapter Nine

TOWARDS morning my aunt sat up and rubbed her startled eyes with the back of her hand.

'What are you *doing*?' she asked. I had my coat on and I was applying make-up in front of the smoky glass of the Holy Picture. It was her make-up, as I had forgotten my own. I had found yellow powder in an old envelope and a worn puff beside her prayer book. There was lipstick too which looked as if it would give you disease, as it was dried-up and smeared with hairs. My aunt must have found it somewhere, as she never used lipstick herself. I was applying it, when she spoke to me.

'I'm getting ready,' I said as casually as possible.

'Ready for what?' she asked, running her hand through her grey hair which was broken in many places, from having been burned too often with a curling-tongs.

'I'm going back,' I said. 'I have to go back to my job.'

'You can't do that,' she said, 'run out and leave me,' and she staggered up. 'Don't go, don't leave me,' she pleaded. 'He'll kill me,' she said. 'To find you gone.' There were tears in her tired eyes. A life of tears. She had had her own sorrows. Her young love had been shot one morning on the Bridge of Killaloe, during the time of the Black and Tans. She had remained loyal to her murdered love and kept a picture of him in a gold locket on her neck. It was impossible to leave her; she was too nice and had made too many sacrifices.

'I'll stay,' I said wearily. Her arms came round me and I felt her damp eyes on my neck.

It was New Year's Day and we should have gone to Mass but she said that God would forgive us, as we had to stay and look after my father.

Then we heard cows lowing as they went towards the yard gate and Maura pounded on the back door. She was a local girl who came to milk morning and evening.

'Mam, are you up?' she called as she lifted the latch and stuck her head in. She grinned from behind new steel-rimmed spectacles.

'Welcome home,' she yelled to me. She always yelled, no matter how near to her you were; she spoke as if against the force of a terrible wind.

'There's a calf hanging out of the cow dead,' she said to my aunt.

'Who's dead?' my aunt said, raising her eyes to the ceiling. Maura's simple-mindedness appalled her.

'The calf is hanging out of the cow dead,' Maura repeated, thrilled at having something important to relate. Then she said that she'd go for the vet, and before we could stop her she ran off. I wanted to go because Mr Brennan, the vet, was Baba's father and I knew that he would help me or that his wife Martha would. I thought of their pretty house with white rugs on the maple floor and a picture of Baba and me on the grey wall. I called Maura back, but she did not heed me. She ran pounding across the front field, sometimes taking great leaps off the ground and letting forth a yell of satisfaction.

We went out to see what was wrong.

In daylight the place looked more desolate. The privet hedge had yellowed from some disease and the wild rose shrubs were trampled. Cows came in and out over the sagging paling wire.

'There's black frost,' my aunt said. Two tea-towels spread out to dry had frozen stiff. Walking past the empty rusted water-tank, my aunt said:

'Do you remember long ago?'

Hickey, our workman, used to stand there on summer evenings, admonishing the cows to drink up. The cows – which belonged to Jack Holland mostly – now drank from cement troughs, farther down.

As Maura had told us, a calf's head hung from the cow. The poor cow was moaning and lashing her tail, but there was nothing we could do for her until Mr Brennan came. My aunt ran back to get hot oatmeal, and while she was away the bus for Limerick passed at the front gate. I cried

87

two solitary tears, knowing that I was doomed to stay among the dead thistles.

The cow would not take the oatmeal, and she kept trying to turn her head around, to see the dead calf.

When Mr Brennan came he got Maura and my aunt to drive her slowly to the yard, and he followed on in his motor-car, taking care to avoid the tree stumps and hillocks of grass on the way.

Walking back alone, I sighed at the sadness of the damp, dilapidated house, and wondered if it was, as my aunt had said, a curse which had been put upon it. Jackdaws flew in and out of the various chimneys. Dada was in the kitchen, searching for his shoes. Nervously, I got them from the coal scuttle and dusted the slack off them with a new goose wing.

'They must have fallen in,' I said.

'Fallen in!' He took his hat off the dresser and did not wait to hear about the sick cow. He wanted to get out for a drink.

I laid the table for breakfast. The tea-spoons were tarnished and they smelt funny. In Mama's day there were boards in the cutlery drawer, marking a division for knives, forks, spoons. Now everything was jumbled in there, cutlery, the old scissors, hairy twine, a tin-opener, butter papers that had gone rancid, and cow horns. They kept cow horns for pouring paraffin oil or machine oil and dosing cattle.

'And how are you, hadn't time to shake hands with you,' Mr Brennan said as he came down later on to wash his hands. I poured water from the kettle into a tin basin and got a clean towel.

'Thanks,' he said, looking at me sharply. He came to the point quickly; I tried to talk about Baba but he interrupted me :

'I saw that letter your father got.'

'It's funny how people want to believe the worst,' I said, without knowing how I said it.

'I'm very, *very* disappointed in you,' he said. 'I thought I could rely on you.'

I felt that I had lost him as a friend but I thought that his wife, Martha, would help me, as she professed to understand about men and love. I was glad therefore when he suggested that I go over home with him, to collect penicillin for the sick cow.

*

Martha was arranging a bowl of roses when we got in to their centrally-heated hallway.

'Here she is,' Mr Brennan said, showing distaste, and left us together.

'My goodness, Caithleen, you've grown half a foot.' She shook hands with me. Tim Hayes, the hackney-car owner, must have said that I came home, because she was not surprised to see me.

'Nice flowers,' I said, feeling uncomfortable. Mr Brennan had given me another lecture in the car.

'Yes, smell them.' They were plastic roses which had been sprayed with some sort of perfume.

'Aren't they pretty?' she said. They were sickening.

'Baba all right?' she asked casually.

'She's fine.'

In the kitchen, she made me a cup of tea. They had papered the walls with new striped paper so I admired it. We had a cigarette.

'Tell me all the news,' she said. I sat at the end of the table and told her about Eugene. I just said that we met a couple of evenings a week and had dinner, and that he was very nice and very good-looking.

'You'd like him,' I said to soften her. Her expression did not change, but she blinked a lot.

'Will you help me to get away from here,' I said desperately.

'Help you!' she exclaimed, and blew cigarette smoke deftly from her delicate nostrils. She laughed, nervously, almost as if she were enjoying it. 'But you must be mad, to think of a man like that. It's out of the question!'

'Oh, please, please, you must listen to me,' I pleaded.

She said, unflinchingly, 'Baba's father and I agree that you should not see this man again.' This was the Martha who once drank gin-and-it with commercial travellers!

89

I laid my head on the plastic-topped table and began to cry loudly as I cried when I was small, and was not allowed to wear one of Mama's georgette dresses for fun.

'Sssh, ssh, the boss is coming in now and don't let him catch you crying,' she said, taking a silk handkerchief which she had tucked in the gold bracelet of her tiny wrist-watch.

'I'll pray for you, honestly. If you ask God He'll help you to bear it.' She seemed to have got very religious.

Mr Brennan had tea with us, and Martha talked of her visit to Oberammergau the previous summer.

'It would do *you* good to see those people,' she said. 'All the men leave their hair uncut for months beforehand, not knowing which one will be destined to play the part of Christ.' She bowed her head as she said 'Christ'.

One small part of me listened for safety's sake, but the rest of my mind puzzled over how I might get away.

Mr Brennan said something. I didn't hear it. I just saw him frown at me.

'She's upset,' Martha explained.

'She'll be all right; she'll get over it in a month or two,' one or other of them said.

I was about to scream but then I saw the expression in their eyes and I laughed instead, to confuse them.

Walking home with the penicillin, I remembered the look in their eyes – bitter, determined. Martha had said that I should stay home and I could go to the technical school with her and learn crochet and tapestry.

I walked very quickly. Above me the clouds raced across a rainy sky and lakelike patches of blue showed between them.

Stay at home! Who was going to be the first to say that I should enter a convent? Why did everybody hate a man they'd never met? All those unhappily married people wanted to be sure that I came home and had it happen to me?

Mad Maura hid behind our wall, watching for me, and I knew with a sinking feeling that my aunt had put her there and had probably paid her sixpence to do it.

*

Nothing else much happened that day, except that my aunt called me aside and asked in a whisper if there was anything wrong with me. She seemed doubtful when I said no.

'But there isn't,' I insisted, outraged by the indelicacy of her question. I thought of how I had failed him in the big, soft bed and I almost laughed at the irony of it.

In the late afternoon I cycled to the village for groceries. My father forgot about housekeeping money when he drank, so I had to spend some of the three pounds which I had stolen out of his pocket in Joanna's hall-stand.

*

The sun had come out after a shower, the wet road gleamed and the hedges sparkled as if diamonds had been thrown on them.

I bought rashers, tea, chicken-and-ham paste, peaches, and then on an impulse I bought a stale iced cake that was going cheap, in the hope that it would cheer us up.

In the village I was sure people stopped to look, wanting to kill me with savage stare-you-out eyes. And school-children began yelling something. Had my father been going round showing the letter to *everyone*?

'Divorce is worse than murder,' my aunt had always said – I would never forget it; that and their staring disapproval.

I rang Mr Gentleman's number to ask for a seat to Dublin but his wife answered the telephone.

'Who's speaking, please?' she asked, and I dropped the phone in terror and rushed out of the booth. The postmistress, who had been listening in at the switchboard, rebuked me for doing such a thing. I never liked her. Once when I was young she asked me if Martha and Mr Brennan slept in twin beds or not. I had not told her. She never forgave me.

I bought two letter-cards so that I could write to Baba and Eugene, and then I hurried up the street to intercede for help from Jack Holland. His pub was closed, the shutters up. In the fading light I read an inked sign under the knocker which said:

Gone on archaeological exploration. Back at eight.

I couldn't stay because my aunt was waiting for the tea, so I went on home. Cycling in the dusk, with the bag of messages knocking against my knee, I thought of Eugene. Sometimes a clear and sudden image of him came to disturb me. I saw the skin of his chest a little reddened underneath the hairs where he had scratched it. I cycled near the ditch to avoid a herd of cows straggling home to be milked.

Then a car came towards me. Its old-world shape told me that it might be Mr Gentleman, so I got off the bicycle, threw it in the ditch and hailed the car. It drove by, but had to slow down anyhow because of the cows. I ran after it breathless. It was Mr Gentleman.

'I was looking for you,' I said when he wound the window down.

'Caithleen!' he said, astonished. I hadn't seen him for two years. He looked thinner, more haggard, but his face still had that strange holy-picture quality that made me think of moonlight and the chaste way he used to kiss me.

'Yes, I'm home,' I said. I rested my elbows on the car window, and my face was almost on a level with his.

'And how is the world using you?' he asked casually. You'd think that we had met only the day before. I put it down to shyness, because he was always shy and slow to start a conversation.

'Not too bad,' I said. I didn't want to tell him the whole story there and then, in case it might hurt his feelings. But did he know it already? Everyone seemed to. Anyhow I knew that he'd ask me to sit in, and maybe take me for a drive.

'I didn't see you in ages,' I said, recalling with shame all the letters I had written to him at his office in Dublin.

'I've been very busy, a hundred and one things, you know how it is.' His voice was the same as ever, a bit foreign (he was half French) and very gentle.

'Yes. I often wondered what happened?' I said. He had persuaded me to go with him to Vienna for a few days, and on the evening that we were to go, he just did not come to collect me.

He looked at me sadly, his face made more plaintive by dusk, and he said, 'It was all for the best really, we would have regretted it.'

'I wouldn't have,' I said truthfully.

He frowned and I knew that he was indeed bitterly ashamed of the times we had been together, in each other's arms, kissing, and saying 'I Love You'.

'You're young,' he said. 'Young people do a lot of foolish things.'

'It wasn't foolish. That was the nicest time in my whole life. . . .'

He sat up suddenly and took a quick breath. 'You're a very, foolish, little, girl, do you know that?'

'You're ashamed of me?'

'No, no, no,' he said with the same impatience as of old. I heard that 'no, no, no' when I asked him to write in my autograph-book; and when I wanted to keep his red setter dog for one night, so as to feel close to him.

'Home for long?'

'Not very long, I'm getting engaged,' I said, wanting to hurt him then.

'Does your father know?'

I heard my voice going hysterical. 'We're going to have a big wedding, caterers from Limerick coming out. . . .'

'That's great news,' he said, and smiled as he looked at his wrist-watch and talked about having to go.

'Let me know what present you'd like,' he said, and his small white hand groped on the dashboard for the car key. He turned the engine on.

' 'Bye,' he said with a touch of the old wounded solitude in his expression. He always gave the impression that he did not want to leave you, but that fate, or duty, or family, forced him away. I don't think I said anything as he drove off.

I knew that he went to the parish priest's house on Wednesdays to play bridge. It was a custom which had arisen in the last year since Mr Gentleman got religious again and carried a big missal to Mass, so local gossip said.

Picking up the bicycle I walked on towards home, indifferent as to whether my aunt waited on tea or not. Night had fallen and I was guided by a full moon. I was trembling with anger and could not cycle. I thought of Mr Gentleman with his pale face, his beautiful, loveless eyes, and I thought of how I used to think he was God. I wished I had some way of hurting him, because of his falseness.

*

The moon made the fields and ditches startlingly bright. Some cows lay under trees, chewing the cud, and one was wheezing. The moon threw my shadow ahead of me, and sometimes I was able to overtake it with the front wheel of my bicycle.

'What kept you?' my aunt called as she came towards me, coughing. She suffered from bronchitis.

'Nothing,' I said. I felt sick and angry with her, and with everyone.

'We hadn't a bit of tea, I thought you wouldn't be so long,' she said as I wheeled the bicycle round the house and threw it against the side wall. She said that Dada had not come in yet.

We made tea, and opened a tin of peaches, but we ate without enjoyment.

Chapter Ten

THREE gloomy days went by. Nothing happened except that my father went out in the mornings and came home late. We suspected that he had raised some money from his uncle or brother.

On the third afternoon we buried the calf because my aunt said that it was beginning to smell. Maura, who could do a man's work, had dug a grave earlier on, and we wheeled the calf down in an old rotted barrow. We went because my aunt said that she could not rely on Maura to do it properly. The calf was in an old sack so that you could not discern its shape or anything about it. It was a bitterly cold day.

I thought of Eugene and wondered what he'd make of this bleak sight – us standing there, watching Maura tip the barrow sideways until the sack toppled in, then reshovelling the earth over it, and pressing it down with the heel of her man's boot. She wore boots and trousers, and all the people in the village called her Micky. She worked for us because she didn't cost much and was useful with milking and doing odd jobs. On the way back the barrow got bogged down in the mud and I had to lift it with Maura to get it free.

'Th'aul' cow is lonesome,' she said. We had put the cow in a house while the calf was being buried, otherwise she would have followed the scent. In the house she was mooing and running around kicking loose stones over the floor. The outhouses were falling down and ivy covered their tumbling walls.

'We're all lonesome,' my aunt said, and Maura grinned and said that she wasn't because there were pictures that night. Travelling pictures came to the village once a week.

*

I had been thinking of some way of escaping, but the thought of their chasing me made me frightened.

95

'This vale of tears,' my aunt said desolately. Burying the calf had saddened her. Death was always on her mind. Death was so important in that place. Little crosses painted white, were stuck up on roadside ditches here and there to mark where someone had been killed for Ireland, and not a day seemed to pass but some old person died of flu, or old age, or a stroke. Somehow we only heard of the deaths, we rarely heard when a child was born, unless it was twins, or a blue baby, or the vet had delivered it.

'Th' evenings will be getting long soon,' I said to my aunt to cheer her up, but she just sighed.

We ate dinner in the kitchen. We had salty rashers, a colander of green cabbage and some potatoes reheated from the previous day. While we were eating in silence, a car drove up and around by the side of the house. My aunt blessed herself as she saw a stranger help my father out.

'Grand evening,' my father said as he came in and handed her a brown paper parcel of meat soggy with blood. The stranger had had some drinks also but did not stagger.

'You're settling down!' he said to me. I tried to ignore him by concentrating on peeling a cold potato.

'I met Father Hagerty over in the village, he wants to have a chat with you,' he said.

My heart began to race, but I did not say anything.

'You're to go and see him.'

I put butter on the potato, and ate it slowly.

'D'you hear me?' he said with a sudden shout.

'There, there, she'll go,' my aunt said and she linked him into the back room. The stranger hung around for a few minutes until she came out, and then asked for a pound. We had no money but we gave him three bottles of porter which had been hidden in a press since Christmas-time.

My aunt put them in a paper bag and he went off, swearing. We had no idea where he came from.

We sat by the cooker and listened for my father's call. At about nine o'clock he cried out and I ran in to him.

'I think I'm going to die,' he said, as his stomach was very sick. The news cheered me up no end – I might get away – so I gave him a dose of health salts.

We went to bed early that night. I slept in the room opposite my aunt's, and when I had closed the door I sat down on the bed and wrote a long letter to Baba, for help. I wrote six or seven pages, while the candle lasted. I had already written her a letter-card, but had no answer. It occurred to me that maybe they had told the postmistress to keep my letters.

A wind blew down the chimney, causing the candle flame to blow this way and that. There was electricity in the house, but we were short of bulbs. I hid the letter under the mattress and undressed. The sight of my purple brassière made me recall with longing the Sunday morning Baba and I had dyed all our underwear purple. Baba read somewhere that it was a sexy colour, and on the way home from Mass we bought five packets of dye. Sneaky old Gustav must have been peeping through the keyhole of the bathroom, because suddenly Joanna had rushed upstairs and pushed the door in.

'Poison colour in the basin,' she shouted as she burst in.

'You might have knocked, we could have been doing something very private,' Baba said.

'Poison water,' Joanna said, pointing to the weird-coloured water in the basin. Our underwear turned out very nice, and some boy asked Baba if she was a Cardinal's niece.

I kept a jumper on in bed. We were short of blankets. I had only an ironing blanket over me and a quilt that my aunt had made. The candle had burnt right down to the saucer as I lay on my side and closed my eyes to think of Eugene. I remembered the night he asked me to do some multiplication for him. He knew all about politics, and music, and books, and the insides of cameras, but he was slow to add. I totted up the amount of money he should get for one hundred and thirty-seven trees, at the rate of thirty-seven and six per tree. He had sold some trees to a local timber merchant, because the woods needed thinning. There were blue paint marks on the 'sold' trees, but he said that at night the timber merchant had sent a boy along to put paint marks on extra trees.

'Nearly three hundred and fifty pounds,' I said, reckoning it roughly first, the way we were taught to at school, so that we should know if our final answer was wildly wrong.

'And out of that he'll make a small fortune,' Eugene said, detailing what would happen to the tree from the time it was felled until it became a press or a rafter. I could see planks of fine white wood with beautiful knots of deeper colour, and golden heaps of sawdust on a floor, while he fumed about the profit which one man made.

I went to sleep wondering if I would ever see him again.

In the morning my aunt brought me tea and said that the priest had sent over word that he was expecting me. I dressed and left the house around eleven. My father had stayed in bed that morning and Mad Maura ran to the village for a half-bottle of whisky, on tick.

Always when I escaped from the house I felt a rush of vitality and hope as if there was still a chance that I might escape and live my life the way I wanted to.

It was a bright windy morning, the fields vividly green, the sky a delicate green-blue, and the hills behind the fields smoke-grey.

It's nice, nice, I thought as I breathed deeply and walked with my aunt's bicycle down the field towards the road.

I did not go to the priest's house. I was too afraid, and anyhow I thought that no one would ever find out.

I went for a spin down by the river road with the intention of posting Baba's letter in the next village.

The fields along the road were struck into winter silence, a few were ploughed and the ploughed earth looked very, very dead and brown.

If only I could fly, I thought as I watched the birds flying and then perching for a second on thorn bushes and ivied piers.

I cycled slowly, not being in any great hurry. It was very quiet except for the humming of electric wires. Thick black posts carrying electric wires marched across the fields and the wires hummed a constant note of windy music.

At the bottom of Goolin hill I got off the bicycle and pushed it slowly up; then half way I stood to look at the ruined pink mansion on the hill. It had been a legend in my life, the pink mansion with the rhododendron trees all round it and a grey gazebo set a little away from the house. A rusted gate stood chained between two limestone piers, and the avenue had disappeared altogether. I thought of Mama. She had often told me of the big ball she went to in that mansion when she was a young girl. It had been the highlight of her whole life, coming across at night in a row-boat from her home in the Shannon island, changing her shoes in the avenue, hiding her old ones and her raincoat under a tree. The rhododendrons had been in bloom, dark-red rhododendrons; she remembered their colour, and the names of all the boys she danced with. They had supper in a long dining-room, and there were dishes of carved beef on the sideboard. Someone made up a song about Mama that night and it was engraved on her memory ever after:

> Maura Neary, swanlike
> She nearly broke her bones
> Trying to dance the reel-set
> With the joker Johnny Jones.

'Who was Johnny Jones?' I used to ask.

'A boy,' she would say, dolefully.

Standing in the middle of the road, thinking of all this, I almost got run over by the mail van. He had to swerve towards the ditch.

'I'm sorry,' I said, shaking all over with fright. He laughed at me. He was a good-humoured boy and asked if I wanted a lift. A notice gummed to the windscreen said, 'No passengers', but two women sat in the back of the car on bags of mail. I thought ridiculously of what would happen if the mail-bags contained turkey eggs from the turkey station or a gilt clock on its way as a wedding gift to someone. I asked him to post a letter for me in Limerick that evening. He drove out from Limerick every morning to deliver mail in the various villages along the way and then went back in the evening, collecting more letters.

'Right you be,' he said, and I gave him the letter for Baba and two shillings for himself.

Then I got on my bicycle and cycled towards home. It was

a downhill ride most of the way, so I did not have to use the pedals much. They were stiff, and needed oiling. The tyres hissed, the spokes hummed, and the road was a winding, tarred ribbon of blue. I was planning what I would tell my aunt, and I did not feel a bit guilty as I cycled up our own field and came in home.

I nearly fell when I saw the parish priest sitting in our kitchen drinking tea from one of the good cups.

'Here she is now,' my aunt said. The priest looked at me:

'Well, Caithleen! I imagined that something had detained you, so I dropped over to see how you were.'

'You were gone when I called,' I said, hastily.

He stared at me very hard.

'If you'll excuse me, Father,' my aunt said, and disappeared, so that he could talk to me alone.

Father Hagerty began at once. 'Caithleen, I've heard some bad news from your father. Sit down and tell me about it.'

I sat opposite him. My aunt had put a cushion between his back and the wooden rungs of the chair, and he looked as if he were settling in for a long talk.

'It's nothing very much, I met a man, that's all,' I said, trying to be casual. He frowned. The frown produced four deep lines on his greyish forehead, and for no particular reason I remembered back to the time when he was collecting funds to build a new chapel and held dances in the town hall on Sundays. He served behind the mineral bar himself, and people said that he drained the dregs of bottles to make new bottles of lemonade. Hickey once handed in a pound for one ticket and got no change and, after that, always brought the exact money, which was two shillings.

'You are walking the path of moral damnation.'

'Why, Father?' I said, quietly, folding my hands on my lap to try and look composed. I longed to cross my legs but still held to the belief that it was disrespectful.

'This man is dangerous company. He has no faith, no moral standards. He married a woman and then divorced her – whom God hath joined together, let no man put asunder,' he said.

'He seems to be a good man. He doesn't drink, or anything,' I said.

'Ah you poor child,' Father Hagerty said with a frank and winning smile which I remembered from my schooldays. He always smiled at children and gave them sweets. On the day of my Confirmation he consoled me with a shilling when my white veil got torn on a spear of the chapel gate.

'More tea, Father?' I said.

'No more,' he said, putting his pale hand over the top of the china cup. It was very strong tea, to which creamy milk had been added.

'Think of your eternal soul,' he said, as if he were giving a sermon from the altar, 'think of the harm you might do to it. We are all under sentence of death, we never know the hour nor the minute. . . .'

That worried me, and I held my head down and could think of nothing to say in reply. You could see yourself in the shine on his black boots.

'God is testing your love; God has allowed this man to cross your path and tempt you, so that you will reaffirm your love for Him. You have only to ask, and *He* will give you the grace to resist this great temptation.'

'If God is good, he won't burn me,' I said to Father Hagerty, quoting Eugene's exact phrase.

The priest sat upright and shook his head sadly from side to side: 'Child, don't you realize that you are speaking heresy! You know that you cannot enter into the Kingdom of Heaven unless you obey the word of God. You're turning your back on God,' he said, raising his voice. I looked into his eyes and wondered what lay behind them – pity, or just a sense of duty. He put his hand to his mouth and coughed politely. He expected me to say something, but I had nothing to say.

The side door opened and my father came in, in his shirt and long combinations. He got a shock when he saw the priest.

'Excuse me, Father, I didn't know you were here,' he said, withdrawing into the hall.

'That's all right, Mr Brady.'

My father got his overcoat then, and came in to the kitchen with his shoe-laces slapping around, and his eyes large and bloodshot. He proceeded to make himself a cup of tea. He said that he hoped Father Hagerty was giving me a real straightening out, and that I was a very stubborn girl and would listen to no one. Stubborn, that's what I'd be. They could talk and rant and talk, but I wouldn't answer; I'd just sit there, fiddling with the cuff of my cardigan, a faint smile on my face – though my father might hit me for being insolent. And that was what I did.

'She won't listen to sense,' Dada said.

'She'll listen to God Almighty,' Father Hagerty said.

'She hadn't even a rosary beads when she came home,' Dada said.

'Oh well, wait a minute,' Father Hagerty said, searching in the pocket of his shabby black coat. 'I brought her a little book.'

It was a beautiful leather-bound volume with gilt-edging – *The Imitation of Christ*.

'Thanks, Father.' I took it and saw one tear of mine drop on to the brown leather cover.

'Oh, that's too good altogether, Father Hagerty,' Dada said, and told me to thank the priest properly. I thanked him a second time and he said that I should read a little of it every day and learn to model myself in the image of Christ.

Then he came to the point that I dreaded. He asked me to promise never to see the divorced man again, never to write to him, never to let my thoughts dwell on the occasions I had been with him.

'Promise me that?' he asked.

'Do what you're told,' Dada said. But I couldn't.

The priest asked me again, and Dada shouted, and I just held my head down and kept silent. Dada shouted louder then, and the priest said, 'Now, now, Mr Brady,' and told Dada to take his cup of tea back to bed and not to get excited.

'It's as big a sin for my father to be like that as for a man to have two wives,' I said to the priest when we were alone.

'I'm surprised at you,' he said, 'to speak of your good father like that. Every man takes a drink. It's the climate.' His eyebrows were very bushy when he frowned.

He asked again: 'Will you promise me not to see that man?'

'I'll think about it,' I said. It was the only way of getting rid of him.

'We'll make an Act of Perfect Contrition, the two of us, together.' And he began, 'Oh my God,' and waited while I repeated the three words. Then he said, 'I am heartily sorry,' and paused for me, and so on, until we had finished. I felt an awful hypocrite, saying words that I did not mean.

He looked at his watch and said it was lunch-time, and when he stood up to go I called my aunt from upstairs, so that she could thank him.

'I'll see you over in the church anyhow,' he said to me. 'There's Women's Confraternity this Sunday, and confessions on Saturday night.'

'All right, Father,' I said, making no promises.

'She'll be all right now, she'll be going to dances in no time,' he said, when my aunt came down. She saw him to the gate, and stayed there until his black figure was out of sight.

'Wasn't it terrible, that we hadn't an offering to give him for a Mass,' she said, when she came back.

We had no money. I thought it funny that two grown people living in that large house hadn't a two-shilling piece between them. A tinker wouldn't believe it if she knocked on the door.

'Well thank God he came,' my aunt said.

She seemed to think that everything was all right now, and that I was out of danger. The funny thing was that I was more determined than ever to get away.

Chapter Eleven

FINALLY, my father asked us to fetch the doctor because he felt faint, not having been able to eat for several days. The doctor gave him an injection and told us to ration the amount of alcohol he had. We sat with him in turns and gave him soda-water with a small amount of whisky in it – a smaller amount each time. I had not heard from Eugene or Baba and I was sick with worry.

'I'm sorry,' my father kept saying as I sat on the bed and held the glass to his lips. His hands shook so that he could not hold a glass or a razor. He cried like a child. Always after drinking, he cried for days and was ashamed to talk to anyone. His depression was frightening.

' 'Tis nice to have you home,' he said. 'Why don't you get yourself a cigarette? Sure all young people smoke nowadays, I know that, I'm a fairly understanding man....' And I thought of Eugene's desk with packets of cigarettes strewn about, and 'Cancer is painful' written in his clear, square handwriting on some of the packets.

'Go on, can't you,' my father said, and I smoked a cigarette to oblige him. I wondered when he would let me back.

'I'm for your good, of course,' he said. 'It nearly killed me the day I got that letter, to think of you mixed up with a hooligan like that.' The word 'hooligan' incensed me but I held my temper.

'I'm in the world longer than you and I know right from wrong.' He spoke apologetically and wiped his crying eyes in the sheet and blew his nose.

'I'll be better when I go back. I'll be careful,' I said.

'What back?' he said, rising up in the bed. 'You're not going back. You'll get a little job here and help Aunt Molly and myself. I was thinking,' he said – and winked knowingly at me, as if he were going to say something of the greatest secrecy and importance – 'I was thinking that we might open a little business down the road, redo the gate-lodge

104

and start something going. We might pull ourselves together and buy this place back.' He was quite serious.

'I'll just go back and get my clothes from Joanna's house,'
I said, trying not to sound too eager. I'd have said anything
to get away.

His grip on my wrist tightened, and he said, 'We'll go to
Limerick some day, the two of us and get you some new
clothes.'

'That would be waste,' I said.

He asked for another drink, and as there was very little
soda-water in the siphon, my aunt suggested that I go over
to Jack Holland's and get some, before closing time. She
was in the kitchen making a soda cake in a big tin basin,
the Cellophane packet of brown caraway-seeds on the table
beside her. We all liked caraway-seeds in the bread, except
Maura who picked them out, thinking that they were insects
or something.

I collected the empty siphons and set off for Jack
Holland's public house.

*

'Ah, my little auburn poem, "Sweet Auburn! loveliest
village of the plain",' Jack recited as I went in to the shop.
He rushed outside the counter to kiss me, and the tip of his
nose was cold and wet.

'Things cooled down at home, temperature normal?' he
asked.

'Yes,' I said, 'we're just clearing up. We'll have a cart-load
of empties for you.'

'And I'll have a big bill for you,' he said, grinning, as he
tapped my chin with his finger. 'You know what your dad
said when I refused him credit?'

'No.' I knew it well.

'He said,' Jack began. ' "Isn't it as good to have it in the
bloody book as in the bloody barrel." Not funny. Not funny
at all. But let me show you an example of something
humorous.' Jack pointed to a white cardboard sign on which
he had inked a message – 'No credit today but all free
drinks here tomorrow'.

I gave a little laugh to make him happy.

It was Monday night and business was very slack. A tinker-woman sat with her back to us, cursing into an empty porter glass. Her plaid shawl was faded. He filled her another pint and had to let it stand for a minute until the froth settled and he could add more from the barrel. It took ages. When he had placed it on the counter and taken her money, he said to me:

'Yours truly is in danger of becoming imminent.'

'Congratulations,' I said. 'What is it?'

Imminent; he'd have to do something about the shop then – a thick dust had settled on the wine bottles, there were fly-papers hanging since the previous year, and great cobwebs in the corners of the shelves. Imminent; he'd have to wipe his nose and wear different shirts. He wore a grey flannel shirt, a tweed waistcoat, and black boots.

'As a result of recent private archaeological exploration made by yours truly in the Protestant graveyard some important objects have come to light,' he whispered, so that the tinker would not hear him. Opening a drawer he pointed to several rusted things which lay on a heap of sugar – two brooches, a pewter mug, a sword, a chamber-pot, and coils of ravelled wire. The tinker got off the form and came across to have a look. He closed the drawer at once and she muttered some insult to the dying turf fire.

'Jack, will you do me a favour?' I asked.

'Ah,' he said, 'you want to marry me now that I am likely to be imminent.'

His long grey face beamed at me and I realized as I looked into his water-grey eyes that he was the only human person in that whole neighbourhood.

'Jack, will you help me?' I begged.

'A very ominous word. How about a little kiss to cheer a bachelor's dry lips?' he said, and he led me in to the snug so that he could kiss me. The snug was a small compartment cut off from the shop and with frosted glass around it so that you could not see in. I kissed him quickly, to get it over with. I did not mind kissing him really, because he was sixty or seventy and I was just twenty-one and had known him all my life. He loved Mama and later he loved me and wrote poems to us. We never saw the poems. He just hinted about them and then hid them between the yellow, fly-marked pages of Bryan Merryman's *Midnight Court*. It was one of two books which Jack kept over the kitchen fireplace, along with rock salt and a horn rosary beads. The other book was *Moore's Almanac*, which gave a list of pig and cattle fairs and so enabled him to have plenty of drink in stock, and porter barrels tapped for the fair days.

At night when the men left his kitchen and walked through the dark village to their little houses Jack sat down to read Merryman aloud. Some local boys once listened outside the window and heard him repeat lines like – 'The doggedest divil that tramps the hill, With the grey in his hair and a virgin still.'

Jack had found his love in that bawdy book and in my bright reddish hair and in Mama's small, shy words of gratitude whenever he pressed a bottle of sherry on her or coyly dropped apple pips inside the neck of her blouse on Sunday evenings.

'I want to go away and they won't let me,' I said.

'Ah the little wanderer, far-away places with strange sounding names are calling, calling thee,' he sang as he kicked an empty cigarette carton with the toe of his dirty boot. He went away and filled me a glass of cordial, never supposing that my taste might have changed with the years. The cordial was sickly sweet.

'I love someone and they're going to lock me up and not let me see him,' I said, exaggerating a bit to melt his heart. It did not offend him to hear me say that I loved someone else, because for him time stood still about fifteen years ago, and I was a child passing the shop window on my way to school, tapping to say hello, leaving a bunch of bluebells on the sill.

'I've heard the whole story, all the town is talking of it,' he said.

He recited at random from 'Lord Ullin's Daughter': '"And I will give thee a silver pound to row us o'er the ferry, come back, come back, he cried in grief, 'midst waters fast relenting, the waters wild went o'er his child and he was left repenting." '

'The walls have ears,' he said, guiding me into the hall and taking a candle with him from a new packet. The candlelight emphasized the pale, unhealthy colour of his face. He stuck his head through the door, to make sure that the tinker was not stealing anything.

'When could you go?' he asked.

'Any time.'

The door latch clicked. Another customer came in to the shop, and tapped the counter with a coin. He returned to the bar to serve. Alone in the dark because he took the candle with him I heard the mice behind the wainscoting. There was electricity in the shop itself, but he hadn't bothered to have the whole house wired up. Too expensive.

He came back in a moment and said, 'We'll make it Friday. Be here at nine o'clock and I'll have a car to take you to Nenagh.'

'And can you loan me money, for the train?' I hated asking. He promised to loan me five pounds on the guarantee that I would return it.

'One last thing,' he added. 'I help you, you help me. What about influencing your dad and Auntie Molly to go back to the cosy cot?'

The 'cosy cot' was the damp gate-lodge, and Jack wanted them back there so that he could let the big house. I promised to do my best, though I knew that my father had no intention of ever leaving.

Jack got me a noggin of whisky and three siphons of soda and he put chaff in the bottom of the bag so that the things would not get broken.

'Save the siphons and give Jack a little kiss,' he said, and I touched his lips and received two or three clumsy kisses.

'Gather ye rosebuds while ye may,' he said, as he kissed his fingers and waved after me.

'You're an angel,' I called, and meant it.

*

Cycling home I considered the various excuses for being out on Friday night. The dressmaker gave me the solution. I nearly ran over her as she emptied a slop-bucket over the bridge into the river. She could only empty it at night when there was no one looking. She asked for my news and I invited her over on Friday night.

At home, as I gave my father two aspirins and some tea, I said:

'I'm going to the pictures in Limerick Friday night, the Brennans invited me.'

When he had swallowed an aspirin he said, 'Might go myself, if I'm up.'

'The doctor said you can't get up until Sunday,' I warned.

'Maybe your aunt would like to go?' he suggested.

'Maybe,' I said, knowing that my aunt would have to stay at home and entertain the dressmaker.

I got his razor and shaving soap and a bowl of warm water. I held the mirror while he shaved.

'What picture is on?' he asked as he scraped the soaped hairs and then put them on a cracked saucer which I had left there for that purpose.

'*The Lieutenant Wore Shorts*,' I said, recalling a title that I had once seen in Dublin.

'That ought to be a good picture,' he said.

*

The next three days dragged on. In my mind I imagined myself at the moment of escape being found out and dragged back. I worked very hard and talked a lot to my father. I rubbed his rheumatism with Sloan's Liniment and brought tea to my aunt in bed each morning.

'You'll have me spoilt,' she said.

'Not for long,' I thought, as I smiled at her. I smiled a lot for those few days, fearing that if I talked I might betray myself. I smiled and worked. I cleaned the downstairs windows with a paraffin rag and scrubbed hen dirt off the yard flags. Maura offered to help me and she scrubbed like a maniac for two minutes or so but then lost interest and said she had to get potatoes out of the pit for my aunt. I swept the seven lonely, empty bedrooms because bat droppings dotted the floors.

'There's two bats upstairs,' I said to my father, merely making conversation.

'Where?' He jumped out of bed and went upstairs in his long underpants, grabbing the sweeping-brush on the way. He routed them out of their brown winter sleep and killed them.

'Bloody nuisances,' he said, and my aunt swept them on to a piece of cardboard and burned them downstairs in the stove. She said that we must do something about the rooms. The walls were all damp and fur had settled on some parts of the wallpaper. But we just closed the doors and hurried down to the kitchen where it was warm.

*

On Friday evening after tea I made up my face in front of the kitchen mirror and then went in to say good night to my father.

'You'll get a ten-shilling note in my britches pocket,' he said, and I rooted and found the note. It had loose tobacco flakes in its folds. A cigarette had burst in his pocket.

'See you later,' I said.

'All right,' he said. 'You can make me a cup of tea when you come in. Wake me up if I'm asleep.' I didn't shake hands or anything in case he got suspicious.

'Well, have a nice chat,' I said to my aunt. She was sitting in the kitchen waiting for the dressmaker. She had her good black dress on and her best shoes. Instead of shoe-laces she used black ribbon to tie her shoes.

'Enjoy yourself,' she said, smiling at me. She said it so nicely that I almost broke down and told her the truth. She looked pretty as she sat there, her face powdered, her hands fiddling with the chain and locket which she wore around her neck. There was a tray set for tea and sweetcake buttered.

'Don't wait up for me,' I said as I kissed her good night and went out.

Chapter Twelve

ONCE outside the house, I ran. I ran across the fields (safer than going by the road) and came out at the stone stile near the creamery. Then I ran the rest of the way to the village.

Jack had promised to leave the hall door ajar for me in case anyone should see me going in to the bar. I pushed the door, and saw it fall in with a thud. It had come off its hinges the night of his mother's wake and had never been repaired since.

He must have heard the noise, because he came rushing in to the hall from the shop, with a candle in his hand.

'God Almighty, it reminded me of the tans,' he whispered, 'the night they burst the door in.'

I took the candle while he propped the door back, and then he gave me an envelope containing five pounds.

'I'll send it back,' I promised.

'All set?' he whispered, and when I nodded he called to the men in the shop, 'Hold on there, lads, till I come back.'

He led the way down the narrow hall and through the kitchen, where two or three hens roosted over the fireplace.

In the yard the candle blew out immediately. A figure coughed and came towards us.

Jack announced: 'Tom Duggan, here's your woman.'

I said, 'Hello,' in a faint voice.

I knew Tom Duggan by name and I knew that he lived up the country and that he had one iron hand. How like Jack to find me an escort with only one hand.

'Where do you want to go?' Tom Duggan asked abruptly. He had the rough voice which most people down there have. It is a voice bred in wind and hardship and it is accustomed to shouting at things.

'I want to go to Nenagh to catch the eleven-o'clock train,' I said, and wondered if Jack had told him the whole story.

'Get in,' he said. I sat in the car and found that my seat sloped peculiarly. Jack wished me good luck, kissed me dolefully, and slammed the door. The gears tore, rattling the windows deafeningly, and we took three or four laboured bounds forward over the cobbled yard, as he swung out recklessly on to the main street.

'Funny hour o' the night to be going somewhere,' he said. I didn't answer him. Suddenly I was afraid of him, because I remembered about this funny sister he had. She was neither a man nor a woman but a mixture of both. She was called the Freak and he was nicknamed the Ferret because he poisoned so many rats. Together they were known as the Freak and the Ferret although this sister was sometimes called 'the Stripper', because some of the local boys said they'd love to strip her and see what she was like underneath.

'This is a nice car,' I said, trying to flatter him. It was a terrible car, a black, battered old Ford that rattled in every corner.

Passing our own gateway I expected to see my father with a shot-gun. I saw no one except a figure going in by the little wicker gate. It must have been the dressmaker.

Soon we were out on the quiet country road, shaving the unkempt hedges as we turned corners. He was a reckless driver and I wished that he had had his two hands.

'What are you up to?' he asked in an insolent voice. I wondered how much Jack had paid him, and if perhaps I should bribe him further.

'Don't ask me,' I said, trying to convey my panic without offending him. It would be no joke if he left me on the roadside.

'Your father is a nice man. Everyone likes him, he's a decent man. I bought a heifer off him the second last fair day,' he said.

'He often talks about you,' I said, lying.

'Does he now?' I could feel his smile, as he said, 'That's a fine head of hair you have; a fine head of hair to spread out on a pillow.' My aunt had washed it with rain-water for me the day before.

I worried that he might twist back his arm and put his iron hand on my knee. I remembered a story I once heard about his sister. The rate-collector told how when he had gone to the Ferret's house to collect the rates, the funny sister had tumbled him in the hay. The rate-collector said that rates or no rates he'd never go near that house again. Maybe it would be better after all if I got out and walked, I thought.

'What age are you?' he asked. I told him that I was twenty-one, since December.

'You'll soon be settling down,' he said, and then he whistled, 'If I were a blackbird I'd whistle and sing and follow the ship that my true love sails in. . . .'

Later he said, 'If you married me, I'd give you tea in bed in the mornings.'

I pretended that it was a joke and asked him how *he* made tea. I could see Eugene scalding the little china pot, swishing the hot water round it, saying, 'One of the first things I have to teach you is to make a decent cup of tea and then we must teach you how to speak properly, softly.'

'We'll have a pint,' this man the Ferret said as he slowed down outside a pub in the lighted street of Invara. There were twenty or thirty bicycles thrown against the shop window, all jumbled together.

'We'll do no such thing,' I said frantically as I touched his shoulder and begged him to drive on. He drove on. A little later he said, 'Would you marry me?'

I remembered then having heard that no woman would marry him because of this funny sister. He had put advertisements in different papers and had even written to a marriage bureau in Dublin.

'No,' I said flatly, wearily. If I hadn't been so worried I might have joked with him.

'I'm not a bad match,' he said, 'I've a pump in the yard, a bull and a brother a priest. What more could a woman want?'

Did he take off his hook in bed and hang it on the bed-post along with his clothes, I wondered, hysterically.

We were climbing a steep hill and the car throbbed and puffed as if she were going to expire. I sat on the edge of the seat, my finger-nails dug into my palms, praying. A luminous sign rising out of the ditch warned us that there were three miles of bends. Three miles of death, I thought, as he was a terrible driver. We passed a group of fellows who stood at a cross-roads, and they yelled to us in that maniacal way which country boys have of yelling at strange cars. He hooted at them, to show that he was friendly.

'Are we nearly there?' I asked.

'Can't be far off it,' he said, and he turned on a light at the dashboard and looked at the speedometer. 'This bloody thing is broken,' he said and tapped it, but it did not tell him anything.

The road widened and there were cats' eyes in the centre and street lights in the distance and the dark spire of a cathedral. We were almost there.

'How is it ye asked me to do this drive, what's wrong with the two hackney-cars in the town?' he asked, as we drove into the railway station.

'It's a secret,' I said, as I got out and gave him a ten-shilling note and asked him not to tell.

I was an hour too early for the train, so I sat in the Ladies' Waiting Room eating damp chocolate from a machine; and every time a porter came by I pretended to be engrossed in a paper which I had found.

About eleven o'clock the train arrived. I had come outside to stand on the platform and I found an empty carriage quite easily. It was a fast train which stopped at only two stations along the way. Both times I hid in the lavatory in case the police should be searching for me. There was a printed sign over the flush button – 'Please do not flush when train is standing'. Someone had written below it, in indelible pencil – 'there it goes again, all down on the poor aul' farmer'.

*

At Dublin I hid until the other passengers had gone. Then I got off the train, moved with my head down close to the wall, and up to the last remaining taxi.

I was at Joanna's within ten minutes and found the house in total darkness. It was about three o'clock, and the baby from the house two doors away was crying for his night feed. Joanna had lids on the milk bottles as usual. Birds used to drink a little of the cream in the early morning, but Joanna soon stopped that.

Our bedroom was in the front of the house so I threw up wet clods of clay from the flower-beds and then a few pebbles and cinders from the path. I whistled and called, but Baba did not waken. Finally I had to knock. Gustav came down in his overcoat, and I looked so frightened that he brought me in without a murmur. He put the electric fire on in the dining-room and went off to make cocoa. The electric fire made crackling noises as if it were about to explode, and my body was shaking all over.

'You in trouble with Mr Eugene?' Gustav said as he came in with the tray and found me crying.

'Is he back?'

'Oh yeh, yeh,' he nodded his head. 'He here with Baba. They were dining out, I am told.' I could feel my stomach grow hollow with a new fear.

'You go to bed, Gustav,' I said, and he went to bed and I dozed on the settee until the hands of the plate clock moved to seven. Then I went upstairs very quietly and wakened Baba.

'Well, well!' she said, yawning. She sat up and buttoned the two top buttons of her sky-blue pyjamas.

'I'm back,' I said.

'I can see you're back.'

'Tell me about Eugene.'

'He's thirty-five and he's going bald.'

'Did he ask about me?'

'Yeh.'

'And I suppose you told him lies. You didn't even send me the money when I wrote to you from home, they kept me locked up, I ran away last night.'

'I sent you two pounds,' she said. I might have known that Baba would send it, because she has a good heart.

'What about Eugene, Baba, please tell me. Do you think I could go to him?'

'You're twenty-one – it's legal for you to put your head

in the gas oven even if it's against the law,' she said, and she got up and gave me some more money and a travel bag to put my things in and some powder for my face. My face was grey and pulpy from worry and lack of sleep. She took her little gold watch from under the pillow and read the time.

'You'd want to hurry, your aul fella will be here with a pitchfork any minute.' And she hugged me before I left.

'Good luck,' she said, ' 'tis well for you.'

Out in the street I cried with emotion because Baba had been so nice. I caught the first bus into Dublin. There were only half a dozen people on it and they looked grey and wretched like myself.

From the General Post Office I sent two telegrams. One to Eugene which said, 'ARRIVING MIDDAY BUS', and the other to my aunt which said, 'GONE TO ENGLAND ALONE DO NOT WORRY FORGIVE ME WRITING'.

I thought that would confuse them and leave me a few days to decide what I would do.

When the nearest café opened at nine o'clock I went and had coffee and toast. When you are frightened you are certain that everyone is an enemy. I suspected every face that morning as I drank coffee to fill in the time and moved from one café to another to avoid being noticed.

At five to eleven I boarded the bus at the quays. I had nothing to read so I looked out the window and when it got fogged up I wiped it with my hand and stared at nothing in particular. I knew that I should rehearse what I would say to Eugene but I could not even do that.

It seemed a long drive but it was in fact only about an hour. When we got there I let the others pile out first, because I was embarrassed about meeting him. I looked through the window but his car was not there. Then I hurried out, thinking he had parked the car up the street. There was no sign of him anywhere.

'What time does this bus go back to Dublin?' I inquired of the driver, who had climbed up on the roof to hand down parcels and bicycles.

'Five o'clock,' he called down.

Five hours to wait. I swallowed my pride and decided that I would go to Eugene anyhow. I knew that once he saw me he would not turn away.

I set out to walk and had gone half a mile when I saw a black-coated tall figure coming towards me.

It's a priest, I thought, or a policeman, and I ran into a gateway and climbed over in order to hide behind the ditch. A stream of water ran down the mountain field and through a pipe in the ditch.

I peeped out and saw the figure approach. It was Eugene. I climbed quickly over the rickety wooden gate and ran to him. He had his arms out to welcome me.

'Hello, hello,' he said, and I fell into his arms and told him everything. I talked rapidly and mixed up the whole sequence of the story because I was so tired and frightened.

'But this is monstrous!' he said, laughing. He thought I exaggerated.

'They'll kill me,' I said.

'Nonsense, it's the twentieth century,' he said, and he took my travelling bag and we turned round to go to his house. The wind blew against our faces and he told me that the motor-car had refused to start.

'I thought I'd never see you again,' I said, and he linked me and patted my wrist, above my knitted glove.

'You'll be all right,' he said. 'We won't let them kill you.'

I wondered if he would let me stay there with him, I wanted to stay, I never wanted to leave him again.

*

When we came around the corner of the drive, my first thought was that his house looked so happy and peaceful. The whitewashed front sparkled in the winter sun and the downstairs windows were a pale gold.

'You see,' he said, 'the sun is shining, you're alive, everything is going to be all right,' and we went inside.

Anna did not bid me good morning; she just took a jar of honey off the kitchen table and went up the back stairs in a sulk.

'*My* honey,' he said out loud so that she could hear it.

We heard a door bang. He said that she was in a bad humour because Denis would not give her the money to send for a rubber corset through the post. Also she didn't like me, because I was not swanky and had no clothes to give away.

'You sit down,' he said, 'I'll cook you a big breakfast.'

He tied a towel around him and I kissed him – just a little kiss – and felt the comfort of being near him again, smelling his skin, and kissing it. He fried rashers and eggs while I laid one end of the big kitchen table. He sat at the head and I sat to one side, facing the barred window and the black cherry tree.

'They kept my letters, Baba sent me money and they kept it,' I said.

'Don't talk about them while you're eating or you'll get an ulcer; just forget about everything,' he said, and he leaned over and stroked my forehead lightly.

'Cheers,' he said, raising a cup of tea to his lips. It tasted of hair shampoo, so did mine. Anna had put hair shampoo in the cups, or cheap perfume. I thought it evil of her. We washed the cups and poured a second lot of tea.

My stomach felt sick with worry and I looked through the window all the time.

'A Jehovah Witness was stabbed in twenty-nine places with a penknife, in the village next to ours,' I said, and his whole face wrinkled with pain. I knew that I had said the wrong thing as he was very fastidious.

In a little while he said:

'You look as if you've been through Purgatory.'

I looked awful and my body felt cold and shivery. After breakfast I went upstairs to have a sleep.

'Get into my bed, it's warmer,' he said. And upstairs I just took off my dress and shoes and got into the tossed bed.

From where I lay I could see the top of a pine tree, its branches stirring lightly, the vegetable garden wall with weeds growing on it and more trees beyond that. I could not sleep.

The door was opened softly and he peeped in to see if I were asleep.

'Hello,' I said.

'Did you not go to sleep?'

'I can't. I'm frightened.'

He came over and smoothed my hair back from my face and then he stroked my hot forehead. It was very hot. He put a damp face-cloth to it and said soothing things while the damp cloth covered my forehead and eyes. It was dark and damp for those minutes, and I liked the reassurance of his voice. But then he removed the cloth and dried my eyes:

'Isn't that better?' he said. I felt anxious again.

'You can get into bed with me, if you like,' I said.

'No, no.' He shook his head, gave me a dry kiss. 'When we make love to one another it will be because we want to.'

'But I want to,' I said.

'You do, but it's for the wrong reason. You want to involve me, that's all. You know that once I've made love to you, I shall feel responsible for you.' He looked into my eyes and I looked away guiltily. My eyes were hot and itchy.

'Oh, don't get cross,' I begged.

'Nobody's getting cross,' he said calmly. 'But you must understand that relationships between people are not as crude or as simple as this. Sex is not some independent thing, it's part of what people feel for each other, and I could no more make love to you in this nerve-racked state than I could chew my old socks. ...'

I thought that he must be trying to get rid of me, so I said quickly:

'Have I to go now?'

'I've been thinking,' he began. ... 'In fact the wisest thing would be for you to go away.'

'I have nowhere to go,' I said.

'Now don't get anxious, keep calm and listen to me, I'm not abandoning you to the wolves, I'll give you the money to go to London for a week or two, and then when everyone has calmed down, you can come back again.'

'I don't want to leave you,' I said as I looked into his sallow face and his large dark eyes. He had a strong, hard body and I wanted him to shield me from them and from everything that I was afraid of.

'Please,' I said.

He tapped his forehead with his fist and said, 'Oh God,' and then he sighed for a minute, and I thought, his heart is softening and he'll let me stay here.

'Listen, listen,' he was saying, and I sat up thinking that it was a car which had driven up outside. But nothing came, and he went on, 'If we both stay here they'll come and perhaps force you away, if we both go to London they'll probably have the police after us. The sensible thing is for you to go away. I'll stay here and talk reasonably to your father if he should come, and then in a week or two I'll come over to London and see you.'

A cold sadness came over me. He was sending me away.

'All right,' I said, wearily, and I put out my hand for his and we sat there in silence.

'Do you think they will come today?' he asked after a time.

'No, not so soon. I sent them a telegram this morning to say I was going to England and that I'd write; so they'll wait for a day or two.'

'All right then, you can have a big rest today; and tomorrow I'll bring you in to Collinstown and we'll put you on an aeroplane.'

I had never been on an aeroplane and I worried about being strapped down. Baba said that they strapped you to a seat.

'You'll write to me?' I asked.

'Every day. Big, long letters.' He took me in his arms and held me there for a long time while I cried and sobbed.

'I bought you a little present when I was away,' he said then, and he ran downstairs to get it.

It was a portable radio and he showed me how to work the various knobs and find the different stations.

'You can take it around with you anywhere.' He turned the knob on and we heard light music. He danced with the radio in his arms for a minute and I wondered how he could be so cheerful.

I got up and washed, and after lunch we went for a walk.

'If anyone calls, don't admit them,' he shouted up to Anna.

'Are you expecting the bailiff?' she shouted down in a cheeky voice.

He frowned – and said that she was getting out of hand.

It was mild outside, the wind had died down and it was spotting rain. Everything was very still and we could hear the men over in the forestry sawing trees. I took off my headscarf and let the rain fall on my greasy hair and on my warm face. Always with lack of sleep, my face and eyelids got warm and itchy. As we walked along he told me about a picture he had seen in London called *Golden Marie*. He told me the story of it and described the blonde, sensual girl who played the part of Marie. I felt so dull and unattractive as he talked of her and moved his hands to outline the shape of her body.

We went down the narrow path that led to the lake wood. A belt of pine trees ran down on one side, like an army of green soldiers following one upon another, and a loose stone wall skirted the other side of the track. Many of the stones had fallen down.

'You'll be able to see that picture, I'll tell Ginger to take you,' he said as he stooped down to pick up three white stones. Ginger was a woman whom he intended to send a telegram to, asking her to meet me. She had red hair, he said, and that was why she was called Ginger. I wondered if she loved him; I couldn't imagine any woman knowing him and not loving him.

'Is she nice?' I asked.

'She's a nice girl,' he said casually. He was so casual about everything – the rain, the white stones, the pine trees swathed in a mountain mist – one thing seemed as important or as unimportant as another. I thought he was a little callous.

'You're not doleful, are you, sweetling?' he asked as he put his hand on my shoulder and told me not to brood. The rain lay on my coat in a pearl-like drizzle. The quietness of everything had an unnerving effect on me. It all looked unreal – the trees wrapped in a quiet, swirling mist so that the trunks seemed to be standing on air; and stretches of mist curtained off the lower parts of the fields.

'I hate leaving you,' I said. We had come out at the edge of the wood near the lake, and loose wisps of floating mist moved in patches over the water.

'It will only be for a couple of weeks,' he said cheerfully as we sat on the flat roof of the boat-house and looked across at the stony fields which ran down to the lake on the far side. The mist had not come down fully and some fields were quite clear.

'You didn't think it was as nice as this, did you?' he said, stretching his hands out to include the lake, the small sandy beach, the pebbles in the shallow water, and, across the way, a white, ivied house with a lightning-conductor on the chimney-pot. He told me that the Miss Walkers lived there.

'It's lovely,' I said, not really caring.

'It's nicer in the summer, I must teach you how to swim.'

'The summer,' I said, as if we would never live to see it. Then I thought of other summers and of how he must have swum in the lake with Laura, and afterwards lain on the tiny beach which was partly shaded by a very wide chestnut tree. Always when I was with him I thought of Laura, just as I always thought of my mother when I was with Dada.

'How long was Laura here altogether?' I asked.

'I don't remember rightly, she must have been here about a year.'

'Could she swim?' Baba could swim and dive but I could do neither.

'Yes, she could swim,' and though I expected him to say something else, he didn't.

It got dark early because of the rain, and the fields looked sad in the smudging light of evening. He helped me climb the hill, by pushing me from behind; and he knew his way by tread and warned me of the various rabbit holes.

'Can I sleep in your bed tonight?' I asked, as we climbed between the army of pine trees and the wall of loose stones.

'I suppose so,' he said, gently.

*

I prayed that something would happen so that I could stay. Something did.

Chapter Thirteen

At tea-time a wind began to rise, and rattled the shutters. Anna rushed out to bring in napkins which she had spread on one of the thorny bushes. A galvanized bucket rolled along the cobbled yard.

I had felt afraid all day, knowing that they were bound to come – but if a mountain storm blew up, it might keep them away. By the morrow I'd be gone.

*

After tea we sat in the study with a map of London spread on both our knees while he marked various streets and sights for me. I was to go early next morning and he had sent a telegram to Ginger, so that she could meet me.

'We ought to lock the doors,' I said, unnerved by the rattling of shutters.

'All right,' he said, 'we'll lock everything.' And I carried the big flashlamp around while he locked the potting-shed door, the back door, and another side door. The keys had rusted in their locks and he had to tap the bolts with a block of wood to loosen them. Anna and Denis had gone backstairs to their own apartments, and we could hear dance music from their radio.

'Tell them if there's a knock, not to answer it,' I suggested.

'Nonsense,' he said, 'they never come down once they've gone up at night. They go to bed after the nine-o'clock news.' He was very proud and did not wish to share his troubles with anyone.

'Now the hall door,' I said. We opened it for a minute and looked out at the windy night and listened to the trees groaning.

'Go away from the window, bogy man,' he said as we came in and sat on the couch in front of the study fire. The oak box was stocked with logs and he said that we were perfectly safe and that no one could harm us.

There was a shot-gun in the corner of the hall, and I thought that maybe he should get it to be on the safe side.

'Nonsense,' he said. 'You just want some melodrama....'

I could hear the wind and I imagined that I heard a car driving up to the house; I heard it all the time, but it was only in my imagination. I rubbed his hair and massaged the muscles at the back of his neck, and he said that it was very nice and very comforting.

'We get on well together, you and I,' he said.

'Yes,' I said, and thought how easy it would be, if he said then, I love you, or I could love, or I'm falling in love with you, but he didn't; he just said that we got on well together.

'We only know each other a couple of months,' he said to the fire, as if he had sensed my disappointment. I knew that he believed in the slow, invisible processes of growth, the thing which had to take root first in the lonely, dark part of one, away from the light. He liked to plant trees and watch them grow; he liked our friendship to take its course; he was not ready for me.

'Do you believe in God?' I said abruptly. I don't know why I said it.

'Not when I'm sitting at my own fire. I may do when I'm driving eighty miles an hour. It varies.' I thought it a very peculiar answer, altogether.

'What things are you afraid of?' I wished that somehow he would make some deep confession to me and engross me in his fears so that I could forget my own, or that we could play I-spy-with-my-little-eye, or something.

'Just bombs,' he said, and I thought that a peculiar answer too.

'But not hell?' I said, naming my second greatest fear.

'They'll give me a job making fires in hell, I'm good at fires.' I wondered how his voice could be so calm, his face so still. Sometimes I rubbed his neck, and then again I rested my arm and sat very close to him, wondering how I could live without him in London for the while – until things blew over, he said.

'The best thing you can do about hell ...' he began, but I never heard the end of the sentence, because just then the dog barked in the yard outside. She barked steadily for a few seconds and then let out a low, warning howl that was almost human-sounding. I jumped up.

'Sssh, ssh,' he said, as I stumbled over a tray of tea-things that was on the floor. He ran across and lowered the Tilley lamp; then we waited. Nothing happened, no footsteps, no car, nothing but the wind and the beating rain. Yet, I knew they were coming and that in a moment they would knock on the door.

'Must have been a badger or a fox.' He poured me a drink from the whisky bottle on the gun bureau.

'You look as white as a sheet,' he said, sipping the whisky. Then the dog barked again, loudly and continuously, and I knew by her hysterical sounds that she was trying to leap the double doors in the back yard. We had not locked them. My whole body began to shake and tremble.

'It's them,' I said, going cold all over. We heard boots on the gravel and men talking, and suddenly great banging and tapping on the hall door. The dog continued to bark hysterically, and above the noise of banging fists and wind blowing I heard the beating of my own heart. Knuckles rapped on the window, the shutters rattled, and at the same time the stiff knocker boomed. I clutched Eugene's sleeve and prayed.

'Oh God,' I said to him.

'Open up,' a man's voice shouted.

'They'll break down the door,' I said. Five or six of them seemed to be pounding on it, all at once. I thought that my heart would burst.

'How dare they abuse my door like that,' he said as he moved towards the hall.

'Don't, don't!' I stood in his way and told him not to be mad. 'We won't answer,' I said, but I had spoken too late. One of my people had gone around to the back of the house, and we heard the metallic click of the back-door latch being raised impatiently. Then the bolt was drawn and I heard Anna say:

'What'n the name of God do you want at this hour of night?'

I suppose that she must have been half asleep and had tumbled down thinking that we had been locked out or that the police had come for me.

I heard the Ferret's voice speak my name. 'We've come to take that girl out of here.'

'I don't know anything about it. Wait outside.' Anna said insolently, and then he must have walked straight past her because she shouted: 'How dare you!' and the sheepdog ran up the passage from the kitchen, yelping. The others were still knocking at the front of the house.

'This is beyond endurance,' Eugene said, and as he went to open the hall door, I ran back into the study, and looked around for somewhere to hide. I crawled under the spare bed hoping that he would bring them to the sitting-room, because he did not like people in the study where he worked. I heard him say:

'I can't answer you that, I'm afraid.'

'Deliver her out,' a voice demanded.

I had to think, to recall who it was.

'Come on now.' It was Andy, my father's cousin, a cattle-dealer. I recalled strange cattle – making the noises which cows make in unfamiliar places – being driven into our front field on the evenings preceding a fair day. Then cousin Andy would come up to the house for tea, and sitting in the kitchen in his double-breasted brown suit he'd discuss the price of heifers with my father. Once he gave me a three-penny bit which was so old and worn that the King had been rubbed off.

'Where is my only child?' my father cried.

She's under the bed, she's suffocating, I said to myself, praying that I would be there only for a second, while Eugene picked up the lamp and brought them across to the sitting-room. Could I then hide in the barn – and take the torch to ward off rats!

'My only child,' my father cried again.

For two pins I'd come out and tell him a thing or two about his only child!

'Who are you looking for?' Eugene said. 'We'll confer in the other room.'

But my father had noticed the fire, and with a sinking feeling I heard them all troop into the study. Someone sat on the bed; the spring touched my back, and smelling cowdung from his boots, I guessed that it was cousin Andy. I recognized two other voices – Jack Holland's and the Ferret's.

'Don't you think it is a little late in the day for social calls?' Eugene said.

'We want that poor, innocent girl,' cousin Andy said – he, the famed bachelor, who had spoken only to cows and bullocks all his life, bullying them along the road to country fairs. 'Hand the girl over, and by God if there's a hair astray on her, you'll pay dear for it,' he shouted, and I imagined how he looked with his miser's face and a mean little mouth framed by a red moustache. He always had to carry stomach mixture with him everywhere, and had once raised his hand to my mother because she hinted about all the free grazing he took from Dada. On that occasion my father in his one known act of chivalry said, 'If you lay a finger on my missus, I'll lay you out.'

'This is outrageous,' Eugene said.

Various matches were struck – they were settling in.

'Allow me,' Jack Holland said, proceeding to make introductions, but he was shouted down by my father.

'A divorced man. Old enough to be her father. Carrying off my little daughter.'

'To set the record straight I did not bring her here, she came,' Eugene said.

I thought, he's going to let me down, he's going to send me away with them; my mother was right, 'Weep and you weep alone.'

'You got her with dope. Everyone knows that,' my father said.

Eugene laughed. I thought how odd, and immoral, he must look to them, in his corduroy trousers and his old check shirt. I hoped that all his buttons were done up. My nose began to itch with the dust.

'You're her father?' Eugene said.

'Allow me,' Jack Holland said again, and this time he performed the introductions. I wondered if it was *he* who had betrayed me.

'Yes, I'm her father,' Dada said, in a doleful voice.

'Go on now and get the girl,' Andy shouted.

I began to tremble anew. I couldn't breathe. I would suffocate under those rusty springs. I would die while they sat there deciding my life. I would die – with Andy's dungy boots under my nose. It was ironic. My mother used to scrub the rungs of the chair after his visits to our house. I said short prayers and multiplication-tables and the irregular plural of Latin nouns – anything that I knew by heart – to distract myself. I thought of a line from *Julius Caesar* which I had once recited, wearing a red nightdress, at a school concert – 'I see thee still and on thy blade and dudgeon gouts of blood. . . .'

'Are you a Catholic?' the Ferret asked, in a policeman's voice.

'I'm not a Catholic,' Eugene answered.

'D'you go to Mass?' my father asked.

'But, my dear man –' Eugene began.

'There's no "my dear man". Cut it out. Do you go to Mass or don't you? D'you eat meat on Fridays?'

'God help Ireland,' Eugene said, and I imagined him throwing his hands up in his customary gesture of impatience.

'None of that blasphemy,' cousin Andy shouted, making a noise as he struck his fist into his palm.

'What about a drink to calm us down?' Eugene suggested, and then, sniffing, he added, 'Perhaps better not – you seem to have brought enough alcohol with you.'

I could smell their drink from under the bed now, and I guessed that they had stopped at every pub along the way to brace themselves for the occasion. Probably my father had paid for most of it.

'Well . . . a sip of port wine all round might be conducive to negotiation,' Jack Holland suggested in his soft, mannerly way.

'Could I have a drink of water – to take an aspirin?' my father said.

'Good idea. I'll join you in an aspirin,' Eugene said, and I thought for a second that things were going to be all right. Water was poured. I closed my eyes to pray, dropped my forehead on to the back of my hand, and gasped. My face was damp with cold sweat.

'I would like you to realize that your daughter is escaping from *you*. I'm not abducting her. *I'm* not forcing her – she is running away from you and your way of living ...' Eugene began.

'What the hell is he talking about?' Andy said.

'The tragic history of our fair land,' Jack Holland exclaimed. 'Alien power sapped our will to resist.'

'They get girls with dope,' the Ferret said. 'Many an Irish girl ends up in the white-slave traffic in Piccadilly. Foreigners run it. All foreigners.'

'Where's your wife, Mister? Would you answer that?' Andy said.

'And what are you doing with my daughter?' my father asked fiercely, as if recollecting what they had come for.

'I'm not *doing* anything with her,' Eugene said, and I thought, he has shed all responsibility for me, he does not love me.

'You're a foreigner,' Andy said contemptuously.

'Not at all,' Eugene said pleasantly. 'Not at all as foreign as *your* tiny, blue, Germanic eyes, my friend.'

'What are your intentions?' my father asked abruptly. And then he must have drawn the anonymous letter from his pocket, because he said, 'There's a few things here would make your hair stand on end.'

'He hasn't much hair, he's near bald,' the Ferret said.

'I haven't any *intentions*; I suppose in time I would like to marry her and have children. ... Who knows?'

'Ah, the patter of little feet,' said Jack Holland idiotically, and Dada told him to shut up and stop making a fool of himself.

He doesn't really want me, I thought as I took short,

quick breaths and said an Act of Contrition, thinking that I was near my end. I don't know why I stayed under there, it was stifling.

'Would you turn?' my father said, and of course Eugene did not know what he meant by that.

'Turn?' he asked, in a puzzled voice.

'Be a Catholic,' the Ferret said. And then Eugene sighed and said, 'Why don't we all have a cup of tea?' And Dada said, 'Yes, yes.'

It will go on all night and I'll be found dead under this bed, I thought as I wished more and more that I could scratch a place between my shoulder-blades which itched terribly.

*

When he opened the door to fetch some tea he must have found Anna listening at the keyhole, because I heard him say to her, 'Oh Anna, you're here, can you bring us a tray of tea, please?' And then he seemed to go out of the room, because suddenly they were all talking at once.

'She could have got out the back way,' my father said.

'Get tough, boy, get tough,' Andy said. 'Follow him out, you fool, before he makes a run for it.'

'Poor Brady,' the Ferret said when Dada had apparently gone out, 'that's the thanks he gets for sending that little snotty-nose to a convent and giving her a fine education.'

'She was never right, that one,' cousin Andy said, 'reading books and talking to trees. Her mother spoilt her....'

'Ah, her dear mother,' said Jack Holland, and while he raved on about Mama being a lady, the other two passed remarks about the portrait of Eugene over the fire.

'Look at the nose of him – you know what he is? They'll be running this bloody country soon,' Andy said.

'God 'tis a bloody shame, ruining a girl like that,' Andy said, and I thought how baffled they'd be if they had known that I was not seduced yet, even though I had slept in his bed for two whole nights.

I heard the rattle of cups as Eugene and my father came back.

'How much money do you earn in a year?' my father asked, and I knew how they would sneer if they heard that he made poky little films about rats, and sewerage.

'I earn lots of money,' Eugene lied.

'You're old enough to be her father,' Dada said. 'You're nearly as old as myself.'

'Look,' Eugene said after a minute, 'where is all this ill-temper going to get us? Why don't you go down to the village and stay in the hotel for the night, then come up in the morning and discuss it with Caithleen. She won't be so frightened in the morning and I will try and get her to agree to seeing you.'

'Not on your bloody life,' cousin Andy said.

'We'll not go without her,' my father added threateningly, and I lost heart then and knew that there was no escape. They would find me and pull me forth. We would go out in the wind and sit in the Ferret's car and drive all night, while they abused me. If only Baba was there, she'd find a way. . . .

'She's over twenty-one, you can't force her,' Eugene said, 'not even in Ireland.'

'Can't we? We won our fight for freedom. It's our country now,' Andy said.

'We can have her put away. She's not all there,' my father said.

'Mental,' the Ferret added.

'What about that, Mister?' cousin Andy shouted. 'A very serious offence having to do with a mentally affected girl. You could get twenty years for that.'

I gritted my teeth, my head boiled – why was I such a coward as to stay under there? They'd make a goat ashamed. Tears of rage and shame ran over the back of my hand and I wanted to scream, I disown them, they're nothing to do with me, don't connect me with them, but I said nothing – just waited.

'Go and get her,' my father said. '*Now!*' And I imagined the spits that shot out of his mouth in anger.

'You heard what Mr Brady said,' cousin Andy shouted, and he must have risen from the bed because the springs lifted. I knew how ratty he must look with his small blue eyes, his red moustache, his stomach ulcer.

'Very well then,' Eugene said, 'she's in my legal care. A guest in my house. When she leaves she will do so of her own free will. Leave my house or I'll telephone for the police.' I wondered if they'd notice that there *was* no phone.

'You heard me,' Eugene said, and I thought, oh God he'll get hit. Didn't he know how things ended – 'Man in hospital with fifty-seven penknife wounds'. I started to struggle out, to give myself up.

I heard the first smack of their fists and then they must have knocked him over because the Tilley lamp crashed and the globe broke into smithereens.

I screamed as I got out and staggered up. Flames from the wood fire gave enough light for me to see by. Eugene was on the floor, trying to struggle up and Andy and the Ferret were hitting and kicking him. Jack Holland tried to hold them back, and my father, hardly knowing what he was doing, held the back of Jack Holland's coat, saying, 'Now Jack, now Jack, God save us, now Jack – oh Jack –'

My father saw me suddenly and must have thought that I had risen up from the ground – my hair was all tossed and there was fluff and dust on me. He opened his mouth so wide that his loose dental-plate dropped on to his tongue. They were cheap teeth that he had made by a dental mechanic.

'I didn't do it, I didn't do it, Maura,' he whispered, and backed away from me clutching his teeth. Long after, I realized that he thought I was Mama risen from her grave in the Shannon lake. I must have looked like a ghost; my face daubed with tears and grey dust, my hair hanging in my eyes.

I shouted at the Ferret to stop, when the door burst open and the room lit up with a great red and yellow flash, as Anna had fired the shot-gun at the ceiling. The thunderclap made me stagger back against the bed with my head numb and singing. I tried to stay still, waiting to die. I thought I'd been shot, but it was only the shock of the explosion in my ears. The black smoke of gunpowder entered our throats and made me cough. Jack Holland was on his knees, praying and coughing, while Andy and the Ferret were turned to the door with their hands to their ears. My father leaned over a chair gasping, and Eugene moaned on the floor and put his hand to his bleeding nose. Shattered plaster fell down all over the carpet and the white dust mixed with gun smoke. The smell was awful.

'There's another one in it. I'll blow your brains out,' Anna said. She stood at the study door, in her nightdress, holding Eugene's shot-gun. Denis stood beside her with a lighted Christmas candle.

'Out you get,' she said to them, holding the gun steadily up.

'By God, I'm getting out of this,' the Ferret said. 'These people would kill you!' I went to Eugene, who was still sitting on the floor with blood coming from his nose. I put my handkerchief to it.

'Dangerous savages,' my father said, his face white, holding his teeth in one hand. 'She might have killed us.'

'I'll blow your feet off if you don't clear out of here,' Anna said in a quivering voice.

'Get out,' Eugene said to them as he stood up. His shirt was torn. 'Get out. Go. Leave. Never come inside my gates again.'

'Have you a drop of whisky?' my father said, shakily, putting his hand to his heart.

'No,' Eugene said. 'Leave my house, immediately.'

'A pretty night's work, a pretty night's work,' Jack Holland said sadly, as they left. Anna stood to one side to let them pass and Denis opened the hall door. The last thing I saw was the Ferret's hooked iron hand being shaken back at us.

Eugene slammed the door and Denis bolted it. I collapsed on to the bed, trembling.

'That's the way to handle them,' Anna said, as she put the gun on the table.

'You saved my life,' Eugene said, and he sat on the couch and drew up the leg of his trousers. There was blood on his shin, where he had been kicked. His nose also was bleeding.

'I'm sorry, I'm sorry,' I said between sobs.

'Oh tough men, tough men,' Denis said solemnly as we heard them outside arguing, and the dog barking from the back yard.

'Get some iodine,' Eugene said. I went upstairs but couldn't find it, so Anna had to go and get it, along with a clean towel and a basin of water. He lay back on the arm-chair, and I opened his shoe-laces and took off his shoes.

'Wh'ist,' Denis said. We heard the car drive away.

Anna washed the cuts on Eugene's face and legs. He squirmed with pain as she swabbed on iodine.

'I shouldn't have hidden,' I said, handing him a clean handkerchief from the top drawer of his desk, where he kept them. 'Oh, I shouldn't have come here.'

Through the handkerchief he said, 'Go get yourself a drink. It will help you to stop shaking. Get me one too.'

After a while the nose-bleed stopped and he raised his head and looked at me. His upper lip had swollen.

'It was terrible,' I said.

'It was' he said, 'ridiculous. Like this country.'

'Only for me where would we be?' Anna said.

'What about a cup of tea?' he said in a sad voice, and I knew that he would never forget what had happened and that some of their conduct had rubbed off on to me.

*

We went to bed late. His shin ached and a cut over his eye throbbed a lot. It was an hour before he went to sleep. I lay for most of the night, looking at the moonlit wall, thinking. Near dawn I found him awake, and looking at me.

'I love you,' I said suddenly. I had not prepared it or anything, it just fell out of my mouth.

'Love!' he said, as if it were a meaningless word, and he moved his head on the pillow to face me. He smiled and closed his eyes, going back to sleep again. What could I do to make up? I wasn't any good in bed, never mind not being able to fire a gun. I'd go back to Baba. I cried a bit, and later got up to make some tea.

Anna was in the kitchen putting on her good shoes and silk stockings, preparing to go to Mass.

'I'm not over it yet,' she said.

'I'll never be over it,' I said, and to myself, they've ruined, and ruined, and ruined me. He'll never look at me again. I'll have to go away.

Chapter Fourteen

SHE came back from Mass, bubbling over with news.

'They think in the village that you must be a film star,' she said as she took a long hatpin out of her blue hat, removed the hat and stuck the pin through it for the next Sunday. She said that I was the topic of conversation in the three shops. My father and his friends had stopped at the hotel for drinks on the way up.

As she put the frying-pan on the range, I noticed the tracks of mice in the cold fat.

'I expect you'll be leaving today,' she said.

'I expect so.'

It was after ten so I made Eugene's tea and carried it upstairs. Standing for a moment in the doorway with the tray I felt suddenly privileged to be in his room while he slept. The hollows of his cheeks were more pronounced in sleep and his face bore a slight look of pain. He had a nice gentle mouth, his lips handsomely shaped.

I drew back the curtains.

'You'll break the curtain rings,' he said, sitting up. His startled eyes looked twice their normal size.

'Oh, hello,' he said, surprised to see me and then rubbed his lids and probably remembered everything. I put a pullover across his shoulders and knotted the two sleeves under his chin.

'Nice tea,' he said as he lay there, like a Christ, sipping tea; his head resting on the mahogany bed-head.

Anna tapped on the door and burst in, before he had time to cry halt.

'I handed in the telegram – it will go first thing in the morning,' she said. It was to his solicitor.

She told me that my black pudding, below on the range, would be dried up if I didn't go down and eat.

'Black pudding!' he groaned.

'Your nose is a nice sight,' she said to him.

137

'Probably broken,' he said, without a smile.

'Oh – not broken!' I said.

'Lucky I don't earn my living with my nose,' he said. 'Or make love with it.'

'Hmmmh,' Anna said as she stood in the middle of the room, hands on hips, surveying the tossed bed and my nightdress on a chair.

'All right,' he said to us both, 'trot off,' and I went but she stayed there. I listened outside the door:

'I saved your life, didn't I?'

'You did. I am very grateful to you, Anna. Remind me to strike you a leather medal.'

'Will you loan me fifty pounds?' she asked. 'I want to get a sewing-machine and a few things for the baba. If I had a sewing-machine we could mend all your shirts.'

'We could?' he said, mockingly.

'Will you loan me it?'

'Why don't you say "give me fifty pounds". I know that word "loan" has no meaning here.'

'That's not a nice thing to say.' She sounded offended.

'Anna, I'll give it to you,' he said. 'A reward.'

'Good man. Keep it to yourself, not a word to Denis. If he knew I had fifty pounds he'd buy a bull or something.'

She came out of the room beaming, and I ran away, ashamed at having been caught listening.

'Tell-tale-tattle,' she said as I hurried guiltily along the carpeted passage. 'Come on, I'll race you down the stairs,' and we ran the whole way to the kitchen.

She read the Sunday papers.

'She's the image of Laura,' she said, pointing to an heiress who was reported as being in love with a barber.

'Fitter changes sex,' she read aloud. 'Mother of God, I don't understand people at all. Do they never look at themselves when they're taking their clothes off!'

She read our horoscopes – Denis's, the baby's, Eugene's, mine, and Laura's. She included Laura in everything, so that by the time she went out after lunch with Denis and the baby, I had the feeling that Laura was due back any minute. It was with this unsettling feeling that I made my first tour of the house. Eugene had gone down the fields to look at the ram pump.

There were five bedrooms. The mattresses were folded over and the wardrobes empty, except for wooden hangers. The furniture was old, dark, unmatching, and in lockers beside the beds there were chamber-pots with pink china roses on the insides of them.

In the top drawer of a linen chest I found a silver evening bag with a diary of Laura's inside. The diary had no entries, just names and telephone numbers. There was also a purple evening glove that smelt of stale but wonderful perfume. I fitted on the glove and for some reason my heart began to pound. There was nothing in any of the other drawers, just chalk marks stating the number of each drawer.

*

Nearing dusk I came downstairs and raised the wick of the hanging lamp which Anna had lit for me before she went out. The rabbit was on the table, as she had left it, skinned and ready to be cooked. Denis had caught it the day before.

'The dinner,' I said aloud, as I got a cookery book and looked up the index under R.

> Radishes,
> Ragout of Kidneys,
> Raisin Bread,
> Raisin Pie,
> Raisin Pudding,
> Rarebit,
> Raspberries.

Rabbit was not mentioned. The cookery book had belonged to Laura. Her maiden name and her married name were written in strong handwriting on the fly-leaf.

'The dinner,' I said, to suppress a tear, and then I remembered how Eugene had asked, earlier in the day, 'Can you cook?'

'Sort of,' I had said.

It was a total lie. I never cooked in my whole life, except

the Friday Gustav and Joanna went to a solicitor's to make a will. I brought home two fish for lunch, one for Baba, one for me. Baba laid the table while I fried the fish. I knew nothing about cleaning them. I just put the grey, podgy little fish on the big frying-pan and lit the gas under it. Nothing happened for a few minutes and then the side of one fish burst.

'There's a hell of a stink out there,' Baba called from the dining-room.

'It's just the fish,' I said. Both fish had burst by then.

'It's just what?' she said, rushing into the kitchen, holding her nose.

When she saw the mess she simply took hold of the pan and ran down the garden to dump it on Gustav's compost heap.

'Phew,' she said, coming back in to the house. 'You should have been alive when they ate raw cows and bones and things. A bloody savage.' And she put the pan into the sink and ran the tap on it.

We went out to lunch to Woolworths. It was a big thrill being able to march around with a tray, helping ourselves to whatever we fancied – chips, sausages, trifle topped with custard, coffee, a little jug of cream, and lemon meringue pie.

Sitting in the big flagged kitchen I thought of Baba and cried. I missed her. I had never been alone before in my whole life, alone and dependent on my own resources. I thought with longing of all the evenings we went out together, reeking with vanilla essence and good humour. Usually we ended up in the cinema, thrilled by the darkness, and the big screen, with perhaps a choc ice to keep us going.

'Oh God,' I said, remembering Baba, my father, everyone; and I buried my face in my hands and cried, not knowing what I cried for.

Three or four times, I went around the corner of the front drive and leaned on the wet, white gate to see if there was a sign of anybody coming. Nobody came, except a policeman who cycled down the by-road, stood at the gate-lodge for a minute, relieved himself, and cycled off again. He was probably keeping an eye out for poachers.

By the time Eugene came back I had dried my eyes; and I wondered if perhaps he expected me to have left discreetly while he was out.

'I'm still here' I said.

'I'm glad,' he said as he kissed me. It was dusk and we proceeded to light the Tilley lamps.

As we sat by the study fire he said, 'Ah you poor little lonely bud, it's not a nice honeymoon for you, is it? Think of nice things ... sunshine, mountain rivers, fuchsia, birds flying ...'

I lay in his arms and could think only about what would happen next. He had put a record on the wind-up gramophone, and music filled the room. Outside, rain spattered against the window, and the water had lodged on the inner ledge of the window frame. It was very quiet except for the music and the rain. His eyes were closed, as he listened to the music. Music had a strange effect on him: his face softened, his whole spirit responded to it.

'That's Mahler,' he said, just when I expected him to say, 'You can stay or you can go.'

'I like songs that have words,' I said to clarify my position. But his eyes were closed and I did not think that he heard me at all. The music still reminded me of birds, birds wheeling out of a bush and startling the mellow hush of a summer evening; crows above an old slate quarry at home, multiplied by their own shadows and by their screaming and cawing. I wondered about my father then, and felt that they would come again, that night.

'But this music has words,' Eugene said, unexpectedly. So he had heard me. 'Words of a more perfect order, this music says things about people, people's lives, progress, wars, hunger, revolution. ... Music can express with as simple instruments as reeds, the grey bodiless pain of living.'

I thought he must be a little mad to talk like that, especially when I worried about my father coming; and feeling very apart from him, I jumped up, on the excuse that I must look at the dinner. We had put on the rabbit.

It simmered very slowly and the white meat was falling away from the bone, gradually. I thickened the gravy with cornflour but it lumped a lot. Little beads of the flour floated on the surface.

'Twill have to do, I thought, as I went away to put some more powder on my face – the steam of the dinner had reddened my cheeks. When I came back to the room he was reading.

I sat opposite him and stared up at the circle of wrecked plaster – the result of Anna's shot. I thought, when I leave here tomorrow it is this that I will remember, I will always remember it.

'I'll go tomorrow,' I said suddenly. The yellow lamplight shone on his forehead and the reflection of a vase showed in the top part of his lenses. He had put on horn-rimmed glasses.

'*Go?*' he said, raising his eyes from the paper which rested on his knee. 'Where will you go?'

'I might go to London.'

'Do you want to?'

'No.'

'Then why are you going?'

'What else can I do?'

'You can stay.'

'That wouldn't be right,' I said, pleased that it was he who suggested it, and not me.

'Why not?'

'Because it would be throwing myself at you,' I said. 'I'll go away, and then when I'm gone you can write to me, and maybe I'll come back.'

'Supposing I don't want you to go away, then what?' he asked.

'I wouldn't believe it,' I said, and he raised his eyes to the ceiling, in mild irritation. I kept thinking that he asked me to stay because he pitied me, or maybe he was lonely.

'Why do you want me to stay?' I asked.

'Because I like you. I've lived like a hermit for so long, I mean, sometimes I feel lonely.' And he stopped himself suddenly, because he saw my eyes fill with tears.

'Caithleen,' he said softly – he usually said Kate, or Katie – 'Caithleen, stay,' and he put out his hand for mine.

'I'll stay for a week or two,' I said, and he kissed me and said how pleased he was.

We closed the shutters and had dinner. The rabbit meat and potatoes were crushed in the flour-thickened sauce, and the meal tasted very nice. He said that he would buy me a marriage ring, so that Anna and the neighbours would not bother me with questions.

'We can't actually get married, I'm not divorced and there is the child,' he said as he looked away from me, towards the crooked ink on the graph paper of the barograph. I followed his gaze – the jagged ink line suggested to me the jagged lines of all our lives, and I said, to hide my disappointment:

'I don't ever intend to get married, anyhow.'

'We'll see,' he said, and laughed, and then to cheer me up he told me all about his family.

He began – 'My mother is a hypochondriac' – he seemed to have forgotten that I met her – 'and she married my father in those fortunate days when women's legs were covered in long skirts. I say fortunate because her legs are like match-sticks. They met going down Grafton Street. He was a visiting musician – tall, dark, foreign, on his way to buy a French-English dictionary – and very courteously he asked the lady if she could direct him to a bookshop. I' – he tapped his chest – 'am the product of that accidental encounter.'

I laughed and thought how odd that his mother should have charmed the stranger so quickly. He went on to tell me that his father had left them when he was about five. He remembered his father dimly as a man who came home from work with a fiddle and oranges; his mother had worked as a waitress to feed them both, and like nine-tenths of the human race he had had a hard life and an unhappy childhood.

'Your turn,' he said, making an elegant gesture in my direction.

Fragments of my childhood came to mind – eating bread

and sugar on the stone step of the back kitchen, and drinking hot jelly which had been put aside to cool. Sometimes one word can recall a whole span of life. I said:

'Mama was in America when she was young, so she had American words for everything – "apple-sauce", "sweater", "greenhorn", and "dessert".'

I thought of incidental things – of the tinker woman stealing Mama's good shoes from the back-kitchen window, and of Mama having to go to court to give evidence and later regretting it because the tinker woman got a month in jail; of the dog having fits, and of a hundred day-old chickens being killed once by a weasel. In talking of it I could see the place again, the fields green and peaceful, rolling out from the solid cut-stone house; and in summertime, meadowsweet, creamy-white along the headlands, and Hickey humming 'How can you buy Killarney' as he sat like an emperor on the rusted mowing machine, swearing to me that dried cow-dung was sold in the shops as tobacco. I watched the grease settle on the dinner plates and still I sat there talking to Eugene as I had never talked before. He was a good listener. I did not tell him about Dada drinking.

*

We went to bed long after midnight. He limped upstairs while I followed behind with the Tilley lamp and wondered foolishly if I were likely to drop it and set fire to the turkey-red carpet.

'So we both need a father,' he said. 'We have a common bond.'

He did not make love to me that night. We had talked too much and anyhow he was stiff from having been kicked.

'There's no hurry,' I said.

He petted my stomach and we said warm, comforting things to lull each other to sleep.

Chapter Fifteen

On Monday afternoon Eugene's solicitor drove out from Dublin. We had a fire in the sitting-room as we were expecting him. He was an austere, red-haired man with red eyebrows and pale blue eyes.

'And you say these people assaulted Mr Gaillard?' he asked.

'Yes. They did.'

'Did you witness this?'

'No, I was under the bed.'

'The bed?' He raised his sandy eyebrows and looked at me with cold disapproval.

'She's getting it all garbled, she means the spare bed in my study,' Eugene explained quickly. 'She hid under it when they came, because she was afraid.'

'Yes, a bed,' I said, annoyed with both of them.

'I see,' the lawyer said coldly as he wrote something down.

'Are you married, Miss Ah ...?'

'No,' I said, and caught Eugene smiling at me, as much as to say, You will be.

Then the solicitor asked me what was my father's Christian name and surname, and the names of the others and their proper addresses. I felt badly about being the cause of sending them solicitors' letters but Eugene said that it had to be.

'It is just routine,' the solicitor said. 'We will warn them that they cannot come here again and molest Mr Gaillard. You are quite certain that you are over twenty-one?'

'I am quite certain,' I said, adopting his language.

Then he questioned Eugene, while I sat there looping and unlooping my hanky around my finger. Eugene had made notes of the whole scene which led up to their attacking him. He was very methodical like that.

I brought tea, and fresh scones with apple jelly and

cream; but even that did not cheer the solicitor up. He talked to Eugene about dupress trees.

He left shortly after four and I waved to the moving motor-car, out of habit. It was getting dark and the air was full of those soft noises that come at evening – cows lowing, the trees rustling, the hens wandering around, crowing happily, availing themselves of the last few minutes before being shut up for the night.

'Well, that's that,' Eugene said as we came back in to the room, and he felt the teapot to see if the tea had gone cold.

'They won't trouble us again,' he said, pouring a half-cup of strong tea.

'They'll trouble us always,' I said. Recounting the whole incident had saddened me again.

'They'll have to accept it,' he said; but two mornings later I had a wretched letter from my aunt.

Dear Caithleen;
    None of us has slept a wink since, nor eaten a morsel. We are out of our minds to know what's happening to you. If you have any pity in you, write to me, and tell me what are you doing. I pray for you, night and day! You know that you always have a welcome here, when you come back. Write by return and may God and His Blessed Mother watch over you and keep you pure and safe. Your father does nothing but cry. Write to him.
                                        Your aunt Molly

'Don't answer it,' Eugene said. 'Do nothing.'

'But I can't leave them worrying like that.'

'Look,' he said, 'this sentimentality will get you nowhere; once you make a decision you must stick to it. You've got to be hard on people, you've got to be hard on yourself.'

It was early morning and we had vowed never to begin an argument before lunch. In the mornings he was usually testy, and he liked to walk alone for an hour or two before talking to me.

'It's cruel,' I said.

'Yes,' he said. 'Kicking me with hobnailed boots is cruel. If you write to them,' he warned, 'they will come here and this time I leave *You* to deal with them.' His mouth was bitter, but that did not stop me from loving him.

'All right,' I said and I went away to think about it. Out in the woods everything was damp; the trees dripped and brooded, the house brooded, the brown mountain hung above me, deep in sullen recollection. It was a lonely place.

In the end I did nothing but have a cry, and by afternoon he was in better humour.

That night, he said, 'We're going into town tomorrow.' And taking a spare wallet from a drawer, he put notes in it and gave it to me. His initials were in gold on the beige-coloured leather, and he said it had been a present from someone.

'We'll buy you a ring and one or two other things,' he said; and then as he had his back to me, hefting a big log on to the fire, I peeped into the wallet and counted the number of notes he had given me. There were twenty in all.

*

Next day, walking down Grafton Street in a bitter wind, I felt as if people were going to accuse me of my sin in public.

'Bang, bang,' he said, shooting our imaginary enemies, but I was still afraid, and glad to escape into a jeweller's shop.

We bought a wide gold ring and he put it on me in the shop – 'With this expensive ring, I thee bed,' he said, and I gave a little shiver and laughed.

We bought groceries and wine and two paperback novels and some note-paper. I asked him in the bookshop if he were very rich.

'Not very,' he said. 'The money is nearly gone, but I'll get your dowry or I'll work. . . .' There was some talk about his going to South America in the spring to do a documentary film on irrigation for a chemical company. And already I worried about whether he would bring me or not.

He had a haircut in a place that was attached to a hotel. He left me in the lounge, sipping a whisky and soda, but the minute he was out of sight I gulped the drink down and fled to the cloakroom in case anyone should recognize me. I washed my hands a few times and put on more make-up and each time I washed my hands the attendant rushed over with a clean towel for me. I suppose she thought that I was mad, washing my hands so often, but it passed the time. My ring shone beautifully after washing and I could see myself in it, when I brought my hand close to my face.

I must stop biting my nails, I thought, as I pressed the cuticles back, and remembered the time when I was young and bit my nails and thought foolishly that once I became seventeen I would grow up quite suddenly and be a lady and have long painted nails and no problems. I gave the grey-haired attendant five shillings and she got very flustered and asked if I wanted change.

'It's all right,' I said. 'I got married today.' I had to say it to someone. She shook my hand and tears filled her kind eyes as she wished me a long life of happiness. I cried a bit myself, to keep her company. She was motherly; I longed to stay there and tell her the truth and have her assurances that I had done the right thing, but that would have been ridiculous, so I came away.

Fortunately I was back in the lounge, sitting in one of the armchairs, when I saw him return. Even after such a short absence as that, I thought when I saw him, how beautiful he is with his olive skin and his prominent jawbones.

'That's done,' he said as he bent down and brushed his cheek against mine. He had had a shave too.

I had put on a lot of perfume and he said how opulent I smelled. Then, as a celebration, we crossed the hall to the empty dining-room and were the first to be served with dinner that night. He ordered a half-bottle of champagne, but when the waiter brought it in a tub of ice it looked so miserable that he sent it back again and got a full bottle. I asked to be given the cork and I still have it. It is the only possession I have which I regard as mine, that cork with its round silvered top.

We touched glasses and he said, 'To us,' and I drank, hoping that I would stay young always.

That night was pleasant. His face looked young and boyish because of the haircut, and I had a new black dress, bought with the money he gave me. In certain lights and at certain moments, most women look beautiful – that light and that moment were mine, and in the wall mirror I saw myself, fleetingly beautiful.

'I could eat you,' he said, 'like an ice-cream,' and later when we were home in bed, he re-said it, as he turned to make love to me. He twisted the wedding ring round and round my finger:

'It's a bit big for you, we'll get a clip on it,' he said.

''Twill do,' I said, being lazy and feeling mellow just then from champagne and the reassurance of his voice in my ear, as he smelled the warm scent of my hair.

'That ring has to last you a long time,' he said.

'How long?'

'As long as you keep your girlish laughter.'

I noticed with momentary regret that he never used dangerous words like 'for ever and ever'.

'Knock, knock, let me in,' he said, coaxing his way gently into my body.

'I am not afraid, I am not afraid,' I said. For days he had told me to say this to myself, to persuade myself that I was not afraid. The first thrust pained, but the pain inspired me and I lay there astonished with myself, as I licked his bare shoulder.

I let out a moan but he kissed it silent and I lay quiet, caressing his buttocks with the soles of my feet. It was very strange, being part of something so odd, so comic: and then I thought of how Baba and I used to hint about this particular situation and wonder about it and be appalled by our own curiosity. I thought of Baba and Martha and my aunt and all the people who regarded me as a child and I knew that I had now passed – inescapably – into woman-hood.

I felt no pleasure, just some strange satisfaction that I had done what I was born to do. My mind dwelt on foolish, incidental things. I thought to myself, so this is it; the secret I dreaded, and longed for. . . . All the perfume, and sighs, and purple brassières, and curling-pins in bed, and gin-and-it, and necklaces, had all been for this. I saw it as something comic, and beautiful. The growing excitement of his body enthralled me – like the rhythm of the sea. So did the love words that he whispered to me. Little moans and kisses; kisses and little cries that he put into my body, until at last he expired on me and washed me with his love.

Then it was quiet; such quietness; quietness and softness and the tender limp thing like a wet flower between my legs. And all the time the moon shining in on the old brown carpet. We had not bothered to draw the curtains.

He lay still, holding me in his arms; then tears slowly filled my eyes and ran down my cheeks, and I moved my face sideways so that he should not mistake the tears because he had been so happy.

'You're a ruined woman now,' he said, after some time. His voice seemed to come from a great distance, because in hearing his half-articulated words of love I had forgotten that his speaking voice was so crisp.

'Ruined!' I said, re-echoing his words with a queer thrill.

I felt different from Baba now and from every other girl I knew. I wondered if Baba had experienced this, and if she had been afraid, or if she had liked it. I thought of Mama and of how she used to blow on hot soup before she gave it to me and of the rubber bands she put inside the turn-down of my ankle-socks, to keep them from falling.

He moved over and lay on his back and I felt lonely, without the weight of his body. He lit a candle and from it he lit himself a cigarette.

'Well, a new incumbent, more responsibility, more trouble.'

'I'm sorry for coming like this, without being asked,' I said, thinking that 'incumbent' was an insulting word; I mixed it up with 'encumbrance'.

'It's all right; I wouldn't throw a nice girl like you out of my bed,' he joked, and I wondered what he really thought of me. I was not sophisticated and I couldn't talk very well nor drive a car.

'I'll try and get sophisticated,' I said. I would cut my hair, buy tight skirts and a corset.

'I don't want you sophisticated,' he said, 'I just want to give you nice babies.'

'Babies —' I nearly died when he said that and I sat up and said anxiously, 'but you said that we wouldn't have babies.'

'Not now,' he said, shocked by the sudden change in my voice. Babies terrified me — I remembered the day Baba first told me about breast feeding and I felt sick again, just as I had done that day walking across the field eating a packet of sherbet. I got sick then and hid it with dock leaves while Baba finished the sherbet.

'Don't worry,' he said, easing me back on to the bed, 'don't worry about things like that. It will come out all right in the end. Don't think about it, this is your honeymoon.'

'The bed is all tossed,' I said, in an effort to get my mind on to something simple. But we were too comfortable to get up and rearrange it. He reached to the end of the bed for his shirt and his undervest which was inside it. I helped him put it on and kissed the hollow between his shoulder-blades, recalling their apricot colour in daylight.

'Are you hungry?' I asked, when he lay down. I was wide awake and wanted to prolong the happiness of the night.

'No, just sleepy,' he yawned, and lay on the side nearest to me.

'I was a good girl,' I said as he put his hand on my stomach.

'You were a marvellous girl.'

'It's not so terrible.'

'No more old chat out of you,' he said, 'go to sleep.' I could feel my stomach rising and falling gently under the weight of his hand.

'What's your diaphragm?' I asked.

'Meet you outside Jacobs at nine tomorrow night, Miss Potbelly.' He was asleep almost as he spoke, and slowly his hand slid down off my stomach.

*

I did not expect to sleep but somehow I did.

When I wakened the room was bright and I saw him staring at me.

'Hello,' I said, blinking because of the bright sunshine.

'Kate,' he said, 'you look so peaceful in your sleep. I've been looking at you for the past half-hour. You're like a doll.'

I moved my head over on to his pillow so that our faces were close together.

'Oh,' I said with happiness, and stretched my feet. Our toes stuck out at the end of the tossed bed. He said that we ought to have another little moment before we got up and washed ourselves; and he made love to me very quickly that time, and it did not seem so strange any more.

*

In the bathroom we washed together. We couldn't have a bath because the range had not been lit and the water was cold. It was freezing cold water which came from a tank up in the woods and I gasped with the cold of it, and the pleasure of it, as he dabbed a wet sponge on my body.

'Don't, don't,' I begged, but he said that it was good for the circulation.

He washed that part of himself without taking off his clothes again; he just rained the rubber tube that was fixed to the end of the cold tap on it, saying that it had had a monk's life.

'Have to make up for lost time,' he said as I dabbed it dry with a clean towel and asked, unwisely, if he loved me.

'Lucky you don't snore,' he said, 'or I'd send you back.'

'Do you love me?' I asked again.

'Ask me that in ten years' time, when I know you better,' he said as he linked me down to breakfast and told Anna that we had got married.

'That's great news,' she said, but I knew that she knew we were lying.

Chapter Sixteen

THE days took on a pattern then. We slept until ten or
eleven, got up and had light breakfast. During breakfast
Eugene read his letters, and sometimes he read them aloud
to me. They were mostly letters about his work and it
seemed certain now that he would have to go to South
America for a few weeks, to make the picture on irrigation.
There did not seem much chance that he would be able to
take me.

'Anyhow, it won't be until April or May,' he said, 'so let's
enjoy this lovely day and not worry about what's to come.
This is life, this *now*, this moment of you and me eating
boiled eggs.'

After breakfast we usually went for a walk. It rained a lot
up there, but we did not mind the rain. He showed me
oak-apples and badger holes, and things I had never noticed
before. He loved being out, along the hedges, among the
trees, watching the river.

'Look,' he sometimes said, and I would turn, expecting to
find a person but it would be an animal, often a deer; or a
shaft of intense green light between the trees. The sky for
ever changed colour – slate-black, blue-black, blue, and
white-green. He clowned to amuse me, becoming an old
man by hunching his shoulders and letting his gloves
dangle, so that the wagging fingers looked like those of a
withered man.

We did some work on the farm – put stones back on a
wall, mended a fence, drove cattle from one field to the next.

'It looks as if you're going to stay, Kate,' he said, one day
out on the hill.

'I'll stay a few more weeks,' I said. I loved being with
him and being in his bed, but I missed going to the pictures
with Baba.

In the afternoons he worked at his desk, while I helped
Anna to prepare dinner. We had stew and potatoes baked

in wood-ashes and sometimes watercress soup. On Sundays we had wine with our meal, and cashew nuts and fruit on Thursdays, the day the groceries were delivered. He liked frugality and did not eat very much.

After dinner if he still wanted to work (he was preparing a short film for the BBC on Spring in Ireland), Anna and I went for a walk, after she had put her baby to bed. She came to like those walks up the drive to the road, telling me loudly the secrets of her private life. Her cherished ambition was to become a cook in a big house, but she had met Denis at a dance and they spent their first night in a hedge. Much, much later of course.

' 'Tis all right for you, Mr Gaillard *talks* to you,' Anna said. Denis had only a kind word for the baby and the sheep-dog; I used to notice him myself not answering her for days, as if he wanted to punish her. I liked her better than at first. She gave up talking about Laura. I'd bribed her with ten-shilling notes and odd nylons. She began a dress for me on the new sewing-machine and was saving porridge packet-tops to get me a necklace. We had porridge every morning.

*

But on the evenings that Eugene did not work I sat in the study with him and rubbed his hair while we listened to records on the wireless. In rubbing his fine hair I kissed his neck to smell it, and we would embrace each other and eventually go up to bed. We undressed very quickly and made love in the dark room, between cool sheets with the owl crying in his usual tree outside. Later we got up again, washed, and had supper before going out for another walk.

I cannot describe the sweetness of those nights because I was happy and did not notice many things. There always seemed to be a moon and that fresh smell that comes after rain. I'm told now that some men are strangers with a woman after they have loved her, but he was not like that.

'Love suits you,' he often said, 'makes you prettier.'

I felt pretty; happy. We walked under trees, and down to the bottom of the wood to see the moon on the lake and on the curving stretch of river that flowed out from the lake to the distant sea. Once we saw a whole troop of deer, but in that split second after they had seen us, so they were already running. A dead, shot deer drifted down from the upper reaches of the lake and Denis helped him to bring it home. We gave away a lot of the meat. It reminded me of long ago when they killed a pig at home and I carried plates of fresh pork to the houses of neighbours and was given sixpence or a shilling – but there was still a lot left for eating, and by the time it was finished the smell of it remained in my mind, no matter where I went.

At night, the bog, as he called it, had a strange quality of timelessness, as if the scrub oak and rushes and little half-grown birches had never been trod on. He got no turf from it; it was just a sanctuary for pheasants and the grey deer. One night we came on the afterbirth of a deer and we looked at it for a long time, under the moon, as if it were something of great importance. It may have been, to him.

After about a month, Baba came unexpectedly, and brought The Body with her. They blew the horn so much as they drove up the avenue that we thought it was the police coming to take me away. It was only Baba, in The Body's battered blue van which smelt of greyhounds. The Body opened the back door of the van to let Baba out (the side door is permanently broken), and a flock of greyhounds tumbled out with her and set off down the field to chase the cattle.

'Who is that?' Eugene said. We were in the front room having tea.

'The Body,' I said, and my heart sank, knowing that the meeting between them would be awkward.

Baba climbed the steps – wearing a green jacket which I had left behind in Joanna's – and The Body came in, full of welcome for himself. He took a whisky bottle off the sideboard and proceeded to drink from it. It was cow's urine which Eugene was to take to the veterinary surgeon later in the day. After the first taste, The Body threw the bottle down, and went over to the fireplace to spit out what was in his mouth.

'Eugene!' Baba said, embracing him. That helped a bit because he liked Baba.

The Body looked at me quizzically and said, 'What have you done to yourself? You don't look the same any more.' He frowned, trying to puzzle out what it was about me that had changed, and I thought slyly, being in bed and being made love to has altered my face, but in fact it was that I looked tamer because Eugene had asked me to make-up more discreetly. He bought me paler powder and narrow, black velvet ribbons for my hair and a pair of flat, laced shoes which I saw Baba eyeing at that very minute. He had showed me diagrams of ruined feet but I still wore high heels when I was going out.

'I know you well,' The Body said to him, 'I often saw you around town and took you for a Yank.'

I was afraid that Eugene might say something sharp such as 'There are no Yanks nowadays', but he didn't; he offered The Body a chair, not a soft armchair but a straight-backed chair. He had told me before that some of the arm-chairs were likely to come to pieces and not to encourage fat people to sit on them. Life with him carried many rules which I resented slightly.

I got extra cups out of the sideboard, and poured some tea, which was still hot.

'Well?' Baba said, looking at me for a full explanation of everything. 'What happened?'

'I almost got kicked to death by a rabblement of drunken Irish farmers,' Eugene said.

The Body winced and I knew that he was saying to himself, what is Caithleen doing with a cynical bastard like that, but I could not explain to him that Eugene guarded me like a child, taught me things, gave me books to read, and gave pleasure to my body at night.

'Show us,' Baba said, and Eugene pulled down his sock and showed her the scabs.

'That's a luscious scab, 'twould win a prize,' she said, mocking a Dublin accent.

The Body picked at his tooth with a match-stick, and looked at me with a smile which asked, are you happy?

The four greyhounds had come to the window, their moist black snouts pressed to the glass as they sniffed and moaned to be let in.

'Are these yours?' Eugene asked The Body.

'They're mine,' The Body said proudly. And pointing to one of them he said, 'She'll make a fortune one day that little lady. Mick the Miller will only be trotting after her,' but Eugene had never heard of Mick the Miller. I had grown up with a photograph of the greyhound pasted on a kitchen calendar. His childhood had not been like that: it was full of rows, and sheet music, and tripe, or sweetbreads for dinner, and his father bringing home oranges, until the time he left them.

The Body slugged the tea down, and told Eugene that he'd like to see the outhouses, and have a breath of air. With relief I saw them go, and heard The Body say, 'Did you ever hear that one about the woman who took her son to Killarney and stayed in a big hotel – "Monty, Monty," said she, "open your mouth wide, we're paying for the air down here!"' He laughed at his own joke. I knew that his next joke would be the one about the Vice-President and after that the incident of how he had been struck by a grandfather's clock in Limerick and had been obliged to break the clock.

'Well, Jesus, you're in a nice mess,' Baba said to me.

'I'm not in any mess,' I said, 'I'm very happy.'

'Are you fixed up yet?'

'Fixed up what?'

'Married, you eejit.'

'That's my jacket you're wearing,' I said, to get off the subject.

'This old rag,' she said, holding a corner of it up to the light, 'you could strain milk through it.'

'Did you bring my clothes?' I had written to her to post me my clothes.

'What'n the hell clothes are you talking about? There are no clothes of yours except a few dish-cloths that Joanna gave to the rag man in exchange for the saddle of a bicycle. She said you owed a week's rent anyhow.'

'Where's my bicycle?' I said. I had put it in a shed with a torn raincoat over it, to keep the mudguard from rusting.

'Old Gustav goes to work on it. You should see him! He'll break his bloody neck some morning; you'd know he was a foreigner the way he sits on that saddle, you'd know he didn't speak a decent word of English.'

'It's my bicycle,' I said.

'Are you preg?' she asked. ' 'Cos if you are, you won't be able to cycle. Your aul fella is writing to me every day to get you back.'

'Is he coming?' My heart began to race again. I hadn't heard from him for over two weeks.

'You'll have to get a layette – lay it – if you're preg,' she joked.

'Is my father coming?' I asked again.

'How would I know? I suppose he'll come some fine day when he's blotto and shoot the lot of you.' She shot at the portrait of Eugene over the fire. 'Blood and murder and then he'll start singing – "I didn't know the gun was loaded and I'm *so* sorry, my friends; I didn't know the gun was loaded and I'll never, never do it again." ' Baba hadn't changed a bit.

'What are you doing with yourself?' I asked in a piqued voice.

'I'm having a whale of a time,' she told me. 'Out every night. I was at an ice-show last night. Terrif. The Body and I are going to a dinner-dance tonight, and someone wanted to paint my picture last week. I met him at a party and he said I had the nicest profile he ever saw. So next day, as arranged, I went along to his den and he wanted the picture in the nude. "Christ sake," says I, "what has your nude got to do with your profile?" He was in a pair of shorts whanging a dog-whip about in his hand. God you wouldn't see me running!' She looked around the room with its brown furniture and shelves of books. 'How long are you staying in this bog?' she asked, and answered for me, 'Till he gets tired of you, I suppose. You're a right-looking eejit in those flat shoes.' She had her black high-heelers on.

'Have you a boy?' I asked. She made me restless.

'Oh def. You can ask Joanna how many cars call now. I've got oodles of men, and John Ford is giving me a screen test this week.'

'It's a lie,' I said.

'Of course it's a lie,' she said. 'Give us another cup of tea; any grog in the house?'

There was a bottle of whisky hidden in the gun bureau but I did not want to open it, as it was not my house. When they came back, Eugene did not open it either and they left soon after, disappointed I suppose because they weren't offered a drink. Before she left, Baba told me that she had heard from her mother that my father was coming to see me along with the Bishop of the diocese. I didn't think that she was serious but in fact she was.

Next day my father came. We were in the study, giving instructions to the local plasterer about doing the hole in the ceiling.

'My father, my father,' I said as I saw the Ferret's car drive up to the hall door.

'Get back from the window,' Eugene said.

'What's up?' the plasterer asked.

Then the knocker was pounded.

I ran down to tell Anna not to answer it, and we locked the back door.

The knocking resounded all over the waiting house, the dog barked and my heart beat rapidly, just as it had done the first night they came.

'Caithleen, Caithleen,' my father's voice called plaintively through the letter-box. I ran to the study and whispered to Eugene.

'If he's alone, maybe we should see him?' His voice calling my name had made me pity him.

Eugene had been looking through the binoculars to see who was in the car and he whispered, 'There's three others in the car, there's a bishop or something, I can see his purple dicky.'

'Caithleen,' my father called, and then he knocked steadily for about two minutes. It was a good thing we didn't have a doorbell or we would all have been deafened.

'I'll settle it,' Eugene said, and he went out and put the chain on the hall door and then opened the door suddenly. It could only open a few inches, because of the chain.

'Anything you want to say to your daughter will have to come in writing to her.'

'I want to see her,' my father said.

I stood behind the study door, praying and gasping. The plasterer must have thought I was going to die. The cement was going hard on him but he couldn't start work because Eugene had told him not to make a sound.

'Your daughter does not want to see you,' Eugene said. The words sounded very cruel when put bluntly like that.

'I just want to have a chat with her. I have a friend of hers here, Bishop Jordon, he knows her since she was a child, he confirmed her. We won't lay a finger on her.' I knew from the pitch of his voice that he was frightened and ashamed.

'Look, Mr Brady,' Eugene said, 'I have written to you, through my solicitors, I do not want you here and I do not want any Monseigneurs meddling in my affairs. I thought that we had made that clear.'

'We're not doing any harm,' my father said, in a desperate voice.

'You are trespassing on my property,' Eugene said, and I wrung my hands in shame. 'She's twenty-one years old and here of her own free will.'

'You think you're very important,' my father said, 'but this is our country and you can't come along here and destroy people who've lived here for generations, don't think that...' But his voice faded, because suddenly Eugene shut the door.

Outside, my father knocked with his fists on the wood, but after a few minutes he went down the steps and then I saw the car driving off. He sat in the back and looked through the back window as they drove off.

That was Saturday afternoon, and for the rest of the evening I cried and disliked myself for having been so cruel to my father. I did not bother about my hair or my appearance, as I wanted to look awful so that Eugene would realize how wretched I felt.

'I'm in love and I'm miserable,' I said aloud to myself. He overheard me and said, 'Take two aspirins.' I couldn't cry, or wash my hair, or talk to myself but he noticed it.

'Will you take me to Mass tomorrow?' I asked. I could feel the goodness going out of me, as I had not been to Mass for five weeks.

'Of course I'll take you to Mass,' he said. He was very unpredictable like that; he would sometimes say yes, when you expected him to say no.

'Of course I'll take you to Mass, you poor little pigeon,' he said as he put an arm round me and patted my shoulder.

'You've got no shoulders,' he said. I had sloping shoulders like Mama's and they were very white and frail-looking.

*

We did not go to the local chapel because I knew that the priest would accost me on the way out, as he had written me three letters. We drove instead to a village eight or nine miles away. It was a new concrete chapel set on a treeless hill and there was a white notice-board outside stating the extent of the debt which the new church had entailed. Although it was a February morning, the sun shone, as it sometimes does in Ireland, to compensate for a whole week's rain. I left him in the sun, sitting on the low mossy wall opposite the chapel gate, reading the *New Statesman*. The inside of the chapel was cheerless, the brown plastered walls had not been painted, and there was scaffolding in one of the side aisles.

I had no prayer book, just the white beads that a nun gave me in the convent, so I tried hard to say a rosary. The people distracted me – their coughing, their ill-fitting clothes, and that sour smell which comes from drying their faces with dirty towels. I could see Eugene's bright eyes mocking me, 'Only egomaniacs see Christ as God come specially to save *them*. Christ is the emanation of goodness from all men' – and I lay my forehead on the new oak rest and thought of the time when I had a crush on a nun, and decided to be a nun too, and another time for a whole week, I had decided to be a saint and kept pebbles in my shoes as a penance, which is what we called 'making an act'.

The sermon was about Grace and I came out from Mass wondering if I had spurned God's Grace once too often. For a minute I forgot that Eugene was waiting for me, and as he looked up from his *New Statesman* and said, 'Did you have a nice Mass?' I realized with slight shock that he was waiting for *me*.

With the sun in my eyes, I said, 'When I came out just now and saw you here, I forgot that you were waiting for me, isn't that funny?'

'No, it isn't funny,' he said, and I thought with panic, I have insulted him and he'll be cold with me now for days.

'So when you're in there, you become a convent girl again,' he remarked. I thought of myself looking like a crow in black shoes and stockings and a serge gym-frock which was never ironed properly, because Mama died before I went away to boarding-school, and I had to attend to my own uniform.

'I was never really a convent girl,' I said, recalling the sky-blue Holy Picture on which Baba wrote the dirty thing that got us expelled from the convent.

'I don't know how you can do it,' he said, remarking on my hypocrisy. 'How can you live two lives? In there' – he nodded towards the concrete church – 'you're deep in it with Crucifixions and hell and bloody thorns. And here am I sitting on a wall, reading about atom bombs and you say "Who am I?" For that matter' – he tapped my chin with his index finger – 'who are you and what are you doing in my life?' He was laughing all the time, but I still did not like what he said. I hung my head, but he recognized the flashes of unhappiness in my face – the mouth drooping at the corners, the slight pout. He jumped over the wall, plucked a branch from a budding chestnut tree and presented it to me with a deep bow.

'What unites men and women is not God or the *New*

Statesman,' he said, putting the sticky bud under my nose. Then he kissed my cheek and we sat in and drove home.

'You won't brood for the rest of the day, will you, sweetling?' he said as we drove along between the rows of winter hedges. The sun shone and old women and children – the ones who had been too old or too young to go to Mass – sat outside cottages and waved to us. The children were in their good clothes, and I remember the pink face and white hair of one albino girl who sat on a whitewashed pier, swinging her legs, wearing patent shoes with silver buckles on them. And I thought to myself, I'll never forget this moment because somehow it is very important to me, even though I don't know why, and I waved to the little pink girl, and said to Eugene, 'No, I won't brood.' But already I had begun to brood and relive the scene outside the chapel in my mind; and from afar I scented trouble and difficulties but I could not arm myself against him, as I loved him too much.

'It's all right for you,' I said helplessly, 'you can think things out, but I'm different.'

'We're all different,' he said as he started to sing, 'I wonder who's hating her now.' It was a song he often sang, and I imagined that it was directed towards Laura. He sang to jolly things up, he said.

'I wouldn't get married,' I said rashly, 'unless I got married in a Catholic church.'

'I'm glad you told me,' he said, 'I'll make a note of that,' the merest hint of sarcasm in his rich voice. A rainbow was arched in the bottom of the sky and looped across the sunny hills. I counted its seven colours; behind it the sky was changing from blue to water-green and I could feel my attitude to him changing, like the colours of the changing sky.

We gave a lift for part of the way to two young men who were making the journey to a youth hostel seventeen miles away. They sat in the back seat, whispering; and when I turned to speak to them, I was conscious only of their knees. They wore shorts and their thick knees were on a level with my face, because the back of the car was so small. They were about my age and it occurred to me that I ought to be with them, walking from one village to the next, worrying about nothing more than the price of a cup of tea. But then I consoled myself with the thought that young men, with their big knees and their awkward voices, bored me.

Chapter Seventeen

WHEN we got home Eugene's mother was there. She came to lunch most Sundays.

She had a little present for me – a hand-embroidered tray cloth. It was a wedding-gift. We pretended that we were married, and anyhow I wore a ring. We drank sherry, and then she sat in the sun until lunch-time.

During lunch a row broke out, because I had put chopped onions in a sauce. She took the tray-cloth back, saying that I must have put the onions in on purpose, knowing that they would make her bilious.

'I knew I could never trust a red-haired woman,' she said to the water jug as we ate in silence. She had pushed her dinner plate away, and was calling the dog, 'Shep, Shep'.

Eugene winked at me, and I went on eating.

'Well things have come down a lot here. Laura was an adventuress, but she knew how to entertain.'

'Have some orange mousse,' Eugene said, but she said that she couldn't trust that either.

'I'll have a piece of bread and butter if it's not too much trouble,' she said; and ignoring the sarcasm, he got her some bread and then disappeared. He always fled from a row. I finished my dinner and got up as soon as I decently could.

He helped me to wash up. He peeped through the dining-room door and saw her eating the dinner, including the mousse, which she had so vehemently refused. No talk of poison now.

'Come here,' he whispered, and I looked through the keyhole and saw her spooning the mousse from the bowl.

'I'll tell you a secret,' he said when we were back in the pantry. 'She'll see us all to our graves yet.' And then he kissed me, and while I was in his arms the warm hum of love began again.

A car drove up as we were kissing and he slipped away to

welcome two guests whom he had invited out from Dublin.

'I'll comb my hair first,' I said, and I went up and put on a lot of make-up to compensate for my social inadequacies, because his friends terrified me. The man was a lecturer in history and wrote poems on Sundays, and he had a pudding of a wife who thought she knew everything. By coincidence a third guest came, another poet, Simon, an American, who had cycled over from Glencree, near by. Eugene's mother wore an Indian shawl and sat in state on the velvet chair beside the fire, telling everyone that onions repeated on her.

Simon the poet said 'Wow', when I was introduced to him, and stroked his reddish beard. I knew from Eugene that he had been a friend of Laura's, and I was frightened of him. He called all women cows – 'a fat cow', 'a thin cow', 'a frigid cow', 'a nice cow'.

'Things went wrong with the food today,' Eugene's mother said to the pudding wife, who sat opposite her wearing green tweed trousers.

I went off to the kitchen to make some tea, and Simon came to help me. Standing in the middle of the flagged floor, his green, close-together eyes looked on me as he said:

'Well, here you are, shining quietly behind a bushel of Wicklow bran.'

'You pinched that,' I said to him, because I remember everything that I have read, 'from James Joyce.'

'Who the hell is James Joyce?' he said, and then asked how I got on with old Eugene and what we talked about and if he was good in bed.

Such impertinence, I thought, and remembered a proverb of Mama's – 'By their friends you shall know them'. I resented Eugene for knowing a man like this.

'Did you measure it?' the poet asked. He winked and looked at me in such a way that my stomach suddenly felt sick.

'What?'

'What! You ask me what! Wow, you need lessons. His you-know-what. All my women measure mine, it's great fun; you should try it.'

I kept my head down so that he would not notice how I blushed, and I hated him, the way I hate people who tell me smutty stories which are not funny. He had sandy red in his beard, and a little Irish somewhere behind his American accent – though he claimed his people were blueblooded English.

'Shall I butter these for you, Caithleen?' He pointed to the sliced currant cake.

'Do.' He said my name too often and was affable and ugly alternately – as wicked people often are.

'How's old Eugene's work going? Any epics coming up? God, how he'd love to make *Moby Dick*, or something great.'

'I don't think so,' I said. Once I asked Eugene if he had secret ambitions to make a famous picture and he shook his head gravely, and said, 'No, not a famous one; I'd like to compile a long chronicle about the injustice and outrage done by one man to another throughout the ages, and of our perilous struggle for survival and self-perfection – but who'd want to look at it?'

'You know what his big ambition is,' Simon the poet scoffed. 'To have a drink with someone in MGM.'

'You're behind the times,' I said, trembling with emotion, as I always tremble when I want to say something that is important. 'He says that what matters is to have a conviction about your work; to do your duty according to your lights.'

'Duty, har, har,' Simon laughed, as if some laughing machine had been wound up inside him. 'Laura would love that. Jesus that's priceless; he's good on propaganda. Duty! God, Laura will love that when she comes.'

'Comes?'

'Yeh. Hasn't she told you? She must be saving it up as a big surprise, because she's sailing for Cobh next week. Now what about some lemon for my tea, Miss Caithleen Brady?'

'It's over there.' I pointed to a bowl of fruit on the dresser. The lemon looked brown and wrinkled but I didn't mind; my legs were trembling, because of what he'd told me.

'There'll be a hot time in the old bed when she arrives. Have you ever seen her? Wow!' And then he began to sing,

'Do not forsake me, oh my darling, on this our wedding day. . . .'

I had seen a photo of her. She had short hair and a strong face. I'd looked at Eugene's pictures one day when he was out. He kept them in a locked box but I found the key under one corner of the carpet where it was not tacked down. There were a lot of pictures of his daughter, and on the back of each one he had written details of where the picture was taken and what the child had been doing – 'Elaine eating bread and jam in high chair', 'Brown Dog sleeping in Elaine's pram'. They distressed me, and putting them away guiltily I wondered when the child's birthday was, and if he sent her presents.

'Old Heathcliff is a bit gone on her still, you know, old hatreds die hard,' Simon the poet said, crashing in on my worried thoughts.

'The tea is made now,' I said, desperate to escape from him. Earlier on he had confided to me that he sucked birds' eggs, which gave him a special virility. 'Alone with nature and the little birds,' he said mockingly.

'The tea is made,' I said again and piled the last few things on to the tray.

'Now there's an efficient girl, that's what I like; an efficient girl and cool. Wow cool! You've got a clever tear in your eye, Caithleen; clever because it's not real. I am a poet and I know these things. After you.' And he carried the tray as I walked ahead of him, up the narrow dark passage, towards the dining-room.

'You've got a nice little ass,' he said, and as usual my high-heel caught in the rat hole along the wooden passage. (Once in a snow-storm a rat had gnawed his way into the house, and Anna said that Laura had stood on a chair and screamed, just as any woman would.)

'You brought the wrong cups,' Eugene said when he saw me unload the tray. They were kitchen cups.

'They'll do,' I said, getting red.

'No, no, no. It's Sunday afternoon, we're entitled to nice cups,' he said good-humouredly as he re-piled the unmatching cups back on the tray and carried it out.

'Well, what can you expect?' his mother said to the big log in the fireplace. 'Country girls. Fresh from the bogs.'

Simon stroked his beard and looked from one to another of us. The other couple sipped their port wine, and the woman smiled, either sorry because of what had happened or to show her pleasure over it.

'Sit down, dear,' she said. I hate people who call me 'dear'.

'Excuse me,' I said, leaving the room. I got my coat and went off to hide in the lady's garden.

For that hour I hated Eugene. I hated his strength, his pride, his self-assurance. I wished that he had some deep flaw in his nature which would weaken him for me; but he had no flaw (except his pride); he was a rock of strength. Then I remembered – as one does in a temper – the ugly side of his nature: of how cross he could be, of the day he shouted, 'You're a mechanical idiot who can't even turn off a tap.' He had been doing something with the water cistern up on the roof and he had explained that I was to turn the tap on and off when he said the words 'on' and 'off'. I turned it on all right but when it came to turning it off I got flustered and turned it on more, and then he shouted that he was being flooded, and I got quite helpless and could do nothing. His jibes and pinpricks leaped to memory – 'Baba, when I have a harem you'll be in it,' 'I'm teaching Kate how to speak English before I take her into society,' and 'Run upstairs on your peasant legs.' For that hour I hated him.

'I hate him,' I said to the early birds who had come to make their nests. They did not so much sing as warble, and make noises to clear their throats, in preparation for their long song of beautiful courtship.

'Courtship,' I said bitterly and wondered who Baba was with; and if she still saw Tod Mead. I thought, or tried to think, of the various men I knew, all simple boys compared with Eugene. I remembered then a story he had told me of how he shared one room with another man somewhere in London and each washed his own half of the floor on Saturdays; and it seemed to me to be a cold, inhuman thing to do. I could not see myself washing half of a floor without letting the cloth slide over to include the other half; but they were methodical, they had a line drawn across the centre of the linoleumed floor. I thought of this and of Simon the poet saying to me, 'How do you feel about breasts?' as he buttered slices of cake and took the foundations from under my life by telling me that Laura was coming back. His high-pitched laugh re-echoed in my mind and I worried because Eugene knew such a person.

I stayed there moping and wishing that he would come for me. There were catkins on the sally tree, white as snow and hanging like tassels, and along the granite sundial there trailed a shoot of winter jasmin, its spare yellow flowers giving hope and brightness to the sad day. Eugene had said that wild thyme would grow there later on and that the garden would be filled with the bouquet of wild thyme. I wondered if I would be married by then.

'He'll never marry you,' Baba had said, and I thought, it's true, because he's a dark horse. The good and the bad of him alternated in my thoughts, as I remembered first his scowling expression and his unyielding nature and then his tenderness – he brought me toast to bed once and put lanolin on a welt of mine, and got three pillows so that I could be propped up to read. For a while I welcomed the fact that one day I would be old and dried, and no man would torment my heart.

*

It got chilly once the sun went down. He came to look for me when the visitors had gone.

'Trying to make little of me in front of people,' I said as he stood over me in the dusk, patting my hair and apologizing. The dark, violet hush of evening had descended.

'I'm sorry,' he said, 'I didn't mean to offend you. I just thought that the cups looked awful and that Mother would complain and that we might as well get the better ones.'

'Cups don't matter.' I almost shouted it. 'Cups are not important; you're always the one that's talking about inessentials – well, cups are inessentials.'

'All right, all right,' he said, patting me to keep still.

'You shouldn't have done that to me, in front of all these people.' It maddened me to think that it happened in front of that wicked poet and the two women who would remember it, no doubt for ever.

'You know no nice people, no sincere people,' I said.

'My dear child,' he replied, almost smugly, 'there are no wholly nice people, there are no sincere people; I mean, a worm is probably sincere, if that's what you want.'

I remembered how 'sincere' had been Mama's criterion for everyone. 'Lizzie is sincere,' she said of some mean woman who asked us to tea and gave us sandwiches with tomato ketchup in them, and rhubarb. 'They're sincere,' Mama would say of mean cousins in Dublin who expected her to send them home-made butter for nothing, all during the war. It was how she judged people.

'And that Simon fellow, talking to me about intimate things . . .' I complained.

'Oh, I should have warned you – his male appendage, I gather, is rather small and some woman once laughed at him.'

He looked up at the violet sky; the birds in the darkening trees singing their night songs, and the calmness in the air, seemed to give him such pleasure that he hardly heard what I was saying. He's happy, I thought, when his friends walk on me and say filthy things to me!

'He's a funny friend to have,' I said.

'He's not a friend,' Eugene corrected. 'In this country there are so few people to talk to that one is thankful for any friendly enemy who can speak one's own language.' He sighed at the dark sky as if he would like to ascend into its calm loneliness.

I broke in on this moment. 'Simon says that Laura is sailing for Cobh.'

'Indeed!' he said, without any apparent surprise. 'I'll be delighted to see her.'

I got off the wooden seat and stared up into his calm, impassive face.

'You what?' I said.

'I'll be delighted to see her, we can discuss things; maybe

I can get a divorce and marry you. We'll share the child.'
(He never said the little girl's name.) 'Laura can come here
and we'll all be good friends. You can wash her hair; she
can wash yours ...'

'You mean ... ?' I began but did not go on. There was
nothing I could say, because I was thinking, he's a prig, an
indifferent, unfeeling prig. I let out some sound of despair.

'All right; I'll write to her about a divorce. I can see that
not being married is injuring your country soul.'

The words stung me. Something – everything – had
struck the whole, laughing pleasure of my life.

*

That night while I sat by the fire reading the opening
chapters of *Anna Karenina*, he typed out a letter to Laura.
I longed to know if he had begun it with 'dear Laura', or
'dearest Laura', or 'my darling', but I could not look over
his shoulder.

We walked to the village to post the letter. The night
felt warm and springlike; the fields on either side were
damp with dew and he did not link me.

Half way along the dusty mountain road we found that
they had begun to tar it, and the tar being fresh, our feet
left marks on its blue-black surface.

'Cheers,' he said, 'we're going to have a tarred road.' It
was the first word he spoke since we set out.

In a sad, doomed voice I said, 'It's not fair, is it? We just
can't be left alone.'

My father had written three times, the local priest wrote,
the head nun from the convent sent me prayers and medals,
and now Laura would be coming.

'Nothing's fair, it's not a fair world,' he said, in a tired,
dull voice.

*

In the village I heard piano music from the lounge of the
one hotel, and it made me lonely for all the gay nights with
Baba, hearing her say, 'Down the hatch', to some man or
other. When he had posted the letter I said:

'I'd love to go into the hotel.'

'You don't want to go in there.' He frowned toward the yellow-sashed building with porter barrels outside, under the window.

'Just for one drink,' I said, and though he sighed, he took off his cap and escorted me in to the lounge bar. The place was crowded, the room thick with smoke and commotion. Someone was singing. They were mostly local people and they all stared at us. It was because we weren't married. He ordered two whiskies. The noise, which had subsided when we came in – while people nudged and whispered – began again and a fat woman continued to play the piano. They had painted the piano white, so that it looked like a wash-stand.

'Do you know any of these people?' I asked, in a low voice. They had not saluted him. Anna had told me that they didn't like him, because he never got drunk or bought free drinks for them on fair days. Some of them drove cattle and sheep into his land at night; and in the morning, Denis drove them out again. A herd of goats kept coming in, and he wrote several times to their owner but she ignored the letters. He would not have minded, if she had asked for permission, but, like most poeple in the neighbourhood, she was dour and unfriendly. Someone had cut the tops off hundreds of small trees in the new plantation shortly after I came there. It was regarded as a big disgrace for me to be there and they used to question Anna, every Sunday, when she went to Mass.

'I know one or two of them,' he said.

'So his nibs's got rid of the American woman and now he has this young one,' I heard one man tell another. I blushed and looked down at the glass-topped table.

'He forgot the soda,' I said to Eugene, as I stared at the yellow paper doilies under the cracked glass of the table. As I was not used to whisky, it tasted awful without soda.

A drunk man came up just then and raised his cap and asked Eugene to sing.

'I can't sing,' Eugene said, and the drunk man then asked if I would sing.

'We don't sing,' Eugene said, and the drunk man hummed a few bars of 'The Old Bog Road', and held his cap out, so that we would put money in it. I did not know what to do; I just felt the blood rising in my neck as I prayed that he would go away and leave us alone. Then suddenly he flicked my wool beret off, and it fell on to the table and overturned my drink.

'Come on,' Eugene said, standing up. We went out quickly, and I heard people laugh, and the drunk calling, 'Pagans, pagans'.

'I'm sorry,' I said when we got outside, 'it was my fault, I didn't realize that it would be like that.'

'Stone Age people,' he said; but he wasn't angry with me, he linked me. Walking home, I said, ' 'Twill be different tomorrow, I'll have cheered up again.'

'It's funny,' he said, 'the difference between fantasy and reality. When I met you those first few times in Dublin by accident, I thought to myself, "Now there is a simple girl, gay as a bird, delighted when you pass her a second cake, busy all day and tired when she lies down at night. A simple, uncomplicated girl." ' He spoke mournfully as if he were speaking of someone who had died.

'I'll be like that again,' I said. But he shook his head sadly and I knew that he was thinking: It was all an illusion, it was the clear whites of your eyes, and your soft voice, and the chiffon scarf around your throat, which gave me the wrong impression. I'm sure he thought something like that; even though he may have put it in different words.

Simon the poet lost no time. Laura's first telegram came on Thursday. Eugene was out when it was delivered, and I opened it because he told me to always open telegrams. It said:

WELL EVERYBODY DESERVES A LITTLE FUN. ENJOY YOURSELF

LAURA

I ran to look for him. Anna said that he had gone for a ramble and that maybe I'd find him on the mountain, helping Denis to bring the sheep down. The sheep were

brought down to the fields near the house weeks before
lambing time. I ran out of the house and through the
woods to the wasteland which led to the mountain. I heard
sheep long before I saw him.

'Is that you, Kate?' he called out as I hurried along a
narrow track, and saw two figures, Denis's and his, herding
the sheep. Denis had a lantern.

'That's me,' I said in an angry voice, and when I was
within a few yards of him I told him about the telegram.
Denis moved away, calling the dog and pretending not to
hear me.

'So that's why you're gasping and blowing,' he said, and
grinned. I handed him the telegram, which I had crumpled,
in my state of outrage.

'I think it's awful,' I said. 'The post office, everyone, has
read it.' Young gorse pricked my ankles and my stocking
caught in a brier, but I did not care.

'It's just a joke,' he said. 'You have no sense of humour.
We'll have to give you one.'

'Humour!' There was a narrow path between the thickets
of gorse but I kept wandering off it.

'There, there, there.' He linked me but I refused his arm.
In the dusk the clumsy bodies of the sheep appeared to be
tumbling down the hillside recklessly.

During dinner he read. Always during a coolness he read;
he could read for days to avoid a scene.

Laura's letter came on Saturday. Her name was on the
back of the pink envelope, his name in fact – Mrs Laura
Gaillard. He did not show it to me, but in the afternoon,
when he went out, I rooted among his papers and found it.
I read:

Eugene my dear,

I haven't written for months. We're both fine and the weather
is just marvellous. Well of course Simon (he *is* an old woman)
has written and told me everything including some trivial little
incident about wrong cups. I always said you had a feudal attitude to women! And since then, I've had your sweet letter in
which you say, 'I have met a girl; she is Irish and romantic and
illogical,' and I say, What is she doing with dat man of mine!

Honestly I was bowled over. Don't fall off the chair or anything but you know we still have a sneaking attraction for one another which defies all the laws of gravity. Sometimes at night when I am in a perfectly empty room (Boo asleep in her cot) and I think 'Gee-wheez, he's a wonderful man and he's funny and has talent and he loves me'. I guess it is love. I have all your letters including the very first you wrote me after the night we met at Snope's party and it's signed 'Heug'. You remember how we used to play with each other's names? Heug for you, and 'Alura' for me. Your letters are in my G file and when I read them I realize how wise and subtle you are and how you once loved me. I'd let you see them, but you must promise to send them back.

The weather is fine – have I ever told you that the climate here is the most beautiful in the world? At night there is a sea mist (do you remember when we all swam naked that time down in Killarney, and you caught a chill?).

Boo-boo is fine and I hate to tell you but she doesn't miss you. We play together for hours and have fun and I envy her the lovely, secure childhood she is having. But she will know you, I'm sure, when you come.

At this point the paper began to tremble in my hand, and I read on feverishly.

When is this film scheduled for and are you going to South America first, or here first? Let me know by return, I want to have everything nice for you. I have painted the walls a powder blue and the ceiling dove grey. You'll adore it. I'm having an exhibition later on and I've just finished a darling picture which I think is IT. It expresses everything I have to say about life, the soul, neuroses, love, and death. . . .

Boo sleeps on her right side with her hand under her cheek and she *is* a doll.

Love and kisses,
Laura

P.S. The thing that worries me is that Mom and Ricki and Jason and everyone thinks we were made for one another.

He did not have to ask what I had been doing when he came in. The letter was in my hand and my lips trembled.

'Oh no,' he said, putting his hands to his eyes. 'I'm so stupid, to leave a thing like that under your nose.'

'It's terrible,' I said, wildly.

'You shouldn't have meddled in my affairs.' He took off his cap and scratched his head in irritation.

'It's my affair.'

'It has nothing to do with you,' he said calmly. 'I didn't intend you to read that letter and you had no right to do so.'

I threw the letter down on the desk. 'I'm glad I did. I now know what I've let myself in for. You going off to America to see her, and not even to tell me.' If I had to bring all the bitterness and hatred of the world into my heart I was going to make him take me; that's how I felt about it in that state of raw and ugly temper.

'So you know it all,' he said. 'Well, that's more than anybody else knows. Every time I look at you, you're crying about something. If it's not her' – he nodded towards the letter on the desk – 'it's your father, and if it's not him, it's something else.'

'Deceiving me,' I said. It was all I could say.

'I beg your pardon,' he said in a very cold and controlled voice, 'am I to understand that my past life has deceived you?'

'No not that,' I tried to explain, 'but the way you do things, you're so independent, and you don't tell me anything.'

'My God!' he sighed, and put his cap on. His angry eyes turned away. 'So you want ownership too, signed and sealed? One hour in bed shall be paid for by a life sentence?'

I lost my nerve and could not look at him. 'It's just such a shock,' I said in an appeasing voice now, because I had vowed to be good, and anyhow I wanted him to take me with him.

'Will you take me with you?' I said, but he did not answer, so I said it again and touched his hand. He took his hand away to remove his cap, and threw it on the desk. It overturned an open bottle of ink, and in a flash I saw it flow on to the maroon carpet and heard him swear and grind his teeth.

'Will you take me with you?' I said, in a last effort to extort a promise from him.

'Oh, for Christ's sake,' he said, going over to soak up the

ink with a sheet of blotting-paper, 'go away and postpone your scene until later on.' It was as if he had flung me out of the room; I walked out quickly, went upstairs and began to pack my clothes into a canvas travel bag – one of his.

I had not very many clothes but still the bag was stuffed to capacity, and the zip-fastener would not close. The straps of a slip and a brassière stuck out, and my three pairs of shoes were on top. I had no money.

'Can I have a pound for my bus fare?' I said, as I came downstairs and tapped lightly on the study door, which was ajar. He was on his knees, washing the ink stain out of the carpet.

'A pound for your bus fare?' He looked up and saw that I had my coat on, and then his eyes fell on the stuffed travel bag.

'I'll send you back your bag,' I said, knowing that he was going to comment on it. 'It's the best thing – to go away,' I said, trying not to break down until I had left.

From the green cash-box he took five pounds and handed them to me.

'One will do,' I said, touched by this last-minute generosity.

'You'll want your bus fare back again, won't you?' he said, giving some sort of smile. Then he looked at the bag (the indecency of it, with underwear straps sticking out), and he said, 'You'll give the wrong impression, you know, leaving in a dishevelled state.'

'I'm sorry,' I said as he put his lips to mine to kiss me good-bye. I don't know why I said 'I'm sorry', it's just that he had this marvellous faculty for being right and I always felt sorry, no matter whose fault it was.

'I'll drive you to the bus,' he said; but of course by then he had kissed me and I was crying and we both knew that I would not leave at all. We put the bag down and we sat on the couch, while he told me in a concerned voice that I would have to grow up and learn to control my emotions. Discipline and control were the virtues he most lauded. These and frugality. In fact, the things I was most lacking in.

'We'll just have a cup of tea. Did I ever tell you my daily motto?' he said, after he had talked to me about being patient.

I shook my head.

'When about to cement fourth wife under kitchen floor – pause, and make tea.'

I wondered if he had told Laura that, after sitting on a chair and lecturing to her calmly about self-perfection and mind-control and things like that. So often she crept into my thoughts, coming between me and what he said.

*

We made tea and ate fancy biscuits, and then we went for a walk and saw the first snowdrop of the year. I felt very happy and elevated by all that he had said to me – I was going to be different – large and placid and strong.

*

That night when he loved me and sank into me I thought to myself, it is only with our bodies that we ever really forgive one another; the mind pretends to forgive, but it harbours and re-remembers in moments of blackness. And even in loving him, I remembered our difficulties, the separated, different worlds that each came from; he controlled, full of reasons and brain, knowing everyone, knowing everything about everything – me swayed or frightened by every wind, light-headed, mad in one eye (as he said), bred in (as he said, again) 'Stone Age ignorance and religious savagery'. Jesus meek and mild show me the right road.

Chapter Eighteen

EVERYTHING was all right for four or five weeks. He wrote to Laura about a divorce; I wrote to my aunt and said, to cheer her up, that I would be married very soon.

Buds like so many points of hope tipped the brown and black twigs – green buds, black buds, and silver-white buds that looked as if they should sing as they burst upon us, waiting. Lambs were born at all hours of day and night, and two lambs whose mothers died were brought in the house and made pets of by Anna. They were a nuisance.

Baba came one week-morning (Sunday was her usual day for coming) just as I was picking daffodils down the avenue. I had conveyed Eugene up to the top of the road to open the various gates for him. He went to a cattle fair to buy calves as we had extra milk now. There were a lot of daffodils in bloom on the grass verge at either side of the gravelled avenue, and on the way back I gathered an armful to pass the time. Their roots were wet as if spittle had been smeared on them and they smelt slightly unpleasant as daffodils do. Then I heard a car, looked through the trees, and seeing that it was a strange car I ran back to the house to hide. I thought that it might be my father; but in fact it was Baba.

'Baba, Baba!' I unlocked the door and ran to her. She wore a white macintosh and a red beret.

'This is marvellous,' I said, kissing her. I wished, though, that she hadn't found me without my make-up.

Her eyes were large and excited, the way they get when she has something important to tell. In the hall the two pet lambs ran up, making baa noises and pretending that they were frightened of her.

'Baa, baa,' she said, chasing them, 'it's like a bloody zoo!' Then she whispered, 'I want to talk to you, it's urgent. Where's Chekhov?'

'He's out,' I said, and we went into the study and I closed the door – Anna expected to be included in all conversations with visitors. I filled us some port into tumblers; the tumblers were dusty but I did not want to go away and rinse them. Baba appeared to be very nervous.

'Are you cold?' I asked her. The ashes from the previous night's fire were still warm and the walls warm to the touch.

'Brace yourself,' she said, touching my glass with hers, 'I have bad news.' My heart started to thump because I thought it was a message from my father.

'I'm in trouble,' she said.

'What kind?' said I, hopelessly.

'Jesus there's only one kind.'

'Oh no,' I said, drawing back from her as if she had just insulted me. 'How could you?'

'Listen to who's talking,' she said. 'What the hell are *you* doing?'

'But you can't,' I said, in a panic. 'You're not even living with anyone.'

'Can't! It's the simplest bloody thing, I mean it's simpler than owning two coats or getting asked to a party.'

'Oh, Baba,' I said, holding her hand.

'Give me a fag,' she said abruptly. She hated pity and that slop of holding her hand.

While I rooted on Eugene's desk she filled out two more drinks. 'Don't,' I said, 'he'll miss it.'

'What? You're not in a bloody monastery.' And then she put the tipped cigarette in her mouth wrongways. We sat down and tried to decide what she should do.

'Whose is it?' I asked, but she wouldn't tell. She said that he was a married man and he worried in case his wife might get to hear of it. I felt certain that it must be Tod Mead. She said that the man had taken it very casually and said good-bye to her on the upstairs of a bus the day before. 'See you around' were his parting words to her.

'I can go to England or I can come here,' she said. The 'come here' made me speechless for a moment. I foresaw a situation where she'd be in our bed and ordering me to get up and cook breakfast. And I did not want a baby in the house. I dreaded babies.

'Can't you do something?' I said.

'Do something!' she shouted. 'It's morbid. I've done every bloody thing, took glauber salts, and dug the garden, and I did so much waxing in that dump that Joanna got rid of the charwoman on the strength of it. . . .'

I almost said, 'It's an ill wind . . .' as I thought of Joanna's half-blind joy at finding Baba on her knees waxing. But Baba was too worried for me to say anything; her teeth chattered, and I sat there consoling her until Eugene came.

'It's morbid,' she kept saying, 'everything's morbid. Some-one filled me up with gin in a basement in Baggot Street. "Baba, you're a noble woman," he said, standing there in his he-man's string vest, and I hadn't the heart to tell him that I'd rather go home. That's me,' she murmured, 'the loser in the end.'

I advised that she should go to England. She had received three hundred pounds from an insurance policy when she was twenty-one and her parents should be made to give it to her.

But when Eugene heard about it he said that if nothing fortuitous happened, Baba might have to come to us.

'We'll have a harem,' he said, joking her, and she cheered up enormously and began to give me impertinence. I wasn't a bit sorry for her, as she sat there in a brown kimono dress with her legs painted tan and her ankles crossed.

'Do you still shave?' she said to me.

'I never shaved. How dare you!'

'Who are you tellin'?' – and she peered closely at my chin. Once in an emergency when we had no tweezers she had bitten two short, black hairs off my chin with her sharp teeth.

*

We had lunch, and though she complained earlier of morning-sickness, she ate like a horse. Then Eugene said that as it was a historic day, he would take photos of us, so we brushed our hair and went out to the lady's garden with him, and waited for the sun to reappear. Baba stood on a stone to be as tall as me.

'This place would give me the creeps,' she said, looking

around the cluttered garden, with one shrub thrusting its way between two others, dew still on the grass and the young rose leaves opening, wine-colour. Only the daffodils were in bloom.

'Cheese,' Baba said as he took the picture, and I still have that picture and look at it in a puzzled way, because I had no idea when he took it that my life would take such a sudden twist.

Driving Baba to catch the evening bus back for Dublin, Eugene assured her that she could come to us if the worst came to the worst and she was at her wits' end.

'*We'll* help you,' I said, trying to have a share in his kindness.

'Yes,' she said to me, 'you were always good at bringing oranges to sick people in hospital.'

He helped her in to the bus with as much solicitude as if she were an old woman, and it occurred to me that if I had a baby he would probably marry me.

'Poor Baba,' he said, 'the poor old bitch,' as we waved to the moving bus and shut our eyes because of the dust it scattered. I did not feel for her in the way that he did – women care mostly for themselves or for their children who are extensions of themselves, or for their husbands who fill their days and their thoughts and their bodies: as he filled mine. Though he was not my husband.

I hoped that we would be married soon; and I was saving up for a trousseau.

'Something old, something new, something borrowed, and something blue,' I used to say as I put ten shillings away each week, in a box.

*

We went home and in a day or two I forgot about Baba, except to worry vaguely about her coming to live with us. It was rainy, lilac, April weather – sun and squally showers and then a wind rose to dry the rain off the hedges and blow the white apple-blossom all about, so that it appeared to be snowing flowers. There were two or three weeks of happiness – I helped him mow the lawn, and the cut grass

183

clung to the soles of my canvas shoes and we could smell it in bed when we had the window open.

One day, as Anna sharpened knives on the stone steps and sang 'How much is the doggie in the window?', we carried two basins out of doors and he washed my hair and rinsed it with rain-water. Afterwards he took photos of me with my wet hair (to finish out the film), and one of Anna sharpening the knives. A heavy shower began to fall; then we went upstairs, he tied my damp hair in a knot so that he would not get entangled in it, and he made love to me, while the rain refreshed the garden. We could smell the rain, cut grass, and primroses and I said, 'What will Anna think of us?'

'She'll think we're going the pace,' he said. And rivers of love flowed into me, through him, carrying long-drawn-out ripples of pleasure which made me cry back to him and, in crying, worry that Anna might burst into the room with a batch of ironing, as the door did not lock.

'All those little seeds we let go to waste,' he said tenderly to me and I made some vague reply about having a baby next year. It must have been while we lay there talking, that the postman came on his pop-pop bicycle and delivered two telegrams. One was for me and one for him.

Mine was from Baba and it said:

CHEERS THE CURSE CAME GOING TO ENGLAND SOON

and I wished that she had worded it more discreetly, as I could not now show it to him.

'It's only from Baba,' I said as I looked and saw his face whiten and his thin lips pressed together in anger. Leaning over I read his telegram:

IF YOU MARRY HER YOU WILL NEVER SEE BOO OR ME AGAIN
I PROMISE YOU

LAURA

(Another instalment for the village to read.)

'It doesn't matter,' I said as I looked at him and feared and also knew that something dreadful was coming to wrench us apart.

184

'It doesn't matter; don't worry,' I kept saying, and I wanted him to come and sit in the room while I made some tea, but he said that he would go out for a while. I watched him go down the front field with his head lowered, the dog following close behind, brushing his trouser leg with her fluffy white tail. And I thought, he's making a choice between me and them, and I wished that I could have a baby in some easy, miraculous way.

He came back later, with a bunch of red and white hawthorn in his arms and I smelled its sickly-sweet smell and said, 'Don't bring it in the house, it's unlucky.'

But he scorned my remark and put it in a big vase on the hall table.

We were kind to one another for that day and the next and I did not barge in on his thoughts or ask what he intended to do in relation to Laura.

His face looked haggard and the lines around his eyes seemed to grow deeper. Neither of us slept well. Nothing is as aggravating as lack of sleep, and by the fourth day we were edgy with each other and he complained about inessential things, like the towels in the bathroom or the worn dish-mop. He worked at his desk, preparing for this picture on irrigation. He had maps and encyclopedias spread out on his desk and I carried his meals in on a tray. Seeing him there, working and looking at me guardedly, I imagined that he was planning to go to Brazil without me; and each time I had to run from the study to stop myself from saying something foolish.

In the evening he listened to music and sat very still. Obviously he was thinking that this was a problem only because I made it so. He gave me the impression that he was sad, not only because Laura had blackmailed him, but because I had allowed it to affect our relationship. Gloom spread over the house as the mountain mist spread over the fields in the wet evenings, and I felt that I had never known him. He was a stranger, a mad martyr nailed to his chair, thinking and sighing and smoking.

*

On Thursday I had a letter from Baba, saying that she would come out on Sunday to say good-bye. She was no longer pregnant. Her prayers had been heard! But she had made up her mind to go to England anyhow.

'I'm leaving this curse of a country, so you can have a few fivers ready for me on Sunday,' the note said, and I thought of the night The Body was flashing twenty-pound notes in the Gresham Hotel, and he bought the biggest bottle of brandy that I had ever seen and tied it around his neck, so that he'd be like a St Bernard dog.

Just as I finished reading her letter, a lorry drove up which seemed to be full of telegraph poles and men in blue overalls. One of the men knocked on the door to tell me that he had come to install a telephone. Ever since the electricity had been put in, in February, we had been trying to get a telephone. I called Eugene and we decided where we would have it – in the hall.

'Won't it be marvellous,' I said, carrying away the vase of hawthorn which had shed most of its petals on to the carpet. Two men worked in the hall, and two others were outside putting a post in the front field.

'It will spoil the view,' he said as we looked through the window at the men working, and at the daffodils, some of which had lodged in a yellow sea from the night's windy rain. I made tea for the men, and watched them work, and longed for the moment when the telephone would be connected and I could ring the grocer or someone.

*

In the afternoon, just as I sat down to read, Simon the poet drove up in an old-fashioned Austin car. There was a girl with him, a tall American girl called Mary. I brought them in to the sitting-room and called Eugene.

'What a beautiful place,' she said. She spoke in a quiet accent, not at all like the American cousins of Mama's who came one summer and shouted and boasted for a full four hours.

'Simon's been telling me about you,' she said to Eugene. 'I think it's wonderful that you should come out here and

186

bury yourself in this haven. So many smart men go to pieces nowadays that it's nice to see someone getting away from it all.'

'The Irish nearly had me in pieces,' he joked, and I hated him for bringing up the subject so unnecessarily.

'The Irish nearly crucified him,' Simon the poet said. sneering. 'Was it hatchets or penknives?'

'Hobnailed boots,' Eugene said.

'Boy, you were darned lucky they didn't cut the balls out of you,' Simon said.

The tall girl shook her head at me, disclaiming all responsibility for what they said. She had long brown hair that looked as if she brushed it night and morning, and she wore black trousers with silver threads running through the black. Her body was neat and well-shaped.

'Wait until the Pope is in Galway,' Simon said to her. 'You know that one about the Cardinal's fainting?' – and she shook her brown hair and asked eagerly that he tell her.

'The last time the Virgin Mary appeared at Knock she revealed that the next Pope would be tortured. Upon hearing this Cardinal Spellman fainted. Ha. Ha.' He had this funny mechanical laugh and she joined him in it, and said, 'What fun.'

'Do you have a comb? I feel as if I'm wild or something,' she said to me, touching the curled ends of her thick hair. I took her upstairs. I couldn't tell her age but guessed that she was about twenty-two – like me. She knew a lot more than me, though. In the bedroom she admired a Renoir print of a girl tying her shoe, and the view of pine trees through the back window, which reminded her of her own New England. She began to describe the place where she grew up and I could have sworn that it was a description she had learnt out of a book; it was all too 'pat', those bits about 'pines thrusting into the sky'.

'I'm afraid my comb isn't too clean,' I said. It was a white comb, which showed up the slightest trace of dirt between the teeth.

'It's fine.' She smiled at it and drew the comb through her

hair and smiled at her image in the mirror. I asked some
stupid questions:

'Do you like Ireland? Do you like America? Do you like
clothes?'

'Sure. I like Ireland and America and clothes,' she
grinned, as she tucked the pink seersucker shirt she wore
down inside her slacks. 'I like sweaters best.' I imagined her
wardrobe full of clean shirts on hangers, and rows of different belts that matched different sweaters. She drew up
one leg of her trousers to scratch a midge bite that was
swelling on her calf. Her legs were hairy, but of course with
trousers on one would not see that. She wore flat shoes and
I felt that everything about her was calculated to appeal
to Eugene.

I was going to say to her then: 'I'm a bit nervous and
unsure, don't hurt me,' but I saw her re-do her lips carefully with a little camel's-hair brush and revive the pink of
her mouth. It came to me that she was hard and clever.

'I've never used a lip brush,' I said. 'Is it very difficult?'

'It's simple. I'll leave you this one,' she said, 'you can
practise.' And she left the gilt case containing the brush on
top of a powder bowl. Then we went down and she was
smiling and pleased with everything she saw, even the 'nice
cobwebs' in the corners of the dark wallpaper along the
landing.

'I simply adore this place – the view!' she said to Eugene
in the sitting-room, looking upon him with straight grey
eyes.

'Come here,' he said, and he crooked his finger and she
followed across to the french window to look at the valley
of birches in the distance, which was now a blur of lime-
green, instead of purple. He opened the window a little and
she put out her hand in a flutterlike movement, as if she
were a white bird about to fly.

She astonished him by saying that she had seen a 'darling
film' of his at the National Film Theatre in London. She
talked animatedly for a few minutes, and then, looking
around the shabby high-ceilinged room, she said, 'It's got
great charm, this house.' I glanced about the room which

he had made, and realized that I had contributed nothing to it – not even a cushion. I went off to make some tea.

When I came back he was playing records for them – that classical stuff that reminds me of birds – and she stood by the window marvelling at everything and moving her body to keep time with the music. He came across the room to take the tray from me, and smiled as I had not seen him smile for several days.

'So you're getting a telephone, Caithleen,' Simon the poet said to me. 'You can telephone all your friends.'

'Yes, I can,' I said. I had only two friends: Baba and The Body, and neither of them had a telephone.

Eugene poured the tea and passed Mary the first cup. Then he came round with the sugar bowl, and standing over me he said:

'Do you take sugar?'

'Sugar?' I repeated sharply as if he had just said 'Do you take arsenic?' and shook my head and glared at him, and said, 'No, I don't take sugar.'

At any other time I would not have minded, but that day I was more touchy than usual.

'Oh, you *don't* take sugar, of course, I was thinking of somebody else,' he said, and grinned as he moved on to hold the sugar bowl for Simon.

'Watch it,' Simon said, and winked at Mary. She asked me some polite questions, such as did I think sugar was fattening.

'How's New York?' Eugene asked, tenderly, as if it were some girl he inquired after.

'New York, that awful place,' she joked, 'I'm never going back there. I like Europe. There's a much greater intellectual ferment here. All you painters and writers and artists are more embodied into your society, I mean I met a bus conductor the other day who'd read James Joyce. Do you like New York?'

'In a way' – he wrinkled his face – 'I suppose I do. I hate it, but I like it also, some of my soul is there. Let's say I spent a lot of money in Brooks Brothers.'

They laughed; but I didn't understand the joke.

'Me too – I never carry more than twenty thousand dollars in cash,' said Simon the poet.

I felt very lonely and did not want to be with them. Eugene and I were all right alone, but when anyone else came I lost him to them, even to the poultry instructress with her knitted stockings. I had nothing to talk about really, except things about my childhood, and he had heard all of that.

'Have you been to America?' Mary asked me.

'Not yet,' I said, 'but I hope to, next year.'

'Over my dead body,' Eugene said. 'I like that old song about stay as sweet as you are.'

Mary told him that he must let a girl travel and that he mustn't be unkind to women because there was a law about it now. They had a moment of teasing each other, and he ended it by saying, 'Would you like to step outside, please?' as she hit him playfully with the knitted tea-cosy.

She looked tall and pretty as she stood there near the window, with her back to the brown shutter. Eugene looked at her and said to Simon, 'She's so like "your woman" that I can't get over it,' and Simon laughed and said that they must both have had the same vitamins.

'They got a system now to grow them like that,' Simon said, and grinned, and I knew that they meant that Mary was like Laura. I felt a lump rise in my throat to choke me, and the pain which precedes tears. I got to the door, muttering something about fresh tea, and was gone before anyone really noticed.

I went to my secret seat in the lady's garden where I sometimes had a cry. So she was like Laura! Laura was like that – bright, talkative; throwing tea-cosies with charm and not knocking anything over, the way I would. Every second of it came to mind, the way he smiled at her and brought her to the window to see the view, the wonder in her voice, the man's wrist-watch outside her sleeve. (Hadn't Anna told me that Laura wore a man's wrist-watch too?)

I cried and felt wretched and swore at everything for being so cruel. It was such a shock to me to know that he could love me at night and yet seem to become a stranger in day-time and say to me 'Do you use sugar?'

Up to then I thought that being one with him in bed meant being one with him in life, but I knew now that I was mistaken, and that lovers are strangers, in between times.

So she was like Laura – tall and long-legged. If Laura came back, it would be like that; or if he went to Brazil and dropped off on the way to see her. It would be like that, only much worse, because there was also his child, the little girl whom he framed a picture of, the day before, and hung it in the bathroom saying, 'I hope this doesn't affect you, any more.'

I cried insanely and walked around, chewing a stalk of grass to calm my temper. And he brought up the whole thing about my relations again. He always did, causing me to suffer over their red faces and their blundering stubborn ways. When he ridiculed them I felt sick and doomed, knowing that one day he would leave me because of them. I foresaw it all in one of those violent flashes of self-illumination which come to us after whole years of complacency, and still crying and chewing that same stalk of tough grass I came back and peeped in through the side of the sitting-room window. What I saw filled me with panic. They were talking, laughing: Mary had her feet curled up under her on the sofa, her shoes some distance away on the rug. To me there is something marvellously dangerous and frank about a woman who takes off her shoes in company – it's almost like taking off her clothes. I can't do it.

They were drinking whisky and he seemed to be telling them some story, because they laughed a lot, and Mary put her hand to her side, seemingly begging him to stop telling her such funny things, because she had a stitch there. Simon sat on the rocking-chair, rocking and laughing. No one missed me.

I went away and cried more and crushed a harmless flower between my fingers, and thought of Laura's letters to him and wondered how he replied to them. I could see the telegram too, the exact wording of it – 'If you marry her you will never see Boo or me again I promise you' – and farther down a sticker which said, 'Send your reply by Western Union'. I had no idea if he had replied, or not. He always did things without telling me.

It would be better for me to go in and talk to them as if nothing had happened, or else to pack my clothes and leave him, but I did neither. When I came and peeped through the window a second time, I saw that he had lit the fire and the tall shadows of flames leaped on the pink wall. The room looked enchanting, as rooms do, in that twilight-time when people are eating and talking and drinking whisky. With all my heart I wished that I could go in and say something casual or funny, something that would no longer mark me as an outsider.

Instead I went in by a side door and up to my room to powder my face. They did not leave for another hour and a half.

'I'll just see if she's here,' I heard Eugene say downstairs. He called my name, 'Kate, Kate, Katie.' And then he whistled. I did not answer. Finally I heard their car door bang and the engine start up. At last they were gone.

He came in to the house calling me and went to the kitchen to ask Anna, 'I wonder where Caithleen is?'

She must have nodded to the bedroom because he came up at once. My heart leaped with anger and relief as I heard him climb the stairs, whistling, 'I wonder who's kissing her now. . . .' It was almost dark and I lay on top of the bed with a rug over me.

'Having a little rest?' he said as he came into the room. I did not answer, so he came around to my side, and bending down he said, 'Are you in one of your emotional states?'

'I am,' I said tersely.

'What the hell is wrong with you?' he said suddenly in a grievous tone. It surprised me, because I had expected him to coax me for longer.

'You just make little of me and ignore me,' I said.

'Make little of you because I have a pleasurable time. Am I to stop talking to people because you haven't learnt to speak yet? If you can't accommodate yourself to seeing me being amused by other human beings, we'd better just both go home right now,' he said rapidly.

'You should never have made me come here,' I said.

'You came. I didn't *make* you, any more than I invited the posse of relations who came after you.'

He was too articulate, too sure of his own rightness.

'I give you everything – food, clothes –' He pointed to my clothes hanging in the wardrobe. Sometimes the wardrobe door opened quite suddenly as if there was a ghost in it. It had opened just then. 'I try to educate you, teach you how to speak, how to deal with people, build up your confidence, but that is not enough. You now want to *own* me.'

'I like it when there is just *us*,' I said, lowering my voice so that he might lower his.

'The world is not just us,' he said, 'the world is this girl coming, and Simon, and all the people you've met, and all the ones you will meet. Honestly –' and he sat on the bed and sighed – 'I don't think I can do it, I don't think I can start from scratch again on a wholly simple level. It's too difficult, there's not enough time left in the world any more, and hundreds of girls, ready-made.' He nodded towards the door as if Mary were in the passage.

He pointed to me.

'Your inadequacies, your fears, your traumas, your father ...' And I began to cry, knowing my inadequacies like the back of my hand.

'Young girls are like a stone,' he said, 'nothing really touches them. You can't have a relationship with a stone, at least *I* can't.'

'But you like teaching me,' I protested. 'You said you did. Some girls wouldn't take it, but I don't mind you telling me about the ice age and evolution and auto-suggestion and the profit motive. Maybe *she* wouldn't like you telling her things like that. ...' I wanted to tell him that her legs were hairy too, but I thought that would betray my nature completely.

'Maybe she wouldn't,' he said, 'but that doesn't prevent me from talking to her, from liking her. ...'

'But you like *me*,' I said, 'you like me in bed and everything.'

'Please!' he said in a strained voice. He put out his hands to catch a moth which had come through the open window, then stood up.

'I suppose if Laura came back it would be the same thing,' I said.

'It might,' he said. 'One relationship does not cancel out another, you're all –' he thought for the word – 'different.'

'Well if that's the case then, I don't know what I'm doing here.'

'I certainly don't know what you're doing here, acting like a barmaid,' he said urbanely, as he walked slowly over to the fire-grate. There were papers and matches and hairs from my comb in the grate.

'I was thinking just now that I'd be better off if I'd never met you,' I said. He leaned his elbow on the mantelpiece, pushed a bowl of primroses in from the edge, and said:

'You are incapable of thinking. Why don't you get up and wash your face and put some powder on? *Do* something. Sink your inadequacy into washing walls or mending my socks or conquering your briery nature. . . .'

I watched him, strong-featured and hard, standing there, speaking to me as a stranger might.

'Are you seeing that girl again?' I asked.

'Probably. Why not?'

'She's with Simon, she's Simon's girl,' I said.

'Oh, for God's sake stop coming priestly ethics on me; nothing's irrevocable,' he said. And I thought, not even us, and I knew as I thought it that if I loved him enough I would put up with anything from him.

'If you see her again, I'll go away and I won't come back,' I said. It was not just her charm and looks that I was jealous of – though there was that too – it was the fact that she reminded him of Laura. I wanted him exclusively for myself.

'In that case you ought to start packing now, because I'm having lunch with them tomorrow.'

'And me?' I said, outraged that he should not have included me.

'And you,' he said, wearily, 'if you can be relied upon to behave with dignity and not indulge in one of your states.' He moved towards the door. 'Look at yourself in the glass – you're like a red, swollen washerwoman.'

'Eugene, Eugene – ' I got off the bed and he turned round to say 'Yes?' but the bitterness on his face made me swallow whatever I had intended to say. I could not reach him.

He went downstairs and put some music on, and I sat there planning what I would do to teach him a lesson. I decided to go away and put him to the trouble of finding me. I remembered a story that Baba had told me of how Sally Mead (Tod Mead's wife) had left Tod once, and he searched the pubs and streets and hotels for three days, and finally a policeman found her, eating an ice-cream, alone, in the back row of a cinema. She spent the days in a cinema and slept in some hostel at night; but I need not do that, because I could go to Joanna's. I could help Baba to pack, and all the time he would search for me and swear never to let me out of his sight again.

Chapter Nineteen

IT was a long night. I got a suitcase from the top of the wardrobe and packed my clothes; I put my jewellery (some trinkets of Mama's and a gold chain that he had bought for me) in a box. At about two I went downstairs to heat myself some milk, and on the way I listened at the study door. He seemed to be moving around inside and a flute was being played, mournfully, on the radio. For one second, I had the temptation to knock and go inside, and beg his forgiveness; and listen to the music with him; but I went on down to the kitchen, heated the milk and brought it up to bed. Anyhow I could always apologize when he came up later on. But that night, he slept in the guest-room; and I minded that more than anything.

In the morning we did not speak, and while he shaved I put the case in the back boot of the car, and the marriage ring he had bought for me in an ashtray on his desk. I had finally decided to go away for a week, to give him plenty of time to miss me. I had a short letter, in my handbag, ready to hand to him when we got to Dublin. In the letter, of course, I pretended that I was going away for ever.

The new telephone was there in the hall, clean and shiny, waiting to be used. Anna looked at it, and said that she hoped it wouldn't ring while we were out. In boredom, she had bleached her black hair blonde, but it was badly done and you could see the black roots clearly. I didn't tell her that I was going away, because I knew that she would implore me either to stay, or to bring her with me.

Eugene and I did not speak half a dozen words as we drove down the mountain, past the brown fields, and down the long rocky hill which led to richer grass and cows grazing, and potato fields blue from a recent spray of copper sulphate.

'Where are we having lunch?' I asked.

'The Shelbourne,' he said, and I looked out the window at

the two crooked chalked signs on a limestone wall –'UP THE I.R.A.', and 'SHUN CYCLING SLAVES', and memorized them, telling myself that I might never drive this way again; telling myself, yet not believing it.

As we passed a grove of Scots pine trees I said, 'Now I know the names of trees,' but he did not answer me. Their limbs were amber in the sun.

When we got out at Stephen's Green, I walked a little ahead of him, towards the hotel. As we came through the revolving-doors I said, 'I'm just going into the cloakroom for a minute, won't be long,' and he went in to the lounge, without answering.

In the cloakroom I took the letter out of the paper bag (I had put it in a paper bag to keep it clean), came out, gave it to a page-boy along with two shillings and asked him to hand it to Mr Gaillard who was in the lounge. Then I ran out of the hotel and felt more exalted than I had felt for ages. I got my case from the unlocked boot of his car (it never locked), and took a taxi to Joanna's. In the taxi I mused over how shocked he would be when he read the note, and of how he would hurry to Joanna's looking for me. The note was short. It simply said:

I love you, but I do not want to be a burden to you, so I am leaving. Good-bye.

In the taxi also, I powdered my face so that when I got to Joanna's I should not look too desolate.

'Jesus, look what the cat brought in,' Baba said, opening the door to me and then going back into the hall to call Joanna.

'Mine Got, have you fill up with baby and that man send you back to us?' Joanna asked, as she saw me standing there with the stuffed suitcase, one latch of which had come open. She wore a summer dress which I had left behind, and it was funny to see her in it. She must have had it let out. Baba wore blue jeans and a sleeveless blouse. It was very hot.

'No, I just came back for a few days to help Baba pack and see her off,' I said cheerfully, and they brought me in.

Joanna was making lemonade from some yellow powder stuff. The kitchen window was open and the flowered curtain ballooned gently under the raised sash. I saw my bicycle outside, and thought with sadness of all that had happened to me since I last rode it. Baba began to question me, and very quickly I broke down.

'My mother is bloody right,' Baba said. 'All men are pigs.'

'True, is true,' Joanna said, because Gustav was out, 'smoking and trinking and start to shout if I go cross. I myself am nerves and I cannot say anythink.'

'Let Cait talk,' Baba said, shutting Joanna up. Baba looked pale from her recent misadventure and she smoked more than ever.

'Come to England,' she said to me. 'We'll have a whale of a time. Strip-tease girls in Soho, that's what we'll be.'

She was going to England the following Friday and her parents had allowed her to take her insurance money out of the bank, having reconciled themselves to the fact that she would never pass an examination now. She had told them that she was going to take up nursing.

'Nursing!' she said to me. 'Shaving people and changing sheets. I'm going to Soho, that's where I'll see life. You should come with me.'

'Ah no, he'll want me back,' I said, telling them about the note which I had given to the page-boy. Joanna put us to tidying the front room, so that the place would look respectable when he came. It was funny dusting a rubber plant on a summer's day, when nice flowers bloomed in the garden outside. There were wallflowers out, and peony roses just opening. I did not expect him until half three or four, as I knew that he would lunch first with Simon and Mary, behaving as if nothing had happened.

'Give her a drink,' Baba said to Joanna at a quarter to four. I sat near the front window, holding the net curtain up. Sometimes I let it drop in the belief that he would come the minute I stopped looking. My hands were shaking and my stomach felt sick.

At half four when nothing had happened, Baba dolled herself up and went out to look for him. I made excuses

and clung to stupid hopes, as one does in times of desperation. I said, 'He didn't get the note,' 'He doesn't know where
I'm gone,' 'He always forgets Joanna's number,' and with
these paltry hopes and egg-cupfuls of Joanna's home-made
Advocaat I passed the time from the window to the door, to
the hall, upstairs and then down again; until finally Joanna
had one of her brainwaves and gave me a pullover to rip.
I foresaw our reunion, and debated whether I should sulk
for a bit when he arrived with Baba or run to him with
open arms.

Meanwhile Gustav came in for his tea and shook hands
with me, and Gianni, the lodger, arrived looking as conceited as ever.

'How do you like the country?' he asked. 'Have you seen
much wild life?'

'Wild life!' I said, and took my cup of tea in to the back
room, where Joanna keeps buckets of preserved eggs and
apples on the window ledges.

'Baba should be back now,' I said to the plaster nymph
in the fireplace whose cheeks Joanna rouged from time to
time because everything got mildewed in that room. The
roof leaked.

Eventually I heard the door being opened and I rushed
out. Only Baba was there.

'Baba, Baba,' I said. Her cheeks were flushed and I knew
that she'd had one or two drinks.

'Come upstairs,' she said, making a face towards the
dining-room door to indicate that she did not wish them to
hear.

'Is he outside?' I asked, as she linked me upstairs to the
bedroom which I used to share with her. We closed the door.

'Where is he?' I asked.

She looked at me squarely for a second and then said,
'He's gone home.'

'Without me?' I was shocked. 'Isn't he coming for me?'

'No,' she said, sighing, 'he's not coming for you.'

'Is that Mary gone with him?'

'That moron! Says everything is "cute and moving". You
telling me *she* was good-looking. Jesus, she's only in the

199

halfpenny place next to us; all *she* has is her underwear and a necklace down to her stomach. I cut her dead,' Baba said, smiling victoriously.

'Where is she? Is she gone home with him?'

'She's a right lookin' eejit, she got the collywobbles, and that spy with the beard had to take her home. "Wow," he says to me. "Bow-Wow," says I back to him. You're too soft with sharks like him!'

'But what about Eugene?' I asked.

'Sit down,' she said, giving me a cigarette.

She began, 'I told him that you were here, and he said, "Naturally!" Then he ordered me a brandy, and when th'other pair went off, I told him that you were having a fit and he said that he'd made up his mind about you. ...'

I trembled all over, and clutched the bed-clothes to prepare myself for the worst.

'He says you're to stay here,' Baba said flatly. 'He says old men and young girls are all right in books but not anywhere else. You're to stay here,' she said, pointing to the two iron beds, 'until maybe you've growed up a bit and he comes back from making his sewage thing in America. Are you up the pole or anything?'

I shook my head and sobbed and gripped the satin bedspread until she thought I'd tear it. Then I lay on the bed face downwards and began to moan and cry.

'Jesus, don't have a nervous breakdown,' she begged as she clutched my shoulders to steady me, 'or convulsions or anything. Don't go off your head.'

'I'm entitled to have a nervous breakdown or go off my head,' I shouted as Joanna came in and said something sympathetic and then told Baba to take the spread off the bed before I ruined it. I had my shoes on, lying there. Baba pushed me towards the edge of the bed and I lowered myself on the floor and pounded the brown linoleum while they folded the bed-spread and put it away in a drawer.

'A little bit hysteric, eh?' Joanna said, and Baba recalled how our friend Tom Higgins got put in Grangegorman for a lot less. He kissed a strange nun on O'Connell Bridge because she reminded him of his dead sister. His sister died of tuberculosis in the bed next to Baba's in the sanatorium; and before that his brother got killed in Spain.

'I'm going to Eugene, I'm going to him,' I said, getting to my knees.

'No, you're not,' Baba said firmly. 'He doesn't want you.'

'He does want me, he does want me,' I shouted, and then Gustav came in, and opened his mouth with shame and wonder when he saw me kneeling and crying on the floor, my hair wild about me.

'Miss Caithleen who is so gentle,' he said, and I thought, yes, I was so gentle and now I am a wild, debased person because of some damn man, and I lay flat on the floor and cried.

They lifted me on to the bed, gave me pills and whisky, and more pills, so that I would calm down. I slept with Baba in the single bed, and once in near-sleep I thought that her arm around my stomach was his arm, and I wakened up, relieved, only to face the truth again, and the emptiness. That was the time I missed him worst. Baba's arm was around me but it was his body I smelt, the sweet and languid smell of his body in sleep, the dark mesh of hairs on his chest, the honey colour of his skin and the warmth which had enveloped us, night after night. I stayed awake then, my mind muddled from pills and crying.

*

Baba had stopped going to lectures, so at about eleven next morning we went up to a phone booth and Baba put a call through to his house. The person in the exchange told her that the telephone had not been connected yet, but to try later.

At home I sat inside the window and looked out at the peony roses which were opening, and at the leaves of the birch tree blown upwards by the wind. Baba brought me tea, and went out three or four times to telephone him but could not get through.

I thought, while this peony rose is opening into a large red bloom, he is on his way to me; but I was mistaken because when Baba finally got through, late that evening,

Anna told her that Mr Gaillard had gone away and taken a travel bag with him.

'He may be in London or somewhere for a couple of weeks,' Baba said.

'Weeks?' I said. 'I'll be out of my mind if I have to wait weeks.'

'I'm going to England this Friday,' Baba said, wagging her finger at me, 'and for God's sake don't stop me, don't ask me to stay here and nurse you. I've wanted to go for months, and I don't want anyone or anything to stop me.'

'I won't stop you, Baba,' I said, certain that he would come in a matter of days. 'He'll come.'

'Supposing he doesn't?'

'But he will.'

'But *supposing* he doesn't,' and she went on like that, and I thought she was disheartening me because she was jealous. She said again that if I wanted to I could go to England with her.

'You'll see him there,' she said. 'He might even be over there now.' It was quite possible, because the various companies he made films for were in London. I thought, however, that most probably he had just gone away for one night to some hotel to do a bit of fishing. When he was worried about something he always went fishing; and I knew well that he was missing me.

That night I did not promise to go to England with Baba, but next day she was on about it again, and I said that I maybe would go, although I did not believe that I really would. Making plans to go gave me something to think about, and also I thought it would prove to him how independent I was. I wrote to him, telling him that I was going away, marking the letter 'Urgent', and 'Personal'.

Meanwhile Baba made plans for us to leave. She rang her mother and got her to tell my father that I had left Eugene and was going to England with Baba. My father was delighted. In a letter he praised me for being so loyal to my family, and to my religion. He sent me fifty pounds reward – collected no doubt from cousin Andy and other rich relations. They wanted me to go home for a few days but Baba told her mother on the phone that there was no time. Baba had already got the tickets. In the back of my mind was the nice thought that I could get a refund for my ticket or give it to some poor person when Eugene came. I felt that he had to come, because if he didn't it made everything between us meaningless.

I wrote to him again and asked him to have a drink with us, to say good-bye. I said nothing about being hysterical because I knew that once he saw me he would love me and want to protect me again. I said to myself that people were like that with me – they forget me easily, but when they see me they are drawn again and somehow feel protecting.

No answer came to that letter; and twice I went into a telephone booth to ring him, but vanity or terror stopped me from trying to get through. Anyhow I did not want to talk to him on the telephone; I wanted him to come and see me. But really I was afraid to find that he had gone away.

Baba and I were out a lot, saying good-bye, getting new clothes and underwear, having our hair done, drinking with Baba's friends. Sometimes in a pub it would come to me that he was outside Joanna's waiting in his sports car, and I would run from my friends and get a taxi home, only to be disappointed again.

*

The nights were the worst: thinking of him sitting at home in his study listening to music, and moving those ivory chess-men on the chequered board, or skimming the cream off the milk so that he would not die of thrombosis at fifty. The inside of my lips were covered with water blisters and these aggravated the craving pain to be with him. And I thought of what he had said about young girls being like a stone and I wanted him to know that this was not true.

Four days and four nights went by. On the fifth day we were due to leave. Baba had booked a double cabin and she had the tickets in a little cellophane envelope. I packed and kept up the pretence that I was really going; but I knew that just as I got on the ship, he would be standing there, mournful; and when he tapped my shoulder and said 'Kate', I would turn and go to him. In a letter I had told him the exact time we were sailing and where from, so I knew he'd come.

Chapter Twenty

On our last day we bought labels and twine. We sent a barm-brack and twenty cigarettes to Tom Higgins, who was in a mental hospital (we were afraid to visit him), and Joanna had chicken for lunch as a celebration.

After lunch, we packed last-minute things and Joanna kept plaguing us to leave her some clothes and perfume in the ends of bottles. Baba half-filled three perfume bottles with water to keep Joanna happy.

When we had packed we hurried from one neighbour's house to the next, saying good-bye, and Baba came with me to say good-bye to Mr and Mrs Burns in the shop where I used to work. Mr Burns gave me a pound and said it was God who had saved me from that awful man. No one except Baba seemed to realize that I wanted only to go back to Eugene.

'Cheer up, when we're in London you can write to him, he's bound to come over and take us out for big dinners,' she said as we walked home, smelling the hawthorn scent that carried in the wind from the bushes in people's gardens. I wondered if he would come or not. Two or three times I thought of asking Baba to ring up again, but I thought that it might spoil everything and stop him from coming.

At home, in Joanna's front garden, the peony roses had opened out – into a deep, glistening red. Joanna had watered them and everything was nicely moist. He still hadn't come. Baba had arranged to meet The Body and Tod Mead in a pub.

A taxi came for us at six, and Gustav helped the driver with the cases. When they had all sat in, I ran back and stuck a note under the knocker – 'Gone to pub opposite boat' – so that he would know where to find us. I didn't want Joanna to know I left the note, because she'd say it gave burglars a fine opportunity to break in.

It was a dark pub, decorated inside to look like a ship, and along the mantelshelf were various-sized ships in bottles; and a picture of Robert Emmett on the wall. I made circles with the toe of my shoe in the sawdust and wondered how long more I could wait without ringing him.

'Come on, Caithleen, cheer up, love,' The Body said, hand-me a drink. It was rum and lemon and I did not like it.

'If you bowl over any publishers, let me know,' said Tod Mead, who had some vague idea about writing a novel and becoming famous.

'How's Sally?' I said. Although I'd never met her, I pitied her a lot, ever since Baba was pregnant that time.

'She's in great form, doing a lot of gardening,' he said, and though I wanted to ask him how she *really* was, I didn't. His slight irritableness stopped you from asking him anything that mattered.

'I wonder how they get those ships into bottles,' he said, nodding at a white ship in a long bottle. That was how he evaded things, always changing the subject to something trivial. I would remember him, blue-eyed and secretly bitter, with an old fawn Crombie coat, and a knot in the belt where the buckle should be, setting himself up as an authority on wine and American writers and ships in bottles.

Two students from Trinity College came to bid Baba farewell and she tried to coax a college scarf from one of them, so that she could show it off in London.

All of a sudden, as I watched her and listened to Tod, I got frantic and stood up. 'I'm going to ring him,' I said to Baba.

'All right, ring him, there's no one stopping you,' she said, as she put the striped scarf over her head.

*

The telephone was in the hall. I had to get a single shilling and some pennies, and then wait for several minutes while the exchange connected me to his number.

Anna answered the telephone.

'No, he's not here,' she said, yelling into it. You'd know that it was the first or second time in her whole life that she had used one.

Then she faded away, giving me the impression that she had turned to say something to someone.

'Anna, I'm going to England and I just want to say good-bye to him. Ask him to come and say good-bye to me.'

'He's not here,' she said again. 'He's out the field, honest to God.' She heard me sobbing and she said, 'If he comes in I'll get him to rush in and see you. Where are you? How long more will you be there?'

I had to shout into the bar to ask the name of the pub, and several people shouted the name to me.

'God, 'tis well for you going to England,' Anna said. 'Love, I'm in trouble, I'm up the pole again, is there any pills you could send me?'

'I'll try,' I said. 'Is he there?'

'He's not here, there's no one here, only me and the child. Will you send me the pills, will you?'

'And you'll send him here, before I leave?'

'If he's here at all I'll tell him!'

'Anna, I wrote to him,' I said.

'I know, there's a pile of letters here on the hall table that he hasn't opened.' It was that quality about him which I admired most, that lonely strength which allowed him to postpone a pleasure or a worrying letter for days or weeks.

I asked Anna if the American girl, Mary, had been to the house.

'No one came, only the rat-man, 'tis like a monastery here since you left. He was away for two nights and since he came back he's like a monk, brooding. Will you send the pills?' she begged, and then my time was up and I said good-bye and came away, feeling worse than ever. I could see his brown eyes as I had last seen them in the hotel, full of sadness, and full of the knowledge that I was not the girl he had imagined me to be. A stone, he'd said. I thought of stones bursting open in the hot sun and other stones washed smooth by a river I knew well.

When we were leaving the pub I left a message that he should follow across to the ship; I still thought that he might come. It was getting late and I imagined him speeding down the mountain in his little car, hurrying to me.

Anna had promised to go out and look for him, but he might be anywhere.

*

The Body knew the superintendent of the ship and managed to get permission for all of them to come on board. He tipped several porters as we all trooped on. Baba held her ticket between her teeth, to show it to the ticket man, as her hands were occupied with flowers and travel bags and a new red raincoat. Walking across the gangway I thought, I can still go back and wait for him; because he's coming. But I went ahead, propelled by The Body's hearty voice and by someone who pushed me from behind with the sharp corner of a suitcase.

Our small cabin was thick with company: Tod, The Body, Joanna, Gustav, and the various bunches of crushed flowers which they had given us. The Body passed a half-bottle of Irish whisky around and urged us to drink up.

'I not get the germs,' said Joanna. She was quite merry from a few sherries, and The Body pushed her hat sideways so that everything about her looked lopsided.

'Jesus meets his afflicted mother,' The Body said to her, reminding me of the night we went to the dress-dance and of later when he tripped on her stairs. And for a minute we all felt sad; but The Body shouted, 'Baba, Caithleen; your health; your fortune; stay as sweet as you are and don't let a thing ever change you' – he sang the last bit, and fondled Baba's bottom and lifted her into the air.

'Jesus,' she said as her head hit the white porcelain lampshade.

A bell rang then and a commanding voice announced that all people aboard who were not travelling should disembark.

'Holy Moses, we'll have to swim the channel,' The Body said and Joanna said, 'Mine Got,' and Tod pulled up the back of his coat collar and made the sign of the Cross in mockery over us. They scrambled towards the door and left us with the crushed roses and the half-bottle of whisky which had the damp of their various mouths on its neck.

'He never came,' I said to Baba and she put her arms round me and we both began to cry.

'I'll go mad, I'll go mad,' I sobbed to her.

'Oh not the loony bin,' she said. 'Wait till we go to England, everything is free there' – and then recollecting that we possessed so much money she said, 'Our handbags; Jesus our money,' and she flung coats and cases off the bed and found both handbags under the numerous brown-paper parcels. At the last minute we had found that all our clothes did not fit in our cases, and we had to make various parcels. Baba said we'd need a wheelbarrow to cart the stuff off the boat when we docked at Liverpool.

'We'll stay awake all night,' she said. 'You wouldn't know who'd come in here and rape us and take our money.'

'I'll never forget him,' I said to her, as I went across to dry my eyes, in front of the mirror over the wash-basin.

'There's no one asking you to,' she said. 'Anyhow cheer up, we'll have a whale of a time in Soho.'

There was another announcement from the ship's loud-speaker, and I listened, trembling, in case it might be him but it wasn't.

'Would you know by looking at me that I had a past?' I asked her. I no longer had to suck my cheeks in to look thin.

She replied to the mirror, 'You'd know you hadn't a decent night's sleep for about six months, that's what you'd know,' and then for devilment she pressed the two bells beside the bunks, just to see what would happen. A steward came.

'Just did it for gas,' she said; and he looked around at the chaos of our cabin – clothes on the floor, flowers on the floor, me crying, Baba nursing the whisky bottle on her lap. He shook his head and backed out.

'If they're wondering how big a tip they'll get tomorrow they'd want to watch out or they'll get nothing,' Baba said loudly.

'A pity beyond all telling is hid in the heart of love,' I said, light-headed as a result of the whisky, and finding consolation in the words.

She put her hands to her ears: 'No, no, Jesus are you reciting those mortuary cards again?'

'He always washed his own socks and made metal things to put in them, to keep them from shrinking,' I said, 'and he boiled his corduroy pants one day and they shrank, so he had to use them on a scarecrow.'

'I tell you something interesting, I think he was touched and you're better off away from him.' She tapped her forehead. 'He'll become a monk.'

The ship began to rumble and I swayed a little and she said, 'We're off, come on, let's wave to them,' and she led me by the hand, as we ran up on deck to see the last of Dublin. The Body and the others were still on the quay, waving hands and hats and evening papers; but there was no sign of him.

'The Body is sincere,' I said to Baba, re-echoing Mama's words.

Baba waved a clean hanky and we leaned on the rails and felt the ship move and saw the dirty water underneath being churned up.

'Like a hundred lavatories flushing,' Baba said, to the foamy water as the seagulls rose up from their various perches along the rails and flew slowly, with us. I could hardly believe that we were moving, that we were leaving Ireland; and through my tears I saw our friends waving us away, and cranes and anchored ships and the long, uninspiring stretch of quay which we rode past. And gradually the City of Dublin started receding in the mauve twilight of a May evening – the city where I first kissed him outside the Customs House; the city where I had two teeth out, and pawned one of Mama's rings; the city I loved. We were both crying.

'Poor Tom Higgins shut up in the loony bin,' Baba said as if it were for him she cried; but I thought she's crying too for that part of herself which she squandered, and for the aloes she took, and for all the bus conductors she flirted with.

We could see Dollymount sands now, where I had been first with Mr Gentleman and then with him – both times in love. I pictured sand dunes with grass growing out of them and swore never to set foot there again, love or no love. We felt chilly, as we had forgotten to put on our coats, and it got dark fairly soon and lights came up on all sides of the bay.

Down below us the people travelling third class carried their drinks outside, as they leaned on the rails and sang.

'We'd have a lot more gas down there,' Baba said. There were mostly priests and married couples travelling first class.

The gulls flew slowly with us, their screaming unwinding the scream inside me. By degrees, the sky darkened; a mist rose from the sea; the stars lit up.

'I brought pills, in case we puke all over the damn ship,' Baba said, so we went inside and took three pills and hoped that we would be all right.

I missed him then, more than at any other time; it was terrible sitting on that bed, knowing that he had chosen not to come for me.

'If I'm sick, 'twill spoil everything,' Baba said as she burped, and then put a hand-towel over her new dress, for safety's sake.

'Remind me to feck a few towels,' she said, and I knew that if anyone was to save me from going mad, it would be Baba, with her maddening, chattering voice.

'We're on our way,' she said, raising her arms exultantly to the ceiling. 'We're on our way, English and American papers please copy.' And the ship named *Hibernia* moved steadily forward through the black night, towards the dawn of Liverpool.

Chapter Twenty-One

I work in a delicatessen shop in Bayswater and go to London University at night to study English. Baba works in Soho, but not in a strip-tease club, as she had hoped. She's learning to be a receptionist in a big hotel. We share a small bed-sitting-room, and my aunt sends a parcel of butter every other week. Baba says that it makes us look like a right pair of eejits, getting that mopey parcel tied with hairy twine, and I keep telling my aunt that butter is not rationed here, but still she sends it. It's all she can do to prove her love.

It is hot summer, and I miss the fields and the soft breeze; and I sometimes think of a brown mountain stream with willows and broom pods hanging over it; and I think of the day I went fishing there with him, and he wore big boots and waded upstream. At unguarded moments, in the last Tube, or drying my face by sticking my head out the window (we aren't allowed in the garden), I ask myself why I ever left him; why I didn't cling on tight, the way the barnacles cling to the rocks.

He wrote to me after I came here – a very nice letter, saying what a nice girl I was, and what a pity that he hadn't been younger (in mind) or I hadn't been older.

I answered that letter and he wrote again, but I haven't heard from him now for a couple of months and I take it that he has gone back to his wife, or that he's busy in South America, doing that picture on irrigation.

If I saw him again I would run to kiss him, but even if I don't see him I have a picture of him in my mind, walking through the woods, saying, in answer to my fear that he might leave me, that the experience of knowing love and of being destined, one day, to remember it, is the common lot of most people.

'We all leave one another. We die, we change – it's mostly change – we outgrow our best friends; but even if I do leave you, I will have passed on to you something of myself; you will be a different person because of knowing me; it's inescapable . . .' he said.

It's quite true. Even Baba notices that I'm changing, and she says if I don't give up this learning at night, I'll end up as a right drip, wearing flat shoes and glasses. What Baba doesn't know is that I'm finding my feet, and when I'm able to talk I imagine that I won't be so alone, or so very far away from the world he tried to draw me into, too soon.

FOR THE BEST IN PAPERBACKS, LOOK FOR THE

In every corner of the world, on every subject under the sun, Penguin represents quality and variety – the very best in publishing today.

For complete information about books available from Penguin – including Pelicans, Puffins, Peregrines and Penguin Classics – and how to order them, write to us at the appropriate address below. Please note that for copyright reasons the selection of books varies from country to country.

In the United Kingdom: For a complete list of books available from Penguin in the U.K., please write to *Dept E.P., Penguin Books Ltd, Harmondsworth, Middlesex, UB7 0DA*

In the United States: For a complete list of books available from Penguin in the U.S., please write to *Dept BA, Penguin, 299 Murray Hill Parkway, East Rutherford, New Jersey 07073*

In Canada: For a complete list of books available from Penguin in Canada, please write to *Penguin Books Canada Ltd, 2801 John Street, Markham, Ontario L3R 1B4*

In Australia: For a complete list of books available from Penguin in Australia, please write to the *Marketing Department, Penguin Books Australia Ltd, P.O. Box 257, Ringwood, Victoria 3134*

In New Zealand: For a complete list of books available from Penguin in New Zealand, please write to the *Marketing Department, Penguin Books (NZ) Ltd, Private Bag, Takapuna, Auckland 9*

In India: For a complete list of books available from Penguin, please write to *Penguin Overseas Ltd, 706 Eros Apartments, 56 Nehru Place, New Delhi, 110019*

In Holland: For a complete list of books available from Penguin in Holland, please write to *Penguin Books Nederland B.V., Postbus 195, NL–1380AD Weesp, Netherlands*

In Germany: For a complete list of books available from Penguin, please write to *Penguin Books Ltd, Friedrichstrasse 10 – 12, D–6000 Frankfurt Main 1, Federal Republic of Germany*

In Spain: For a complete list of books available from Penguin in Spain, please write to *Longman Penguin España, Calle San Nicolas 15, E–28013 Madrid, Spain*

Edna O'Brien in Penguins

THE COUNTRY GIRLS

Edna O'Brien's famous first novel introduces us to Kate and Baba, the delightful heroines of an engaging trilogy.

GIRLS IN THEIR MARRIED BLISS

Tearful Kate – bored with her grey husband in their grey stone house in the country – is driven to indiscretions she can hardly handle without Baba's help. And Baba already has her hands full – keeping one step ahead of the unpredictable passions of her rich and vulgar builder . . .

Also published:

August is a Wicked Month
Casualties of Peace
Johnny I hardly knew you
The Love Object
Mother Ireland
Mrs Reinhardt and Other Stories
Night
A Pagan Place
A Scandalous Woman and Other Stories
Some Irish Loving
A Fanatic Heart